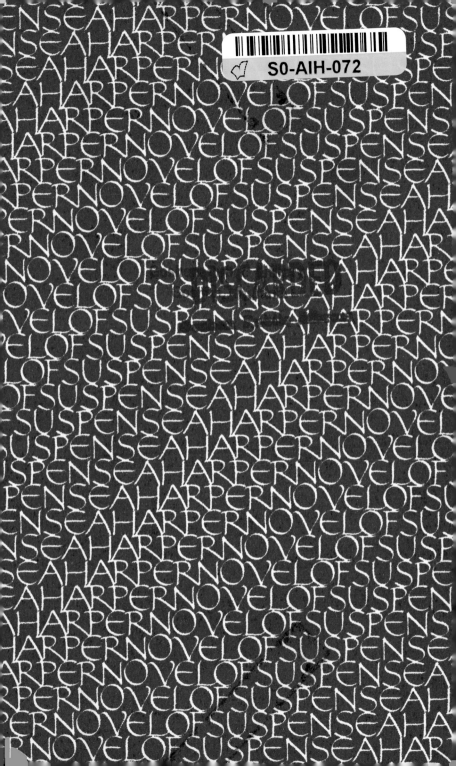

GIVEN THE
AMMUNITION

A
JOAN
KAHN
BOOK

BOOKS BY HARRIETT GILBERT

Given the Ammunition

An Offense Against the Persons

Hotels with Empty Rooms

I Know Where I've Been

GIVEN THE
AMMUNITION

Harriett Gilbert

HARPER & ROW, PUBLISHERS

New York, Hagerstown, San Francisco, London

Fic
GIL
M

FIRST U.S. EDITION

Library of Congress Cataloging in Publication Data

Gilbert, Harriett, date.
  Given the ammunition.
  I. Title.
PZ4.G4645Gi3   [PR6057.I515]   823'.9'14   76-5535
ISBN 0-06-011514-9

76 77 78 79 10 9 8 7 6 5 4 3 2 1

GIVEN THE
AMMUNITION

1

On the Monday of that week, it still appeared to be summer.

Even at half past eight in the evening the air was tepid, lulled by the warmth stored up in bricks and paving stones; and the middle-aged man coming out through the front door of a Chelsea house, locking the door, and turning to hail an approaching taxicab wore only light trousers, a shirt, and a tie. There was, however, a jacket across his arm: a discreet, expensive, neatly folded jacket.

As soon as the taxi had come to rest beside the pavement, the middle-aged man lowered the copy of the *Evening Standard* with which he had hailed it and descended the steps to the street. His movements were complementary to the evening: relaxed and sure. His face was tanned. His gray hair touched his collar. His forehead was high and his features were straight.

"Evening, sir. Where to, sir?"

The driver of the taxi, as others had been before him, was impressed by Edward Mannion.

Mannion, having given the name of an established, fashionable club in Mayfair, smiled, walked to the nearside passenger door of the cab, stepped inside, and unfolded his newspaper. As the taxi eased away from the pavement, he did not look up.

Farther down the same street, another taxi began to move. During the previous two hours, it had been parked in the shadow of a chestnut tree, its driver chewing gum and flicking the pages of a thriller, its passenger tapping the plastic upholstery with yellowish, quick-bitten fingernails. Now it rattled into life and, scattering leaves with exhaust gas, followed its predecessor through the purple, lamplit evening.

"Excuse me."

"Yes, sir?"

Edward Mannion's taxi-driver twisted his head toward the gap in the glass partition.

"What was it, sir?" he asked.

"I wonder if you'd mind terribly just cutting a few corners. I'm in a bit of a hurry. I was supposed to be meeting my daughter at half past eight."

The voice that transmitted this request was deep and smooth. The smile that accompanied it charming. It crinkled the skin around the speaker's blue eyes and folded the flesh beneath his mouth into pouches of good nature.

" 'Course not," said the taxi-driver. "Mustn't keep a young lady waiting, must we, sir?"

"Thank you," said Edward Mannion.

Then he settled himself back in his seat and turned to the fifth page of his evening paper. The print, shaken by the vibrations of the cab, jerked before his eyes, but he was used to reading while moving and had learned to soften his focus. He skimmed over one article on the alarming increase in juvenile crime in Inner London and another headed "SECRETARY GIVES KIDNEY TO SAVE LITTLE PAUL," then slowed down to absorb more deeply the piece in the top right-hand corner. It was about Pieter van der Walt.

Van der Walt was the young expatriate leader of a left-wing terrorist group, mainly concerned with the abolition of apartheid in South Africa, who had achieved recent notoriety in connection with an explosion in a Midlands factory, as a result of which a night watchman had died. The report was of his trial and of his sentencing, that morning, to fifteen years' imprisonment.

". . . did not deny that he had placed the bomb in the factory's warehouse," Edward Mannion read, "nor that he had failed to give sufficient warning of its presence, but claimed justification for this illegal act on the grounds that the company concerned 'makes a substantial part of its profits from trading with that most perverted of all criminals: South Africa.' In his summing-up, the judge, Mr. Justice ——, said that the defendant's childish and ridiculous excuses did nothing to mitigate the atrocity of his crime. The three other people arrested with van der Walt, but later released with the charges against them dropped, were not in court for the trial."

The news was offered without apparent emotion and thus, by this reader, was it received; or, at least, with no more than a sigh of resigned and unspecific disapproval.

Having reread the article once, Edward Mannion shook his head, squeezed his lips together, then turned through a crackle of paper to the bridge problem.

The taxi that bore him dipped its snout and plunged into the white-light tunnel of the Piccadilly underpass.

To be followed, twenty seconds later, by another taxi, whose passenger strained forward in his seat and gripped his denim-covered knees with nicotine-stained fingers.

2

The doorman was debating with himself whether or not he should ask her to move along. Olivia realized this. Until a few minutes earlier, he had seemed unaware of her presence as she leaned against the wall beside him. Scurrying from canopied passageway to pavement's edge, opening car doors, hovering and smiling and joking, he had not given her a glance. Now, however, he was tossing infuriated looks in her direction, scowling at her scissors-hacked hair, her draped and belted dress, her down-at-heel boots, and twitching his head at her as though he were a pigeon and she either a worm or a cat.

There had been a time (in her last term at school, in her first term at university) when Olivia had enjoyed creating this kind of confusion, had enjoyed entering expensive department stores in bare, dirty feet and paying for her small purchases with checks from a merchant bank, had enjoyed the pendulum swing of reaction from disdain to servility that, by such simple devices, it had been possible to create. She had felt herself to be in the vanguard of a battle against hypocrisy and prejudice.

When the fallacy of this belief had dawned on her, when she had understood that the current uniform of urban, middle-class youth makes not one jot of difference to the prejudices of the nation, she had been sad. And now—seeing the look of resentful mistrust on the face of the doorman as his attention spun from the latest arrivals, in their chauffeur-driven Mercedes, and back to her again—she was angered by the same sadness.

He would neither invite her to wait inside nor shoo her away like a gypsy. There would be no revolution or confrontation, only hostility, as though *she* had cheated at cards and *he* (aware of her guilt, yet unable to prove it) must shuffle on, in the hope that she would leave the table of her own accord.

Olivia raised her heels and bent her knees so that she squatted against the wall on which she had been leaning. Soon her father would arrive (her father who was a member of the club of which this man was a servant), and she would get to her feet and precede him along the green-and-gold canopied passageway, and the doorman would know who she was. Then he would smile at her and bow to her and open the door of the bar for her. And she would smile at him and thank him and despise him, despise them both: him for betraying his class to her father's money, herself for having nothing to betray.

She was no more allied to this man than she was to her father. Were she to go across to him now and speak with him, he would hear at once from which stratum of society she came, and would treat her accordingly. They would patronize each other, condescend to each other, and (if she insisted too hard that there was no barrier between them) finish by hating each other.

Still squatting, Olivia fumbled in the small velvet pouch that she carried and took from it her tobacco tin. She rolled a cigarette on the shelf formed by her thighs.

A sensation of loneliness washed over her, of bobbing without direction on foggy water between invisible landing stages. Often in her life she had had this feeling, but in the last three months, since leaving university, it had come to her more and more often and with greater and greater strength.

Sometimes she could dismiss it, could ascribe to it petty and logical causes, but at other times it would overwhelm her with its terror, so that material objects and everyday actions and familiar faces became like grotesque apparitions, jeering at her through the mist, swimming toward her, then dissolving into nothing. When this happened, even her own logic would turn traitor, would melt beneath her grip, and she would cry out within herself for a wave to drown her.

She did not want to commit suicide. (Such an act had never occurred to her in relation to herself. It was too concrete. It implied a belief in something, or in nothing, but a belief.) She wanted only a solidity to dispel (in whatever way; it did not matter) the apparitions; an apparition that, to her, could seem to be solid.

Molding tobacco and paper into a cylinder, she clenched her eyes shut, then opened them again. Her hands, wide and strong with pale oval fingernails, moved with ordinary competence about their work. Beneath her feet, the pavement was steady. She was in control of herself. She was not mad. Yet it occurred to her that madness might be preferable to this limbo state between it and sanity, which others could not see and which *she* could neither explain nor justify.

She lit her cigarette and threw the match into the gutter.

At quarter to nine, it occurred to Olivia that her father was late. Having lifted her watch to her ear to insure that it was working, she frowned, then felt a heaviness lift from her stomach.

"He's forgotten."

She would have liked to leave then.

The dinner date had been arranged that morning at breakfast. She had come down to the kitchen at quarter to ten, certain that he would be gone, to find him still there, sipping tea and completing the *Times* crossword.

"Good morning," she had said and he, an actor putting on a mask, had lifted his royal-blue eyes to meet hers and replied, "Good morning. Sleep well?"

"Yes, thank you," she had said.

"Good. Er, won't you—?"

His right hand and forearm had waved a semicircle above the table.

6

"Thanks. Yes. I'll make myself some coffee."

"Of course. Coffee. I'm not sure . . . Mrs. Clifford always hides it."

"That's okay. I'll find it."

Their conversation had, as usual, been polite.

Olivia had never known how to talk with her father. Until her mother's death nine years before, this knowledge had seemed unnecessary, her mother having acted as interpreter on the few occasions when communication had been called for. Since then, like all skills that are tackled too late, it had been impossible to acquire.

From boarding school and summer camp, from university and the houses of friends, Olivia had written to her father in fluent, cheerful paragraphs. From New York and Paris, from Beirut and London, he had replied. Their letters had described a relationship of relaxed concern and respect, made only more admirable by contrast with that other, spoken relationship, between the schoolgirl and the man who came to visit her on Open Day, the student and the man who slipped her thirty pounds before she left for a vacation job in Cannes.

These two—talking to each other, using sentences without the benefit of premeditation, being forced to accompany their words with facial gestures—were unhappy strangers.

And for three months now, for the three months since Olivia had taken her final examinations in Modern History, these strangers had been enclosed together in the house in Chelsea that, through thoughtlessness, they both referred to as home.

Olivia had poured hot water onto instant coffee and lifted the cup to her mouth.

Her father had said, "Aren't you going to join me?"

She had replied, "Yeah, fine."

After this they had sat, one at either end of a scrubbed pine table, for several minutes, in silence.

When the *Times* crossword was finished, he had asked her to join him at his club for dinner.

"He's forgotten."

Yet she didn't leave.

Behind the curtained windows of the club, salt biscuits and apéritifs were being swapped for Parma ham and wine. Along the street, few cars came. In the air a breeze had begun to flutter the previous warmth, yet Olivia didn't leave. She remained squatting against the wall, shoulders hunched, knuckles compressing her lower lip, because to leave would be cowardly. To run away now, when she knew that her father had not forgotten his appointment with her but was merely being his customary, status-establishing few minutes late, would be as pathetic as had been her passive acceptance of the initial invitation. What she should have said then, she must say this evening. It had already been too long delayed. If any action of hers was to rescue her from the mists and dark water, it would be this, this confrontation.

The taxi drew up before she had had time to change her mind.

"My dear, I'm so sorry."

Olivia levered her body to the vertical position.

"Keep the change," her father said to the cabdriver. "And thank you. I don't think I've ever done it so fast. . . . Now . . . Oh, I really am very sorry. You must be absolutely ravenous. Come. Shall we go in?"

Edward Mannion extended his right hand toward the small of his daughter's back.

As though he had completed the gesture, as though he had touched her, Olivia Mannion twisted the strap of her velvet bag around her wrist and moved forward toward the green-and-gold canopy, the doorman, the centrally heated club.

Farther down the same street, another taxi drew up. Its passenger got out, glanced once toward the club, drew from the pocket of his denim jacket a fold of one-pound notes and gave several of them to the driver, then backed into the doorway of the nearest block of flats. There he folded his arms, relaxed one knee, and let his body slump against a pillar. He looked as though he meant to stand in that position for some time.

3

The sole was good. Its flesh slid from glistening bones and dissolved like cream in the mouth. The wine that followed it down was also good: a light, dry muscadet with pin-prick bubbles clinging to its surface.

Edward lifted his glass toward the light and looked with admiration at the globules of molten gold that were thus revealed, suspended in sunshine.

Across the table from him, his daughter was not speaking. She was poking with her fork at an expensive piece of tournedos en croûte, her dull brown hair obscuring her face, her left elbow on the table, the fist supporting her forehead. The sleeve of her dress had fallen back to reveal a pale arm encircled by various bands of metal.

Edward asked her, "Is it good, the steak?"

"What?"

She lifted her eyes toward him. They were blue, like his, only lighter and marked with crow's-feet at the outer edges. Her forehead, too, was lined, as though by worry or short-sightedness.

His daughter's appearance was a source of aggravation to Edward. Not that it was unattractive. On the contrary, the combination of *his* height and strength with *Caroline's* neatness of feature had been a successful one. A high forehead and a strong chin added dignity to the upturned nose and the soft pink lips, and long limbs stretched plumpness into firmness.

Perhaps it was *because* of this, because the basic material was so good, that he resented the lack of attention paid to it. A good haircut, discreet make-up, and clothes that did not come out of a jumble sale seemed the least due to such natural advantages.

"What?" asked Olivia.

"The steak," said Edward. "All right, is it?"

"Yes, thank you."

"Good."

Edward hesitated, then picked up his knife and fork to ease the last, pearllike flakes from the skeleton on his plate. Shortly afterward, a waiter appeared.

Olivia said, "You can take mine, too. It was great, but I really can't manage it all."

"Very good," said the waiter.

Then Olivia rummaged in her bag and extracted a tin, from the contents of which she proceeded to make herself a cigarette.

"Do you have to?"

Edward had not meant to say this. He had intended to ignore the strands of jaundiced tobacco as they scattered on the white linen, the rag of paper licked along the edge, then rolled between finger and thumb. He had not wanted to make an issue out of things so peripheral and, having done so, he felt doubly annoyed. It was as though he had been challenged by an upstart to ludicrous battle, then been tricked into accepting the challenge.

"It's okay, I've finished," said his daughter, cramming the offending articles back into their tin and dropping the tin into her bag.

Leaning forward to light the cigarette at a candle, she said, "It's cheaper than buying them ready-made."

Edward said, "No doubt. But it really is rather disgusting. You look like a workman."

Again he wished that he had not spoken, as she asked, "Is that so terrible?"

"No, no. Not in itself. Of course not."

He tried to make the words sound final. Reaching for the menu, he wanted to convey that the conversation was closed.

"Okay. Well, then, why did you say it?" asked Olivia. "I mean, don't you see, that's just the trouble. We all say these things, these clichés, we don't really mean and we—well, other people, anyway—end up believing them. Living by them. Living up to them. 'Workman,' for instance. 'Worker.' Most people work for their living nowadays. So what did you mean? Building laborer or something?"

"Yes, I did mean a building laborer. And what's more, one actually at work on a site, not one out at dinner in an expensive restaurant. You don't imagine they roll their own cigarettes then, do you?"

He wished that he could sound more calm, certain that she said and did these things not through ignorance or stupidity but to provoke him.

"Now," he said, "let's drop the subject, shall we, and tell me what you'd like for afters?"

"Nothing, thank you."

"Are you sure? Look at the trolley. There seems to be lots of exciting things there."

He jutted his chin toward the center of the room where a two-tiered rolling table was camouflaged by sweetmeats: caramelized oranges glistening under a varnish of golden sugar, figs and peaches, chocolate gateau, and flans layered thick with yellow cream and downy bitter raspberries.

"Surely you'd like something."

"No, really."

"Not even a piece of fruit?"

"No, thank you. I'm full."

"Well, I'm going to. I'm going to have a slice of that cake with the cherries. You're sure you won't join me?"

He hovered, knowing, however, that she would not change her mind, then lifted a finger to the trolley attendant and beckoned him to them.

4

"Daddy?"

"Yes?"

He had forgotten she was still there. He had been rolling brandy around his mouth, enjoying the trickle of fire as it slid down his throat and reconsumed the meal he had eaten. The feeling this gave him was pleasant, not only in its physical self but in the associations that flowed with it: of business dinners well concluded; of tête-à-têtes with friends; with Caroline. It upset him that these had been polluted by his daughter's voice. The whole evening, he felt, had been like this: like a picnic set on edge by the rasp of a wasp.

"Yes?" he said. "I'm sorry?"

"Look . . ."

Olivia was constructing another of her cigarettes. Her lips were parted, her teeth clenched in what might have been concentration.

"Look, I know I've buggered up your evening and I'm sorry, I really am. It's just that it all seems so . . ."

A strand of hair was obscuring her eyes and she moved it, returning her fingers at once, however, to the twisted cylinder of paper and tobacco they had formed. Her gaze, too, stayed anchored to the table.

"So false," she said. "I mean, not just here, tonight, but everything since I've been back. You know: eating out somewhere practically every evening or going to the cinema with those people of yours—what's their name? Dick and Sally

Hastings—or shopping for things I don't need or visiting the art galleries together. . . . It's as though I were on just another summer vacation and you were trying to *cram* it with things to do, so I wouldn't have time to get bored or . . . think. Oh, I know I'm sounding ungrateful and I do appreciate, really, how annoying it must be for you, having this strange woman around all the time, disturbing your habits and mucking up your life. But it's no good pretending I'm not here, is it? Or that if I am, I'm just the same little child I used to be. I mean, when you sent me to all those wonderful schools and when you encouraged me to go to university, you must have realized they'd change me a bit. . . . Fuck it! All I'm trying to say, and I don't care if it sounds stupid, is that I'd like to get to *know* you."

She looked at him then, but as her face lifted, Edward lowered his. He had been embarrassed by the bathos in her voice and did not want to see its physical manifestation.

"I'd like to find out what you're really like," she said. "And for you to find out what I'm like, too. I'd like us to be able to discuss things. Oh, of course we'll disagree on practically everything. We're bound to. But at least if we could touch each other, affect each other, instead of behaving like actors in some long-running drawing-room comedy. I mean, after all, you're my *father."*

She stopped and Edward had to make a joke.

"Well, that's what your mother always insisted," he said. Then he added, "But anyway, I thought 'the family' was a thing of the past. I thought you modern young revolutionaries didn't approve of things like that. I thought you believed in community living and free love and having anyone over the age of thirty exterminated."

"For God's sake."

"Well, don't you? I mean to say, *you* seem to have rejected damn nearly everything your elders believe in. You dress like a gypsy. You use language that'd shame a barmaid. You lie in

13

bed till all hours of the morning, and when you *do* get up, it's only to lounge around looking bored out of your mind or smoking those vile cigarettes or listening to some God-awful row on the wireless."

"Okay. All right."

"No, it is not all right."

"Well, it's not important."

"Maybe not. But what is important, what really worries me, if you want to know, is this self-satisfied, know-it-all attitude you seem to have toward life. As though you'd got the faintest idea. As though you *could* have the faintest idea."

"What do you mean?"

"You know what I mean. Those slogans you keep coming out with. Those naïve, studenty pronouncements about 'workers' and 'capitalists' and 'underprivileged' and 'revolution.' As far as you're concerned, if something or somebody's anti-establishment, then they're right. Yes, that's just about as much thought as you've given it. I mean . . ."

Edward leaned over and picked up the copy of the *Evening Standard* that lay on the floor beside his chair.

"I mean, I dare say you think that just because this fellow van der Walt's a left-wing subverter, he had every right to blow the head off some innocent old night watchman. If it were a policeman who'd killed someone, however inadvertently, you wouldn't be so ready to defend him."

"I've never defended van der Walt."

"And what makes me laugh," Edward continued, "is that all your so-called opinions are based on absolutely no experience whatsoever. From the cradle onwards you've been protected from any sort of reality. Poverty! Repression! Corruption! You've only read about them, talked about them. Nice, neat theories from the lips of a sociology undergraduate or the pages of a Marxist textbook."

"Then perhaps you've given me the wrong education."

"What?"

"Perhaps you've given me the wrong education."

Olivia's eyes were sparkling. Her teeth, behind parted lips, were clenched.

Edward understood these signs, yet did not think of braking his attack on their account. Rather, they encouraged him. After all, wasn't it Olivia who had declared war in the first place? Hadn't she, ever since her arrival in his house, been goading him into just such an onslaught, with her assumptions of intellectual superiority, her nicely phrased criticisms, her disdainful, sighing silences, her blatant lack of gratitude? Well, then, now that she had finally got her way, had made him lose his temper, his dignity, must she not accept the consequences? If she thought she could retreat into tears and feminine emotionalism, she was very much mistaken, he thought.

"You know damn well you had the best bloody education money could buy," he said. "But speaking a couple of languages and knowing the economic causes of the Second World War doesn't mean you know the first thing about life. You only learn about that the hard way: by living it. So just wait till you've done a bit of living, will you, before you try to teach those of us who have what's right and what's bloody wrong."

"I'm not trying to *teach* you anything. Not *teach*. Just discuss. Just share."

"Oh, aren't you? What about last night before the cinema, the way you kept on and on, pontificating at Dick Hastings and me about the 'immorality' of selling arms! Have you any idea how childish you sounded? Or how rude you were being? Oh, and I'm quite sure you tell all your friends your father's a crook, too. I'm sure you regale them with how evil I am and how ashamed of me you are. Well, that's all right, but I'd find it slightly less impertinent if you didn't happen to be living off my 'immoral' earnings—in fact, if you had any sort of a job of your own."

He stopped. He picked up his brandy glass and dripped the contents down his throat.

Olivia said nothing.

All summer she had dreamed of such a confrontation with her father. Each day, each listless day as they had skirted round each other's feelings and let the heat evaporate their respective indignations, she had imagined just such an awakening. Yet now that it had happened, her emotion was one not of relief but of acute disappointment.

Nor was this disappointment only with her father. His responses to her request (his ridiculous, cliché-shaped misconceptions about "the young," his aggressive defensiveness) had not astonished her. What had been unexpected was that she, given the longed-for chance to justify her faith before him, should have been reduced to sullen, inarticulate self-pity.

Were she to speak now, as her attacker beckoned for the bill, she knew that her voice would crack between the strain of words she did not mean to say. Therefore she breathed deeply in and out and stared ahead of her and up at a dark shape on the cream-painted restaurant wall.

"Do you want to go to the ladies' room before we leave?"

"No, thank you," she said.

She heard the rustle of notes being unfolded, the ring of large coins dropping on a china plate.

"Shall we go, then?"

"All right."

She stood up. Across the table from her, her father stood up. Then, one behind the other, they moved between scattered, dying meals, like exhausted soldiers stumbling from a field of battle.

Outside, the air had begun to chill.

5

"At last, my little pigeons. At long, fucking last."

His left hip ached to the point of non-endurance and his gut was tight with impatience, yet as he muttered these words to himself, Michael O'Keefe grinned.

"At long, bloody last," he said, and the numbness that had been like a pad between his right shoulder and the tall paint-flaking pillar he had been leaning against expanded into living pain.

They were on the far side of the street from him: the man and his daughter. They stood a foot or so apart from each other, in the center of the pavement, he pulling at his shirt cuffs so that they should protrude beyond the end of his jacket sleeves, she with her arms crossed and her hands clutching her waist. After a few seconds they began to walk down the road, east past Shepherd's Market.

As they did so, Michael O'Keefe cast an imaginary line between himself and them. He waited until the line's angle across the road was at forty-five degrees; then he puckered his lips, spat a half-smoked cigarette to the ground, and stepped forward from the shadow. He did not need to look directly at his quarry in order to keep track of it. It was sufficient to glimpse a moving reflection in glass or a blur of activity on the periphery of his vision.

Not that Michael considered such precautions to be necessary. He had been following Edward Mannion for forty hours now and, during that time, had come to the conclusion that Mannion was too self-confident, too self-opinionated a bastard to dream that there might be those who wished him ill, or, if there were, that they would dare to realize their wishes: he stood and moved in an aura of security whose substance was money and power, and the longer this aura was left unassaulted, the stronger it grew, propagating itself like an amoeba.

The disjointed procession moved right, south between the railings and red-brick façades of Half Moon Street and toward Piccadilly. Michael decided that they must be heading for Green Park underground station. Two taxis had passed them and they had stopped neither. He was surprised, but not displeased.

His stomach, however, was still like a knotted rope inside him. Patience was not a quality with which he had been born, nor one he had grown to acquire. When expedient (as in the thirty years of his life it sometimes had been), he could convey a good impression of the virtue, could smile with his lips and curb the agitation of his limbs, but this performance gave him little satisfaction. On the contrary, its successful completion always left him with the taste of bile and a furious sense of self-disgust.

Tonight, however, it was more than ever critical that he repress himself, that he control the need to hurry events to their climax, to grab the reward for the hours he had spent lurking on street corners (while Mannion ate and drank, and was warm in a West End cinema) or trailing like a dog at the heels of his unaware master.

He had to keep the poison of waiting in, to swill it round and round his unopened mouth, because he appreciated (and this much more than the others had done) how important it was that his timing tonight should be perfect.

6

He had suggested that they travel home by underground.

Walking half a step behind him, listening to the syncopated echo of their footfall on the pavement, Olivia wondered whether this was meant to be a gesture of peace. It was an absurd idea, yet not inconceivable, that her father should have proposed a public method of transport as a concession to what he must see as her plebeian life-style. And it was certain that his tone, when now he spoke to her, had mellowed from shrill attack to easy conversation.

He said, *"Have* you decided what you're going to do now? I know it's not easy with an arts degree to find the right sort of job, but you must have some idea."

"I don't know. I need time to think about it, I suppose. I mean, I could always get a job in an office for now. You know, if you'd like some money towards the housekeeping, and so on."

"No, of course not. I didn't mean that at all. I'm sorry if it sounded like that—what I said earlier. It's really not what I meant at all."

"Okay. Sure," said Olivia. She knew that he was speaking the truth, yet knew, at the same, that he was lying.

He was not an ungenerous man, and there was a daughter whom he would have been delighted to support, to pamper, to shower with gifts and proud affection. That daughter, however, was not herself. She was another girl: more brilliant, more beautiful, more confident, less quarrelsome and questioning and rough. She would love Edward as a father, without considering his qualities as a man. She would be grateful to him. Oh, she would shock him sometimes, sometimes upset him, but whatever rules she broke, they would always be the rules of *his* game. It would have been so much easier to have been that daughter.

Edward's hand reached back to touch Olivia's elbow, and the two of them turned left, into Piccadilly.

There buses swayed past them, their illuminated windows exposing passengers not as the corporate mass they were in daytime but as vulnerable, isolated individuals. Between the buses, cars made their way home from the West End. Along the pavements, groups or pairs of middle-aged tourists strolled back to their hotels, the women in mink, the men in moccasins and checkered jackets.

Olivia thought, Perhaps I shouldn't have come back home at all.

Yet the decision to do so had not been made without care. She had guessed that there would be difficulties, disappointments, in any attempt to lay the ghost of a relationship that the letters between herself and her father had evoked. Their previous, amateur-theatrical encounters had warned her of this.

On the other hand, it had seemed right to try—important that the charade they had both been playing, for each other's benefit and their own, should be exposed to the daylight of reality. Thus might its tawdry artifice be seen for what it was, and possibly, she hoped, be cast aside in favor of a truer understanding.

There had been other reasons for the homecoming, expedient reasons: such as the need for a place to live until she found a job; the need of an environment free from university associations where she could sift the contents of her mind; the fact that Simon had left her, having been compelled to spend the summer with relatives in Canada. (Simon: whom she knew, through an acquaintance, to have been back in London for at least three days now and who still had not rung her.) But the desire to come to terms with her father had, she was certain, been the deciding factor.

For the last nine years she had been an observer of other people's families (the guest who was one of Jane's or Peter's "more agreeable friends," who was good with the younger children, who helped with the washing-up, who did not mind her meals on a tray in front of the television), and from this position she had come to appreciate the family unit more, perhaps, than those enmeshed within it.

As an amused, intrigued, and envious outsider, she had learned to love the qualities of loyalty, interdependence, tolerance, and respect that she sometimes saw therein; had learned also to loathe the cruelty, the exploitation, the bitter division that she had, from time to time, perceived.

Olivia had no brothers or sisters. Her mother was a photograph in a silver frame, a trunkful of folded, faded dresses, a ruby engagement ring (its gold worn thin) wrapped up in cotton wool. Her father alone was her family. Because of this, because he was not just a man but also a collective, he had assumed a symbolic nature alongside his personal one. To Olivia, particularly in the last two or three years (as the jolly, comfortable myth of the letters had coarsened into burlesque), he had become partially abstract: had become heritage and tradition and status quo.

And it was to *this* Edward Mannion, as much as to the man who had procreated her, raised her, given her blue eyes and a square chin, that she needed to establish her relationship.

7

At the far end of the platform, a drunk was singing. His voice reverberated around the tiled tunnel, sometimes harsh and clear, sometimes low and wordless like the gurgling of a water heater.

The song that he sang was a popular one of the day, intended for the lips of a young girl and concerned with the joys of being pregnant by the man one loves. Alternately vomited, then dribbled, from cracked purple lips, it was obscene.

> "How good to feel our love within me growing.
> How good to know it's safe within my womb."

At one moment, the hideous vocalist staggered three steps toward the rails, then three steps back, as though performing a dance. Edward was reminded of an old print he had once seen of a baited bear.

There were two slatted wooden seats on the platform. At the nearest of these, Edward stopped, watched while his daughter sat down, and placed himself beside her. Then he would have liked to wait in silence for the train. He would have liked to let his mind withdraw from the present and wander through carpeted halls of thought. He would have liked to leave the drunk, the blowing grit, the trampled cigarette butts, and the crumpled, shifting chocolate wrappers.

It was not that he found the underground station any more disgusting than the inside of a taxi. (A taxi had plastic seats and choking ashtrays and gave him no aesthetic pleasure, but was more convenient than the public transport when one was in a hurry; that was all.) It was that he regarded an underground train as a means of locomotion between two points, and was therefore impatient with those of its appendages that did not directly serve this function.

This evening, however, he could not ignore them. He had to remain conscious, because Olivia might interpret silence as a reopening of hostility. And Edward wanted to forget the unseemly row in the restaurant, to pretend it had not happened, to help his daughter believe it had not happened. He knew that the existence of an object or a person or a situation is dependent upon that existence being acknowledged.

Leaning forward and peering along the darkening curve of the tunnel from which the train would emerge, he said,

"Shouldn't be long now. Although you can never be sure these days. I believe they've got an acute labor shortage or something."

For a second he was worried lest even this mundane remark should have proved too provocative, should have provided Olivia with the ammunition for yet another sociological outburst, but his anxiety was needless.

Olivia said, "Yeah, I know. I read that."

"And the moment we get in, I'm going straight up to bed. I've got a meeting with the accountant at nine tomorrow, and at my advanced age you need your eight hours' sleep."

Edward left an automatic pause, but there was no reaction to the semi-joke.

"Anyway," he continued, "what are your plans for the morning?"

"I hadn't thought about it."

"Isn't that boyfriend of yours back yet?"

"What?"

"That young man you introduced me to in the spring. The one who had such intriguing theories about suicide. Isn't he back from—where was it? Australia?"

"Canada."

"That's right. Yes, that's right."

Edward leaned back in the wooden seat, raised his arms, and clasped the back of his neck with hands intertwined. A light had ignited in his head: an explanation (so obvious that he was amazed at his failure to see it before) of his daughter's boorish and anti-social behavior.

She was missing her boyfriend. Her boyfriend had been away for some weeks on a visit to relatives, and she was missing him.

Edward was warmed by a flow of pity for the girl beside him, who was not only lonely for her lover but who, in spite of an arrogant fluency in the languages of sex and biology and politics, was incapable of voicing the words that would describe and therefore make bearable her loneliness.

"I expect you'll be pleased to see him again, after all these weeks," he said.

The indicator board above the track still gave no sign of an approaching train, but Edward was happy now to wait.

It looked as though there would not be a train for a minute or two, at least. With the exception of a drunken old Irishman, Mannion and his daughter were the only people waiting on the westbound platform. On the eastbound were a pair of lovers (she with her back against the wall, he with his mouth on hers and his hands spread-eagled across the tiles above her head) and a huddled, hopeless black woman in a green wool coat.

Michael O'Keefe was riding the "down" escalator from the ticket machines to the platforms, and as the roof above him leveled out, as the situation below him clarified itself, his mind underwent a metamorphosis.

Instead of twisted frustration, a cool, sharp, quivering alertness began to sing through his skull. External sound became refined to a single, high-pitched note. Vision was blurred at the edges, yet at the center was more intense than before. Feeling drained from the surface of his skin to concentrate itself within him.

At school, the only sport that Michael had enjoyed was swimming. Poised on the uppermost diving board, focusing on the one point in the water that his body would hit, he had experienced an elation identical to this present one.

"This is it, lad. This is what you've been waiting for. Just him and her and no one to interrupt us till I'm done."

He filled his lungs. He closed his eyes; then opened them and stepped from the escalator onto the platform.

Olivia noticed him coming toward her, heard the padding of his soft-soled shoes, saw the blue of his denim. She did not, however, register his presence as a thought; her head was too full of herself. When he stopped in front of the bench on which she was sitting and began to speak to her father, she assumed, as though in a dream where improbable things pass unquestioned, that they must be business acquaintances or friends. It was her father's reaction that warned her otherwise.

"No, I would *not,*" she heard him say, and the indignation in his voice awoke her, so that she saw them both.

The seated man was drawn into himself and up, his shoulders back, his fists clenched on his thighs. Across his for once unguarded face was just such an expression of disdain as a comic might project through trickling custard pie.

The standing man, feet apart, hands in the pockets of his jeans, swayed backward and forward and thrust his chin in the air. On the chin was a short, dense beard. Above it, red lips, flared nostrils, a high forehead, and receding, shoulder-length hair.

"Come on, man," he said.

Olivia said, "What does he want?"

"Nothing," said her father.

"That's not right."

The newcomer turned to face her. Olivia saw that his eyes were small and brown, yet glowing, like topaz with light behind it.

Removing the hands from his pockets and holding them, palms forward, an inch or two from his body, he said, "I asked the guy if he'd like to give me a cigarette."

The "a" in "asked" was pronounced as the "u" in "bus" should be, and there was a general flatness in the voice that, without amounting to an accent, went some way toward locating its owner both socially and geographically. Olivia gathered that he came from the Midlands, or possibly the North, the educated son of an uneducated family. She heard something else in his voice, a dissonance between the meaning of the words and their sound, a pressure beneath the calm.

Puzzled, she looked from the younger man to her father, who said, "It's all right. I've told him that I've no wish to give him a cigarette, and now he's going to leave us alone."

Olivia opened her mouth to protest. Her father did not smoke. He could, with honesty, have told the younger man this. There had been no need for him to be insulting.

Some rein, however (a sense of loyalty, a fear of appearing naïve?), checked her. She drew her lips together.

"Are you telling me to piss off?" the bearded man asked.

"That's right," said her father.

Then the bearded man said, "I wouldn't do that if I was you, Mr. Edward Mannion."

The silence that followed this remark lasted no longer than two or three seconds, yet its depth was absolute. Even the drunkard had stopped his singing, and leaned, head slumped forward, against a fire hose.

Olivia remembered a car crash she had once been involved in with Simon, remembered the moments between the first, almost unnoticed skid and the final sickening metal-to-metal bang.

This time there was no explosion, nor were the changes wrought by the bearded man's pronouncement of her father's name as obvious as those suffered by Simon's friend's car. The bearded man was smiling now, that was all, and her father's attitude, when at last he spoke, had twisted from aggression to defense.

"What's that supposed to mean?" he said.

"What's what supposed to mean?"

"Don't be so bloody clever. You just tried to threaten me."

" 'Tried,' Mr. Mannion?"

"All right, we've already established that you know who I am. Now, what's it all about?"

"Nothing. Nothing, Edward. Why? What *should* it be about?"

"How the hell should I know?"

"Exactly. How should you?"

There was a second silence, longer than the first, more fidgety. Olivia's initial bewilderment began to sort itself into several distinct emotions.

The first and predominant of these was frustration. It was as though the scene being played out before her were taking place behind glass, behind a television screen, with herself an important spectator powerless to do or say anything that would alter its fantastic course.

The second was disgust at the stranger's aggressive and apparently calculated rudeness. The third, for her father's lack of dignity when confronted by such rudeness, shame.

The fourth, for no one reason, fear.

She said, "For God's sake! If you've got something to say, say it."

The bearded man said, "Okay," then extracted from the breast pocket of his jacket a cigarette, which he lit.

"Okay."

He sat himself down on the bench. He blew a slow barb of smoke across the faces of his audience.

He said, "Okay. How about . . . guns?"

"Now, look here," Edward said.

"Beirut?"

"I'm . . ."

"A little fat Arab called—?"

"I'm warning you."

"But, Edward! It was your daughter asked me to talk."

"You know damn well this has got nothing to do with my daughter."

"Well, that's up to you."

"Is it?"

Lips pressed, Edward glanced at the indicator board, then up the empty escalators.

"All right," he said. "Olivia, you'd better go. Take a taxi. I'll see you later, at home."

"Why?" she asked.

"Just go."

"Look, haven't I got some sort of right—?"

"I'll talk to you later."

He flipped open his gold-edged pigskin wallet and withdrew a note from it.

"No, thank you," said Olivia, standing up.

"Now, come on. There's no need to be childish."

"I'll see you later, then."

She took a couple of steps backward, turned, and walked along the platform, then up the moving staircase, past the ticket machines, and out into the street.

8

The number 9 bus route did not pass through Chelsea. It lay about a mile to the north, along Knightsbridge, the Kensington Road, and High Street Kensington. Olivia was aware of this fact, yet when a number 9 bus, its progress thwarted by a jam at Hyde Park Corner, drew to a halt beside her, she hesitated only a moment before climbing aboard it.

She had scarcely reached the upper deck when the traffic began to move again and she was pitched into a rearward seat.

The conductress, who had been sitting up at the front, her arms limp, her fat legs sprawled apart, heaved herself to her feet and rolled along the gangway.

"High Street Kensington, please," said Olivia.

"Which bit, love?"

"Just before the cinema."

"That'll be ten."

The ticket machine whirred. The relevant coins exchanged hands.

"Feeling all right, are you, love?"

Olivia nodded her head and smiled.

"Yes, thanks."

The conductress acknowledged the lie without resentment. There was, after all, no help that she could have offered. She descended the circular staircase. Olivia listened to her go.

The loneliness that had choked her as she waited outside her father's club now rose with greater concentration in her throat. She understood how much she had been counting on a successful outcome to this evening's conversation with her father. She had told herself that it did not matter, that the important thing was to *make* the stand, to discover, once and for all, the nature of their relationship. But now that she knew it, the emptiness of it, the hypocrisy of it, she was frightened.

She had made no preparation for such an eventuality. She had not believed enough that it would happen. The incident in the underground station, however, with its disgusting conclusion, had been like a miracle play staged to eliminate doubt. No rescue would come from that quarter. She was alone; and the bus lurched on past expensive flats and, to the right, the leaf-mottled gray of the park.

9

The poem was an abortion. He had written it down too soon. Succumbing to the temptations of an ingenious phrase, he had deprived the thought of its rightful gestation time, the result of which was fourteen lines a schoolboy would have been ashamed of. Simon Shaw puffed through his nose and tore into pieces the paper on which he had been writing.

Beside him on the floor was an ashtray. Having stuffed its bowl with the paper pieces, he took from the rim a cigarette of marijuana and tobacco. For a while he smoked and, alternately, drank white wine from a mug.

The room upon whose carpet he sat, his back supported by the drop of a sofa seat, gave an impression of spaciousness unrelated to its size. The principal cause of this illusion was a lack of furniture: the sofa, an armchair, a phonograph, a gate-leg table, and some built-in bookshelves, which were light with a few impersonal paperbacks, were all that the place contained. In addition to this, the walls had been painted white and, from baseboard to ceiling molding, were distinguished by no other features than one blocked-in fireplace with a mirror above it and two high windows.

One of the windows was open at the bottom. Through the space thus formed, the soft night fluttered and hummed, not entering the room, not forcing its way across it as a draft would, but confining its activity to dusty windowsill and pleated curtains, like a dying insect.

When the joint had become too hot to smoke, Simon extinguished it, pushed himself upright, and walked to the phonograph. From a slim pile of records, he selected "L'Après-midi d'un Faune" to put upon the turntable. A few seconds later the music of Debussy crackled into its life of stirring spring sexuality and Simon returned to the sofa. There he closed his eyes.

He did not think. He found it difficult to think when not in motion. (The now discarded poem had been conceived while pouring wine, while buttering bread, while walking up and down the kitchen, eating.) Instead, he indulged in his favorite form of non-physical masturbation: imagining himself to be stretched out, semiconscious, across the cotton sheet of an enormous double bed, while a woman, whom he could not see but whose voice was deep and whose smell was expensive, stroked her hands over his body and commented to some third person on its unbelievable beauty.

"Look at his hips, how slim they are, and the way his flesh pulls tight across his stomach. And oh, the poor boy"—running her fingertips along his forehead—"where can he have got that terrible scar?"

In fact, Simon's face was marred by nothing more interesting than a couple of moles, but in his fantasy existence a blue-white, jagged furrow ran deep from hairline to eyebrow, arousing pity and desire in all who saw it.

"And see how his mouth—"

The doorbell brayed. Simon sat up. Still flushed, he reached the intercom in the hall.

"Hello?"

"It's Olivia."

"Livvy?"

"Yes. Please can I come up?"

He pressed the button that would release the lock on the front door of the flats. He waited to hear her footsteps on the communal stairs. Then he returned to the living room and stood in front of the mirror, not with the intention of rectifying his appearance but of remembering it.

"Simon! Your door isn't open!"

"Okay. I'm coming."

10

The flat had changed.

It had not, in any obvious way, been altered, yet Olivia knew that it had changed. Its temperature had lowered, its texture had smoothed itself out, its color had purified to monochrome.

In the days when Simon's sister had inhabited it and had allowed the two of them to spend weekends there while she was staying with friends in the country, there had at least been an impression of homeliness about the place. Posters had been fixed to the walls with tacks, clothes had bestrewn the floor, plates smeared with old risotto had lurked beneath tables and chairs. The bathroom basin had been stuffed with eternally soaking washing and the bedroom had overflowed with half-packed suitcases and scarves and boxes of internal sanitary protection.

It was true that, at the time, Olivia had been disdainful of these signs of hectic femininity, had despised the lack of books, the superabundance of trivia. Yet now, seeing the impersonal, station-waiting-room alternative, she remembered them with nostalgia.

Tonight it was as though Simon and she had met by accident in some far transit camp: people who had loved each other once but whom the callousness of war had dragged apart. Even the music coming from the phonograph was strange, was unrelated to their common past.

She would have commented on these things had she not sensed that Simon was a part of them. More, that he was the cause of them, that they emanated from his person. She wondered how she would have found the flat had she warned him of her arrival.

Doubt came to her, a sense of guilt, as though it had been wrong of her to come unannounced. Her logic denied this, said that it was Simon who was in the wrong, who should have let her know that he was back, but doubt prevailed.

Searching, probing, she said, "I didn't know you liked Debussy."

"What?"

They were sitting side by side on the sofa, their bodies turned in toward each other, but not touching.

"Debussy," said Olivia. "I didn't know you liked him."

"Oh, well, so-so. Hey, some more wine?"

"No, thanks."

32

"Been getting pissed with the old man, have you?"

"Not really. Anyhow, how was it? Canada?" she asked.

"Oh . . ."

He told her: about Toronto and Red Indians and hamburgers and cheesecake, about Montreal and speaking French and the Niagara Falls. He enjoyed describing things and, from time to time, succeeded in making Olivia smile. He also moved closer to her, touched her with his uneasy body, held one of her hands between his long, hard fingers. Olivia was not misled by these gestures, however, knowing that Simon used physical contact as a method of eliminating tension rather than creating it. She realized that, once again in their relationship, it was she who would have to be the protagonist if any kind of forward motion was to be achieved. Simon had always preferred to tread water than to swim against unfavorable currents.

Therefore she said, "This evening—I only came here on the off chance. Someone said they'd seen you, but, of course, I didn't know."

"Oh, yeah. Yeah. Yeah, that'd've been Teddy Royce. I bumped into him in that pub round the corner. You know, the one with the terrace outside, where they've got such fantastic food. No, I've been back about a week now, I suppose. You're not annoyed I didn't ring you? Are you, Liv? I mean, you know what it's like, readjusting and all that. And anyway most of this time's been spent at my parents'. I really had to see them a *bit*. I really couldn't just pop down there for the afternoon and say, 'Well, hello, here I am, back safe and sound from the other side of the world. How are you? Goodbye.' Could I? *Could* I? Well, you know. It's the same with you and your father. Isn't it?"

"Okay. But you were actually intending to get in touch with me sometime?"

"Of course I was."

Olivia said, "Why 'of course'?"

"What on earth are you getting at?"

"Nothing. It's just that you made it sound like a duty, you know, or a habit. Not something you wanted to do. I mean, if that's . . . if you *don't* want to see me, then you know I'd be much happier if you told me."

"Oh, really, Liv."

"Well?"

"Well, of course I . . . What's the matter with you? What is it? I refuse to believe it's just because I didn't ring you you're so upset. After all, you must've known I'd've gone down to Kent first. I had to collect the keys to this place, apart from anything else."

"Don't they have telephones in Kent? We do in Chelsea."

"I've already explained, I wanted to get myself sorted out. You know what it's like when you've been away a long time. And there were people I had to see: aunts and uncles and so on, to tell them how their beloved offspring were getting on in the young country. You know: what sort of neighbors had they got, and did the grandchildren speak with horrid American accents? That sort of shit. Well, it just seemed pointless ringing you up and saying, 'Hi, I'm back, but I can't see you yet.' No? I mean, it'd've been so . . ."

Squeezing his lips together, he drew a lot of air into his lungs, then, smiling, released it.

"Oh, messy, I suppose," he said. "Untidy. You know what I'm like. I wanted to get all the bothery little things out of the way before seeing you, so that then I could concentrate on you properly."

This speech should have reassured Olivia. Not because it contained a convincing explanation of why Simon should have allowed seven days to pass without getting in touch with her (which it didn't), but because it was the kind of speech that the old Simon would have made, the Simon whom she had last seen, nervous and affectionate and wearing a striped silk scarf she had bought him, by the automatic sliding doors of the Cromwell Road air terminus. The ingredients were all so familiar: the pleas for approbation, the escape into humor, the use of logic to explain illogicality. And they should have reassured Olivia.

But they didn't. Instead, like a sound of tapping half heard through the moaning of wind and the slamming of doors on a stormy night, they illuminated in her imagination a dread so vivid that all else (the sense of proportion, the awareness of probability to be seen there as a rule) was plunged into obscurity.

While this state of artificial lighting lasted, Olivia saw that she had never known Simon, that he had always lied to her, that her relationship with him had been as untrue as that which she had with her father; that when he had said, "I love you," he had meant, "It's socially both acceptable and convenient to have a girl friend and you fulfill that role as well as anyone else, for the moment"; that those qualities *she* had admired in *him* (his tolerance, his gentleness, his laughter, and his clean good looks) were shells behind which carelessness and cowardice and selfishness and narcissism hid.

This vision, or delusion (for after it was gone she was not sure which it had been), didn't stay long, yet it left its memory behind. The photograph of its happening was printed on Olivia's vision in such a way that the strangeness of the flat's appearance ceased to be important, since even the room she had shared with Simon while at university, with its Indian cotton bedspread, its substructure of books, its skylight, and its illustrated walls, would, through her present eyes, have seemed unfamiliar.

"You're pretty angry, aren't you?" asked Simon.

"No, I'm not angry."

"Well, upset."

Awaiting an answer, he watched the muscles clench and relax, clench and relax, in Olivia's face. The accusation implicit in these quiet gestures of unhappiness annoyed him. It was as though he were being criticized for having failed in a responsibility that he had never agreed to undertake, that he had been careful to *avoid* undertaking. That he and Olivia were lovers was not (and they had agreed on this) a contract of exclusivity. She had no right to condemn him for having fulfilled a natural duty toward his parents.

Yet it was not just condemnation that he saw in the girl's troubled face. There was something else: a turning away, a series of shutters dropping behind the eyes.

Anxiety replaced annoyance. If she refused to put her accusation into words, then he would be unable to defend himself without implying an awareness of the crime. Yet it was important that she understood him to be in the right.

"Come on, Liv, what's up?" he asked.

By withholding the full extent of her blame, she was insulting him. She was turning away from him not in pain but in contempt.

"Do you think I'll shout at you?" he said. "Or laugh at you? Surely you know me better than that."

"I don't know."

"What do you mean, you don't know?"

"I don't know how well I know you."

"Oh, for God's sake, if you're going to be metaphysical. . . . No, all right, I'm sorry. But it's not easy, you know, with you behaving like a tragic muse and me not certain what I'm supposed to do about it."

He reached for the bottle of Yugoslav Riesling and divided the last of it between her mug and his. He pressed his mug to his lips and stared at her over its rim.

He said, "Do you hate me?"

"Hate you?"

"Yes. I mean, while I've been away, perhaps. Have you decided that you hate me?"

"Don't be silly."

"All right, we're both being silly. But if it isn't that . . . Has something *happened* to you, Liv?"

"No, I don't think so. I don't know."

"It has! Well, why didn't you tell me? Do you think I'm such a heartless bastard? Okay, don't answer that. But why didn't you say?"

Simon smiled and squeezed Olivia's square, strong hands between his.

"What is it, Liv?" he asked.

A happiness welled up in him, a sense of impending victory, of balance about to be achieved. When she said "For God's sake, Simon, please, just don't go on asking those stupid questions," it was as though, at the start of an erection, she had kneed him in the crotch.

Pain, humiliation, and, most of all, a sense of frustrated intent left him breathless. His throat tightened. Tears leaped to the back of his eyes. His mouth jerked in small electric movements as he fumbled to his feet and turned his back on her, as he took a cigarette from the arm of the sofa and lit it.

He knew that he was overreacting, that Olivia had not intended so great an injury. (She was clumsy sometimes, but never cruel.) This knowledge, however, did nothing to lessen his pain.

"Darling, I'm sorry. I didn't mean it to sound quite like that. It just came out. I am sorry. Really. Simon?"

"Yes?"

He forced himself to smile. He couldn't bear that her apologies might solidify into pity, or scorn.

"Simon? Okay?"

"Of course," he said.

He turned to face her.

"You were absolutely right," he said. "I was behaving like the Spanish Inquisition on a wet Monday. It was unforgivable of me. I can only say that 'I don't know what come over me, Your Honor.'"

"It was just that I've had a bad evening with Daddy. . . ."

"Oh, well, then all is explained. Heaven protect us from our families. I mean, mine's delightful, but a few days in close proximity with them's enough to last one quite a while. All those rituals and heightened emotions. And that terrifying loss of privacy."

"Well that's not quite—"

"No, I know. It's not *quite* the same for you. But I should think one father could get just as claustrophobic as two parents and three siblings if he put his mind to it. Especially *your* papa. Would you like some more wine? There's another bottle in the kitchen somewhere. Or, at least, I'm pretty sure there is."

"No, thank you."

"Coffee?"

"No, I . . ." Olivia groped for her velvet bag and stood up.

Simon watched her, searching her light blue eyes for a sign that the shutters against him had lifted.

When he saw that they had not, anger stabbed him, reawakening the pain that he had thought anesthetized by chatter. For a moment then he hated her, with a hatred that wanted to drag her toward him, not let her escape.

"You're not staying the night, then?" he asked. "I mean, of course, you don't have to. I just wondered."

"No. No, I think not. I think I ought to get back."

"Fine. Well, have you got enough money for a taxi?"

"Yes. Thanks."

"Good. I'll see you downstairs, then."

"It doesn't matter."

"Well, that's all right."

He moved ahead of her to the door of the flat and opened it. She tucked her hair behind her ears and came toward him. As she reached him, he said, "Jesus, I'm mad, I'd forgotten. Teddy Royce told me to ask you and I'd . . . Well, it just went clean out of my head. He's having a party, tomorrow, at his place. You'll come, won't you?"

"Yes. All right," she said.

"Well, fine. Look, I'll pick you up at your place, shall I? About nineish?"

"If you like."

"Why not? It seems sensible."

He followed the line of her gaze and saw that his arm was stretched across the doorway, blocking her exit. He lowered it.

"See you tomorrow, then," he said.

"Yes."

She went past him, into the echoing dark of the comunal hallway and staircase.

"Night, Liv," he said.

"Good night, Simon."

She didn't turn. She didn't kiss him.

11

Edward Mannion's study was on the top floor of his Chelsea house, at the back, overlooking the garden. On the same floor were his bedroom and intercommunicating dressing room. Below, there was a bathroom, a spare room (at present occupied by Olivia), and, below that, at street level, a drawing room and dining room. The kitchen was in the basement.

Edward had bought the house a year after his wife's death, the matrimonial home in Cliveden Place having proved too large, too reverberant with memories, for a widower. It had, in the early nineteenth century, been a workman's terraced cottage, narrow, with small rooms stacked one on top of the other, and a straight simplicity of style. Edward had had it modernized and decorated, had moved in, and had lived there ever since, returning to it from his trips abroad—as a cuckoo, having called the hour, slides back into its clock.

He didn't love the place. The furniture, modern and meaningless, had been chosen by an interior designer. The pictures, for all that some were original and most were expensive, aroused in him as little emotion or thought as did the curtains, carpets, and chair covers. There were no ornaments: no unofficial souvenirs of people or events. All was tasteful, smart, and tidy, and if by chance some breakage or disruption did occur, it was restored to this state, without delay, by Mrs. Clifford, the daily cleaning woman.

The study was the one exception to this rule. Here Edward had allowed himself to expand beyond the confines of his body, to spread in fans of closely written paper across the desk of his young manhood, to bespatter mantelpiece and chest of drawers with photographs (of a wartime group of Royal Engineers, of restaurant tables crowned with smirking faces, of his wife), to line the shelves that climbed from floor to ceiling with volumes of firearms and novels by Galsworthy. There was a key to the door of the study. Mrs. Clifford never entered that room.

At five past midnight on the morning of the Tuesday of that week, Edward sat in the heavy, curved-back swivel chair that he had bought for seven and six in 1939 and drummed with his fingers on the embossed-leather top of his desk. He had not taken off his jacket, nor had he changed his shoes for patent-leather slippers as he usually did upon returning home at night. Between his eyebrows a vertical line was sunk. His lower lip was lifted across the upper.

It was not the threat of the young man in the underground that was upsetting him so, but his impudence, the fact that he had had the *impudence* to threaten. It was as though a mouse had strolled onto his shoe, had settled there, and had refused to move.

No, that was wrong. It was not as ridiculous as that, not as quaint or amusing.

Edward thrust with his feet against the floor and, arms still stretched toward the desk top, tilted back in his chair. He stared through the top pane of the window in front of him. A sky like crude oil slid thick and black across the moon, smearing it, and he thought, No, not nearly so funny.

He knew, were it to come to a showdown between them (himself and the young man who had refused to give his name), that it would be he who would emerge the winner. He knew his hand was the stronger of the two, his skill and experience greater. This same experience, however, showed him that the game would be neither easy nor clean. The end result might be inevitable, but the playing that led to this end would be difficult, dangerous, and, possibly, destructive enough to debase the cup of victory from silver to hollow tin.

"Damn him, the cocksure little bastard!" he said to himself.

Nor was it only the young man's effrontery that annoyed him, but his bad taste, his lack of style, the way he had dropped his hints about people and places with the crudity of a drunkard explaining an already obvious, never amusing joke. And after Olivia had been sent away, he had continued to crow. He had become a horrible, gloating child at a card table: "I've got a king. And an ace. I bet you didn't know *that.*"

Edward had been forced to acknowledge that he had not known, that he had not even been aware of his opponent's existence. Yet now that he did, it was absurd to expect him to be frightened.

He was, however, upset. He *had* been inconvenienced. There was no point in pretending that these things were not true.

Slamming the seat of his chair into its horizontal position, he reached out for the desk telephone extension, tucked the receiver between his shoulder and chin, and dialed a series of numbers.

"Dick?"

"Speaking."

The voice at the other end of the line was furry with sleep.

"Did I wake you?"

"Edward?"

"Yes. Were you in bed?"

"Still am. Still am."

"Sally there?"

"Was when I last looked. Still, you never know your luck."

There followed a grunting and puffing and mumble of words.

"Dick," said Edward.

"I'm with you, old chap."

"Good. Now, listen. Don't say anything, just listen. I want you to find out everything you can about this fellow I'm going to describe to you. All right? Okay. Middle height. Say, five foot ten, eleven. Brown hair. A beard; though of course that could be recent. Round about twenty-nine or thirty and a northern sort of accent. He wears jeans and so on. You know, long-hair-and-dirty-fingernails brigade. And's a bit of a hustler. Now, he must have some connection either with our business or someone who knows about our business. Don't know what it is, but there's got to be a link. All right? Do you think you can do that for me?"

"Yes, right you are. But . . . I mean, you don't mean right now, do you?"

"No, of course not. Only, I'm not going to be in the office till late tomorrow and I'd like you to get cracking on it first thing."

"Oh, fine. And anything in particular?"

"What d'you mean?"

"To find out. Anything in particular?"

"Just *anything*. Look, I know it's not much to go on, not even a name, but see what you can ferret out. Work on the Middle East angle. He either knows or has heard of Khalil, so he could be in the drugs game. Old fatso's got his fingers in a lot more pies than ours, you know. Or . . ."

Edward moved the telephone receiver to his other ear and, with his right hand, drew an invisible circle on the desk top.

"Or you could try Jo'burg," he said.

"Oh. Oh, I see. Oh, it's . . ." The voice on the other end of the line trailed off.

"Yes. So you'll see what you can do, won't you?"

"Right you are."

"And I'm sorry about waking you, Dick. Please give Sally my deepest apologies. Good night."

Edward replaced the receiver in its cradle and, for half a minute, sat silent, watching it lie there. Then he shook his head, stood up, and walked to the study door.

He had entered his bedroom and was preparing to set the alarm clock that stood by the pillow of his single bed when he remembered that Olivia had not yet returned to the house. He listened. No sound came from the residential side street below him. Farther away, like a river, the city's traffic rolled, but around him was only ticking, radiator-dripping silence. Not four feet away from him, behind plaster and lath, a person was probably sleeping or reading or making love, yet to Edward, at that moment, nothing was real but the silence.

He was used to being alone. Since Caroline's death, and in spite of an active, business-generated social life, he had been more often alone than not. Yet at that moment, as the alarm clock ticked and cooling water dripped in the radiator pipes, there sprang from his stomach, up his throat, and along the roof of his mouth, a ridiculous need to call out, "Someone, come, talk to me, touch me, help me."

He considered ringing Dick Hastings again, heard the sleepy, puzzled, attempting-to-be-jovial reply, and the desire passed. Instead, he got undressed, put on his pajamas, his slippers, and his dressing gown, and went downstairs to await Olivia's return.

12

She had walked. Although she had had enough money for a taxi, she had walked.

Arms swinging, feet pounding, thoughtless and without sensation, she had walked from Simon's flat to her father's house.

Having reached the front door, she leaned against it and fumbled in her bag for the knot of string that held her keys. A wash of tiredness broke over her and, stepping inside the entrance hall, she welcomed it.

"Olivia."

She spun. She hadn't noticed, from outside, that the drawing-room light was on. A wall smacked hard against her shoulder blades as she answered, "Yes?"

"Is that you?"

His footsteps preceded him, soft across Axminster carpet, his footsteps and the swish of loose material.

"That you, Olivia?" he repeated as the slit of light from the drawing room grew wider, to reveal a faceless silhouette.

"Hello, Daddy," she said.

"Have you any idea what time it is?"

Still she couldn't see his face, only hear that his voice was constricted, only feel the ether-coldness of emotion suppressed. These signals startled her more than the sound of his calling had done. Forgetting her exhaustion, she removed her weight from the wall and took it back onto her feet.

"No," she said. "No. Is it very late?"

"It's bloody nearly one o'clock. But that's hardly the point, is it? You seem to forget that the last time I saw you, you were leaving Green Park underground station with—or so I assumed—every intention of coming straight back here. That was nearly two hours ago. What happened?"

Olivia frowned. Her father's presence was beginning to materialize, to solidify (from sound and shadow and waves of feeling) into the shape of a fifty-six-year-old man. She saw that he was wearing a navy-blue silk dressing gown, drawn together above the waist by a knotted sash; that his legs, protruding below, were covered by striped pajamas; that his ankles were white; that his otherwise flattened hair was lifted above his forehead in a crest. She saw that the skin around his mouth was bloodless. The alarm that had revived her a minute before now, under the warmth of this recognition, softened into compassion and regret.

At first, however, she was surprised at the dimness with which these feelings came to her, as though they were farther away than she had known. She tugged them closer, reproaching herself for her lack of consideration, reminding herself that her father was not, after all, a young man, telling herself that she *might* have been overhasty, even vicious, in her condemnation of him.

An incident, dating from the period between her mother's death and her own subsequent departure for boarding school, rose to the surface of her memory. She was in the master bedroom of the house in which, at that time, they had still been living. Her father and she were fighting.

Olivia felt the burning of his grip around her wrists, the swelling of veins in face and neck as they struggled against each other. Then she felt her head go down, felt her teeth sink into an area of flesh exposed on her opponent's arm, her teeth trying to meet through that flesh. And then one of her hands was free. She was swinging it upward. She was staggering back, as he, her father, moaned and clasped his face, blood squeezing in scarlet bubbles between his fingers. She saw how his eyes were rimmed with tears from the pain she

45

had inflicted on his nose. She experienced the nausea as triumph somersaulted into regret, as victory curdled into guilt, as freedom became loss.

She said, "I'm sorry, Daddy."

"I'm not asking you to apologize. I'd just like to know where you've been. For all I knew, you might've been killed, run over—anything."

"Yes, I know. I didn't think."

She walked toward him and he stepped aside to let her pass into the drawing room. When she had reached the leather, chrome-based armchair and had dropped her body into it, he followed. He stood in the middle of the room, six feet away from her.

"Well?" he asked. "Where *have* you been?"

"I went to see Simon. The boy you were talking about before."

"You said he hadn't come back yet."

"I didn't know if he had. Someone, a friend, said they'd seen him. . . ."

"Where does he live?"

"Oh, quite near here. His parents have got a place off High Street Kensington."

"And you went there? When you left me, you went straight there?"

"Yes."

"And you didn't even know if he'd be in?"

"No. He was, though."

"Well, I can only hope he was pleased to see you."

"Not particularly," said Olivia.

She looked across at her father. "I know I shouldn't have just *gone* there," she said.

"I must say, if someone hadn't bothered to get in touch with *me*—"

"No, I didn't mean that. I meant . . . I meant I shouldn't have just gone there without telling you. It's just that after that—scene at the underground, I felt so angry and . . . Oh, I felt slighted, I suppose, and rejected, as though you couldn't trust me. I mean, I'm sure I was being stupid and that you couldn't possibly start explaining then and there. . . ."

"I see."

Toward the end of Olivia's speaking, her father had moved away from the center of the room and gone to stand by the velvet-curtained window that spread across one end of it, so that now, when he answered, it was with his back to her.

"I see," he said, and it was as though he were addressing not her but himself.

Olivia leaned forward in her seat. She did not believe that he had, in fact, understood her. If he had, what reason could there be for his attempting to escape from her like this? If he had seen that she was apologizing to him, why should he want to avoid acknowledging the apology?

She said, "I'm just trying to say that I know it was stupid for me to go rushing off to Simon like that, like some sulky little girl. Only, you know, I was pretty upset."

"Of course. That's quite understandable."

He was looking at her again. His head was nodding and his eyes were half closed in an expression representative of acceptance. Yet still Olivia had the impression that he was slipping away from her, was removing himself from the circle of her influence. She would have gone to him and touched him had such an action not been unimaginable. As it was, any connection between them would have to be made with words. Words, which had proved so treacherous in the past.

Staring at him, she tried to project onto the nodding, enigmatic face the face that he had shown her in the hallway, but in vain. The features were the same. The hair still rose askew above his forehead. Yet, added together, these things no longer totaled up to a hurt and worried father, but to a competent man in the process of extricating himself from an unpleasant situation.

"Well, you are going to tell me what it was all about, aren't you?" she said. "I mean, now. What was he after, that guy?"

"Oh, him!" said her father; then, in the tone of one describing an ill-behaved but treasured puppy, added, "The stupid bastard."

Olivia was horrified.

She had given her father a second chance, had offered him her trust for a second time, and he, for a second time, had brushed it away.

"Oh, him. The stupid bastard."

Did he believe that she could be satisfied with such cheap sweets, or didn't he care?

"Is that all you've got to say?" she asked.

"What do you mean?"

"I mean, *is that all you've got to say?*"

"There's no need to shout. I heard you the first time. Now, pull yourself together, stop behaving like an hysterical idiot, and tell me what the hell you *think* he wanted?"

"I don't *know.* How *can* I know?"

"But you were there. You heard what he said."

"No I didn't. Well, only that he seemed to know your name. And something about—I don't know—guns. And Arabs."

"Exactly. There's nothing more to it than that. The fool—goodness knows how, but somehow—had heard that part of my business is conducted with Arab countries. And he didn't approve. He's a fellow-traveling Zionist or something, I suppose. Anyway, he'd decided he was going to insult me about it, that's all. Well, I dare say *you* think he was quite within his rights."

"What do you mean, 'insult'?"

"Oh, get heavy, get tough, throw his weight about. Accuse me of being an anti-Semite. Call me a Nazi."

"What did you do?"

"What d'you think I did?"

"You didn't hit him, did you?" Olivia asked.

The idea that her father might have done this appalled her, yet, remembering the lack of verbal control he had exhibited toward the young man in the underground, a similar lack of physical control did not seem impossible. Also, she understood how little a man with her father's war experience would appreciate being called a Nazi by someone too young to remember what the word had once meant.

Thirdly, if there had been a fight, then this would explain her extempore and hurtful dismissal from the scene of action.

"Did you?" she asked.

"Yes. Yes, I showed the puppy just how far he could go."

In the second after her father said this, there flowed through Olivia's body a stream of great warmth. She didn't approve of what he had confessed to, but her disapproval was extinguished at birth by the rush of sensations accompanying it: by the relief of enlightenment, by the sympathy of understanding, by the pride of trust.

Then her father moved his head.

It was an unimportant gesture, intended as punctuation between the end of one subject of conversation and the beginning of another, yet as he made it Olivia saw that, once again, he had been lying to her. She could not have explained what, but there was something in his eyes or in the movement of the head itself that caught and amplified the falsehood that had echoed through everything he had said to her since they had entered the room that early morning.

She could not even have sworn that he had, in fact, lied. She only knew that if it was the truth he had given her, then it was an incomplete, a censored, a flawed truth.

And there was nothing that she could do about it. Any question she asked now, any answer her father gave, would resonate with that same foul echo. She had known it before, but the confirmation was at least as horrible as the original knowledge.

"So, anyway, now we've cleared that one up, how about us both getting a bit of sleep?" said Edward.

"Yes, okay," said Olivia.

"All right?"

"Yes."

They went out into the hall, Edward turning the lights off behind them.

13

The coffee was a pale dun color and lurked in a cup as insipid as itself: a light blue, gold-rimmed, fluted cup of inferior china, with part of its handle missing. Michael O'Keefe studied the coffee with dislike.

"Who made this?" he asked.

He was sitting at one end of a rectangular varnished wood table, in a kitchen where economy and conservatism, rather than imagination or taste, had decided the décor.

At some time, not recently, its walls had been painted with a crude orange gloss, whose radiated light did nothing to enhance the other features: cupboards made of fiberboard, formica, and opaque corrugated glass, hanging above a yellow plastic sink; a fiberboard-and-formica dresser, its hinged shelf open to reveal an assortment of jam jars, cereal packets, medicine bottles, vegetables, and glasses; metal chairs with rubber-tipped legs and speckled plastic seats; curtains, not wide enough to cover the French windows in front of which they hung, printed with a garish geometric design, sagging from too few rings irregularly spaced; a calendar torn away to December of the previous year, advertising a local Chinese restaurant, transfixed by a thumbtack to an otherwise empty wall. The central bulb in the room was shaded by pink plastic, and it was beneath this that Michael O'Keefe sat, his cup of coffee turning cold in front of him.

There were two other people in the kitchen, that Tuesday morning at one o'clock. The first, at the far end of the table from Michael, was a long, thin woman in her early thirties, with gray-streaked hair held back in an elastic band and bony fingers spread around her face. She wore a patterned blouse, darker beneath the armpits, and trousers of a style no longer fashionable: narrow, tapering trousers, whose bottle-green legs ended an inch or so above the ankle. The skin of her face was devoid of make-up, which was unfortunate, for, thus exposed, one could see that it was neither altogether healthy nor altogether clean. Her eyes were more attractive than their setting, being large and a deep violet blue.

Behind this woman and leaning against the drainboard was the second person: a youth of twenty-four, tall, slim-hipped, broad-shouldered, his body encased in faded jeans and a white short-sleeved undershirt.

Michael O'Keefe looked from one to the other, then pinged the coffee cup with his fingernails and asked again, "Who made this muck?"

"Oh, for Christ's sake, what's wrong with it now?"

The woman had a hard, almost masculine voice, but not deep, the impression of manliness being conveyed more by rhythm than pitch.

Michael said, "It's horrible."

"Then don't drink it. Though if you ask me you're just being bloody fussy. Malky and I've been chucking the stuff down ourselves for the last two days and it doesn't seem to have done *us* any harm. What's wrong with it?"

"It's too weak, for a start."

"Oh, for God's . . . You're only supposed to put one tea-spoon in. What do you want? Three, I suppose. Here, give it to me."

"It doesn't matter. There any whisky left, Malcolm?"

"All gone," said the youth.

"Great! Haven't you two had anything better to do since

I've been away than fill your bladders with coffee and bloody whisky?"

"What do you suggest?"

The woman had stood up, stretched across the table, and swung Michael's cup away from him into the sink. Now she crouched between standing and sitting again, her hands clasping her thighs.

"What d'you fucking suggest we could've done?" she said. "We weren't to leave the house, we hadn't got a television, we hadn't got a radio. What did you expect us to do with ourselves?"

The youth, Malcolm, gave a laugh like a bark, then closed his eyes, and smiled.

"And you can shut up, for a start," said the woman.

"All right, all right. Sit down, Barbara."

Michael drew a packet of cigarettes toward himself and shook one onto the table.

"Now give us a light and stop screaming the place down," he said. "Of course it hasn't been any fun for you, just dragging your heels for two days, but this isn't meant to be a holiday, is it? It's work. And with this type of work, the hardest bit's more often than not the waiting. I mean, don't think my part's been a bundle of action-packed excitement, because it bloody hasn't."

"You still haven't told us about that, have you."

It was Malcolm who said this, and as he did so, he flexed his arms, straightened them, lifted his body into the air, and deposited his buttocks on the drainboard. He performed this sequence of movements with self-conscious strength and control.

"I'm just about to," Michael answered him.

He did not, however, begin to speak immediately. Instead, he waited for a silence of sufficient length to segregate the story from its introduction, then narrowed his eyes, inclined his torso forward, and struck the palm of his right hand with the fist of his left. Performing these ritual actions, he was pleased to notice how the members of his audience responded to them without thought, leaning toward him as he leaned toward them, refining their previous, impatient curiosity into tunnels of concentration that terminated in his person.

"Okay," he said, at last. "Now this is the situation. To begin with, it was dead easy finding out where Mannion lives. He's in the directory, same as anyone else, and there's only three or four with his initial. The first one I rang turned out to be a woman. Well, a 'frightfully sorry' Harrod's housewife, actually. You know . . ."

Here he raised the note of his voice and drew back his lips in such a way that his vowel sounds became elongated into a whine not dissimilar to that of an ambulance siren.

"'Air, am fraffully sorry, am afraird you must hef the wrong number. My name's *Elizabeth* Mennion.' That sort of shit," he said. "Anyway, the second one was him."

"Great!" said the woman, Barbara, tapping the end of her cigarette although there was no ash on it. "And it was actually him you spoke to?"

"Aha."

Michael smiled, tilted his chair onto its hind legs, and placed his feet on the crossbar of the table.

"Now this is where it all becomes *most* interesting," he said.

"How?" asked Malcolm.

"If you'll just shut up for a second, I'll tell you. No, it was not Edward Mannion who answered the telephone, but yet another lady. Only, this time the lady was Mannion's daughter."

"So?"

"Well, did *you* know he had a daughter?"

"Of course not," interrupted Barbara. "We didn't know anything about his private life. Just his name and that he operated from London. That was all Pieter—"

"Exactly. But he has. Quite a young one. And, as I subsequently discovered, she appears to be all that he *does* have. Anyway, there's been no sign of a wife, or other kids, in the last forty-eight hours, and though they could just be away somewhere, I don't think so."

"All right. But what difference does that make?"

"My dear Barbara, doesn't it suggest possibilities to you? Little possibilities of leverage? Oh, for Christ's sake, no wonder Pieter got busted. You lot've got less forethought than a pack of bloody Boy Scouts."

"Leave Pieter out of this."

"He is out, sweetheart. And I'm in. Remember? Look, it was you who asked me. 'They've caught him, Michael. What are we going to do?' I mean, I was quite happy just helping you out, fixing you up with crash pads and dope and simple things like that. For which 'association,' may I add, you nearly got *me* done."

"Okay," said Malcolm. "But you weren't. And nor were we."

"No, thanks to a bit of cool on my side. Not to mention a bloody expensive alibi. Anyway, like I said then, I'll help you. If you want to make a noise and perhaps get Pieter out, I'll help you. I've got nothing to lose. But we're going to need one hell of a lot more fireworks than you used at the factory to make *that* kind of a bang, so this time, buying the stuff's out. And that's where Mannion comes in. Right? Thanks to Pieter's little filing cabinet of information, Mannion's going to *give* it to us."

"Yes, okay," said Barbara. "You've explained all that and it's fine. But what's this daughter—?"

"This daughter might—just might—prove another carrot to encourage Mannion's generosity. I don't know yet. It'll need some working out and when I've worked it out I'll tell you. In the meantime, let me get on with my story."

Michael paused. He relaxed his shoulders. He had not realized, until then, how tense they were. His newly acquired position of leadership was still vulnerable, but he must cling on to it.

He said, "So, having discovered from this young lady that her father was in the bath, I told her not to worry, it wasn't important, I'd ring him at the office on Monday. All right? Then, as soon as I'd put the phone down, I went round to the address, which happens to be in Chelsea, and there, unrelieved I may say by whisky or coffee or any of the other pleasant things in life, I waited. For seven bloody, boring, uneventful hours."

"But that's ridiculous," said Barbara. "Why the hell did you have to do that? You knew he was there. Why didn't you just ring at the door and ask to speak to him?"

"Look, I may not be any more experienced in this kind of thing than you two, but I have been living off my wits in other ways for a bloody sight longer. Now, look, it's taken me over an hour to get from the telephone box to Chelsea, and in that time anything could've happened. Mannion could've got out of his bath and left the house. People could've arrived. For Sunday lunch? Anything."

"All right. But that wouldn't have mattered. You could've called back, or said you wanted to talk to him on his own."

"Yeah, yeah, that's right, I could've done that. I could've written him a letter, asking for an appointment, too."

Michael let his chair drop forward again. He extinguished one cigarette and lit another. He looked from the woman to the young man.

She still leaned toward him, but her face had tightened into lines of resentful incomprehension and battered pride. He was withdrawn, his shoulders resting against the wall, his eyelids low. After a moment's deliberation, Michael decided to maintain his obvious line of contact with Barbara.

"Look," he said to her, "I don't think you understand just

how dangerous a position we're in. I'm sorry if I'm being brutal—really I am, love—but one of us has got to keep a hard head about all this. You and Malcolm, you're too emotionally involved. You're all caught up with your cause and with getting Pieter released and and—well, of course, you'd like everything to happen fast. But the fact is, for everything we've got on Mannion, he could get just as much on us.

"It's like a game of poker, if you want. We've been dealt a bloody good hand, but he could pick an even better one. So we've got to rely on bluff. We've got to play a sort of psychological game. And part of that, you see, was to make sure that when I finally spoke to Mannion, he was both unprepared and on his own. You see, I wanted him to feel threatened, exposed, vulnerable, and he wasn't too likely to feel that in his own home, or his office, surrounded by a bunch of cronies, was he?"

"No, I suppose not," said Barbara.

Michael saw her shoulders slump downward as the resistance flowed out of her body. He laid his right hand on her left one, played with the gold ring on her third finger.

"So that's why I waited," he said.

His voice was low now. It was one with the hum of the refrigerator and the distant passing of traffic. Above it, cigarette smoke hung like a velvet canopy.

"And at about six o'clock in the evening, some people did arrive," he said. "A man and a woman. I thought, at first, he could be Mannion. Ex-army type with a bristly mustache and a red face. He wasn't, though, cause a few minutes later they both came out again, with a man who *had* to be the owner of the house and a girl, very out of place, all scruffy to their Sunday best, who *had* to be the daughter. Anyway, they got into a taxi and made off to the West End, with me following—"

"In a taxi?" asked Malcolm.

"What?"

"You in a taxi, too, of course?"

"No. Me running along beside them at thirty miles an hour. What d'you bloody think?"

"I was just asking. Only, they're not cheap, taxis. Still, you must've known what you were doing."

"Oh, Malky, don't be so damned petty," said Barbara.

Michael said, "Thank you," then, "It's all right, Malcolm, I'll give you my expenses sheet at the end of the week."

"That's okay," said Malcolm, his face bland, humorless, like that of a well-fed cat.

"Anyway," said Michael, "I shan't bore you with all the details of my high living during the past two days, all the stories about sleeping standing up against area railings and living off chocolate and fags. I'll just tell you what happened tonight when I finally got him, when I finally got Mannion the way I wanted him."

Without exaggeration or elaboration, he narrated the final chapter of his story.

When he had finished, when the ashtray was piled high with folded cigarette ends, when the temperature in the room had chilled to its pre-dawn low, he said, "Of course, I never thought the bastard'd say 'yes' straightaway. I told you he wouldn't. But you see now what I meant about the daughter. O-liv-ia. In fact, it's even better than I first thought. It's not only that the old man'd do a lot to keep her in the dark about his little extramural activities, but also, and I'm usually pretty good at picking up this sort of thing, I got the distinct impression that she's ripe for being used against him in more —how shall I put it?—direct ways."

Barbara stirred. She tucked a fallen strand of hair behind one ear.

"I'm sure you're right," she said, "only I don't quite see how . . ."

"Well, never mind about that now," said Michael. "Tomorrow I'm going to put my little hunch to the test, and if I'm right, I'll tell you all about it in the evening."

"Tomorrow evening? So how long's it going to take? I mean, it's all very well, but surely we haven't got time to—"

"Please. I do realize we've got to move fast. But this—this girl could be the one card we need to turn our good hand into a winning hand. Now, will you trust me? Will you, Barbara?"

"All right," said Barbara. "All right. But . . . Yeah, yeah, of course, Mike."

"Malcolm?"

He did not look at the youth as he asked this.

"Yeah, sure," said Malcolm.

He sounded more amused than compliant, yet Michael did not protest. It was the assent alone that mattered, not the spirit in which it was given.

"Okay," he said, and stood up. "Well, then," he said, "I'm going to get a bit of kip. Wake me at eight, will you, Barbara?"

She, too, stood up.

"Of course," she said.

"Night, then, both of you," said Michael.

At the door of the kitchen, he hesitated, tempted to swing around and catch the unguarded faces of the couple behind him. Before the pause had time to become visible, however, he continued on his way.

14

Olivia lay face down on her bed, her hands gripping the sides of the mattress, her legs stretched taut, her toes pointing to the floor. She lay as though she were on a raft in a violent sea.

It was half past eleven in the morning and, through uncurtained windows, sunlight blinded her bedroom, flaring off glass and yellow wallpaper, draining the color from tousled sheets and blankets, spreading in mirage pools across the floor. Sounds, too, invaded the room (of cars parking and cars moving away, of women chattering, of birds) and smells (of furniture polish, of burned toast). These were the waves that assaulted Olivia, that tossed her from side to side, that attempted to wrench her from her bed.

Yet even before their uprising, her hold upon sleep had been tenuous. Even during the calm hours of the night, reminders of consciousness had lapped and lapped against the shore of her mind, draining the blackness of oblivion to gray. She had not been in a state of limbo. Rather had she moved from one extreme of wakefulness to the other with such velocity that the two had appeared superimposed. And, like a vile smell wafted in a breeze, her dreams had blown around this movement, sometimes vivid, sometimes blurred, always unpleasant.

In the first days after coming down from university, finals over, Olivia had been charged with a new energy, a whiplash of release. She had gone to bed late and waked (whether alone or with Simon) early. Searching for a temporary job, she had run from interview to interview and had written letter after letter with regard to a permanant one. She had seen several of those friends of hers who had not gone abroad for the summer, going to the cinema with them, or the pub, or driving with them to the country.

Then Simon had left for Canada, and although this had made no immediate difference to her life, it seemed, in retrospect, to have been the trigger for a growing lethargy, a heaviness, a sense of being suffocated by a wave too high and wide and slowly curving for escape.

She had recognized the wave. All her life it had rolled behind her. She had seen its reflection sometimes, sometimes heard its roar. It was black and hollow and bottomless, and if she had learned in childhood how to keep ahead of it (how to ward it off with scorn, how to shrink it with learning, how to hide from it in friendships and in love affairs, how to set herself goals in order to keep moving from it), still she knew that it was there.

Now, for the first time, she had faltered long enough for it to overtake her. Running too fast, she had stumbled and it had curled itself above her.

News had come to her that she had got her history degree. A firm of encyclopedia publishers had offered her a job. Simon had continued to send her his long, entertaining letters. Her father had taken her out, had introduced her to his friends, had given her presents and spared her his time. Yet none of these things could have, any more, the strength to rescue her. She had understood this. They were brightly painted corks, too small now for her great weight.

The night before, in desperation, she had swum toward one of them, and twice it had sunk beneath her.

This morning, she clutched at the papier-mâché buoy of sleep, feeling it disintegrate, feeling its support departing, gathering strength to remain afloat without it.

"Oh, I'm so sorry. Miss Olivia? I'm so sorry. I didn't realize you was still up here. Did I wake you up? I am sorry."

"Mrs. Clifford . . ."

"Yes, dear. Did I wake you? I didn't know you was up here. I'd've never come in if I had."

"That's all right."

"I thought you'd gone out, see. I was certain you had. Your father's gone out. Gone before I came."

"Has he?" said Olivia. "Was he? Yes, that's right, I think he had to see someone."

"I expect that's what it was. He's usually here when I come, of course, but not always."

Mrs. Clifford was a short, plump woman, with tightly permed white hair and her chin tucked into her neck; she wore flowered dresses and starched, flowered aprons. She stood in the doorway of Olivia's room, her eyes behind their bright glasses flickering disapproval of the untidiness and of the girl's still being in bed.

Olivia pulled herself into a sitting position, then, seeing the other's disapproval narrow into disgust, remembered that she was wearing no nightclothes. A moment of laughter came to her and died, strangled by the events of the previous evening.

"Well," said the woman, "I'll leave you to it, then. You know I'd never've come in if I'd known you was still here," and, walking backward as though to memorize each detail of the scene for future narration, she left.

A minute or so afterward, Olivia climbed from her bed. She wrapped her body in the top sheet, unable to find the enthusiasm for an act of private defiance. A duller feeling than fear, than despair, clung to her like sticky summer dirt.

She walked across the landing and ran herself a bath, but the steam that rose from the water made her face sweat, so that when she got out and dried herself she felt no cleaner than before. She brushed her teeth, but beneath the peppermint she could still taste a yellow sickness. She dressed and went down to the kitchen, where she made herself a cup of coffee, which she did not drink.

The air in her father's house oppressed her. She felt as though she were gasping beneath it, as though her lungs might crack beneath its fetid thickness. She tried to sit still, to relax, to think, but couldn't. The sound of Mrs. Clifford using a vacuum cleaner above her, the sight of her father's crisp linen table napkin folded in four on the scrubbed pine table pressed in upon her senses. She poured the undrunk coffee into the sink. She went upstairs, collected her bag, and ran out into the street.

Still moving fast, although walking now, not running, she made her way along roads whose names didn't register, chest heaving as she drew in the outdoor freshness.

Arriving at the Brompton Road, she stopped and leaned face first against a lamppost.

"I've got to think. I've got to think," she said.

She closed her eyes and listened as her breathing quieted to a rasp. She opened her eyes and raised her face from the rough, cold stone.

Women and men drifted past her and around her, their progress unimpeded by her presence. Olivia felt as though she had come to rest against a cinema screen and that all around her (the people, the cars, the buildings, and the sweet September sunlight) were the shadows of a film being projected across her body. She felt alone in a way that she had never before experienced.

For a long time (at least since her mother's death), she had been aware of herself as distinct from, different from, her environment. Of course, being an orphan had, in itself, given to her the status of a foreigner, had caused her school friends to consider her as glamorous, eccentric, beyond the common law, had caused herself to adopt these attributes, but it had not been in this alone that her sense of separateness had rested. From being the only child of unwilling parents, from being the infant-school pupil more interested in reading than playing, from being the fat, plain teen-ager unconcerned by film stars or boys, she had learned to recognize, to accept, to glorify in, her individuality.

The word "different" had acquired for her the secondary meaning of "superior." Circulating from place to place, from situation to situation, she had persuaded herself that her alienation from them was more to be praised than pitied.

There had, however, been a paradoxical rider to this belief, an assumption that, within her alienation, she was not alone. She had always been certain that there were others like her, that there existed, somewhere, other misfits too big for the everyday mold, and that one day she would find them.

Then, in her first two years at university, she had thought

this goal achieved. It was not that her fellow students had, as individuals, been greater people than those she had known before. Many she had disliked; many, even amongst her friends, not admired. But the context in which their vices and stupidities had been set, the background (of intention and understanding and values) against which they had stood, had seemed, during those first two years, to be a home in which Olivia's vagrant spirit might rest and grow strong.

In the third year, disillusion had crept in and a growing sense of isolation. She had tried explaining this to Simon.

"Of course," he had said. "Everyone gets pissed off towards the end. Though, personally, if it weren't for the exams, I wouldn't mind staying here forever. But you're right; it's a small community and people are bound to get bored with each other. And all those ideas we had—well, I suppose they *do* get stale in the end, churning round and round in the same confined space. You're ready to move on, that's all."

"Where?" she had asked. "Where am I ready to move on to?"

"Well, depending on your degree, some sort of job, I suppose. That's if you're talking on a practical level. Otherwise . . . I don't know. Life?"

"What was *this*, then? What were my last twenty years? Pastimes?"

"No, of course not. Preparations, if anything."

"Yes—well, 'if anything' seems to me the right description. And of the next twenty years and of the twenty after that. Or are those preparations, too, for death? God, I wish I could at least believe that. I wish I were a Christian or a Buddhist. I wish I'd left school at fourteen and gone straight into a factory and married a drunken husband and had ten kids. I wish I'd been so bloody busy I'd never had time to think about why I was doing it all, about why I was bothering to stay alive."

"You wouldn't if you were."

"Of course I wouldn't. But . . . God, Simon, don't you ever
. . . I mean . . ."

She had been unable to convey to him the fear that she had
felt then, the sense of having run too far for her energy, of
having allowed herself to be dragged, to be beguiled along
corridors lined with illusory mirrors and of having collapsed
against one of them in her exhaustion, to see it smash and
reveal a nothingness beyond.

She had, however, allowed him to charm it away, to kiss
her and hold her and talk to her about things they would do
as soon as finals were over.

Today she knew that the fear had returned too strong to
be made to vanish by such gentle magic.

"I've got to think!"

She had begun to walk again, crossing the busy road without attention to its traffic. Although everything was visible to
her, although she heard every sound, still she had the impression that they were disconnected from her reality. Had her
path coincided with that of a delivery van, neither of them,
she felt, would have been affected by the contact.

Ahead of her rose the wide steps of the Victoria and Albert
Museum. She climbed them and entered through a revolving
doorway.

Thirty seconds later, Michael O'Keefe climbed the same
steps and entered through the same door.

At first, he thought that he had lost her. The foyer was
chaotic with tourists and students and schoolchildren, with
swarms of camera-clutching Japanese, with girls in jeans,
carrying sketch pads underneath their arms, with mothers
pleading, teachers shouting, with uniformed adolescents eating chocolate and ice creams.

Then, at the top of a short flight of marble stairs, he saw the
flash of copper that was her dress.

An illuminated plan of the museum hung from one of the foyer walls. Michael pushed his way toward it, glanced at it, committed the relevant details to his memory, and set off in the same direction as that in which Olivia had been going, but on a lower level, still on the ground floor.

The crowd that had dominated the entrance hall now dispersed and became insignificant in the mosaic-floored corridors and the large, high chambers, with their glass coffin showcases, their dead-eyed statues, and their soft-footed custodians. Entering the new atmosphere, Michael was amused by an involuntary slowing of pace and a tightening of the stomach. It was as though, in these august surroundings, the hunt had taken on a ritual nature.

Shaking his head but smiling with his eyes, he hurried on through galleries filled with stone and marble, up stairways hung with wooden bas-reliefs, along a corridor where cases of cameo portraits stood.

"Oh!"

"I'm sorry? Oh, I *am* sorry. How unfortunate."

"What are you doing here?"

"Look, it's—"

"What are you *doing* here?"

"Okay. All right. Much the same as you, I dare say. I came to see the manuscript exhibition. And now I'm just wandering about."

"Manuscript?"

"Original manuscripts. Poems, novels, plays. Up on the second floor."

"Why?"

"Why?"

"Yes. I mean, why? Why that? Why here?"

"Oh, I see. Well, I know by rights a good working-class lad like me should be down the betting shop, or in the pub, but, you know, I thought I'd give myself a bit of culture like. It's difficult, of course, not being able to read the long words . . ."

"I didn't mean . . ."

"Look, it doesn't matter. If I'd've seen you was in here, I'd never've come in and embarrassed you. I'd've turned around and gone back the way I came. I don't expect you to be delighted to see me, not after last night. Only, you know, you *had* got your back to me and I really wasn't to guess you'd be here, was I? Any more than you was me."

"I suppose not."

"Anyway, I won't annoy you any longer."

Michael's path had coincided with Olivia's in a room dominated by a garishly colored, sixteenth-century German altarpiece. Apart from this, there were only some cases filled with small medieval statues and a couple of nuns whispering over a guidebook.

"Anyway, I won't annoy you any longer," said Michael, then squeezed his lips together and smiled, contrived to look apologetic while smiling, and began to step backward to the corridor whence he had come.

He was a fisherman. As he moved, he felt his line for tension and, sensing that it was not yet attached to anything, that its hook still floated free, after a couple of paces stopped and cast out again.

"I—" he said. "I mean, before I go, now that I have bumped into you like this, I would like to say I'm sorry about last night. Fuck! That sounds like an awful line from some romantic novel, doesn't it? What I mean is, I know you were upset and—and I'd just like to say I'm sorry it had to be like that."

"But *why* did it?" said Olivia. "And *what?* Who *are* you?"

"He didn't tell you? Your father?"

"Oh, I don't know. . . ."

"Here, do you want to go somewhere and sit down?"

"No, thanks."

"He must've said something."

"He said that you insulted him. He said that you called him a Nazi because he sells arms to the Arabs. And he said that he hit you."

"Is that all?"

"Is it true?"

Michael half turned. Lowering his face into shadow, he took from the pocket of his jacket two boxes: one of cigarettes and one of matches. Opening the former of these and proffering it to Olivia, he said, "Yes, it's true."

Then he waited, his hand extended, his eyes fixed on those of the girl. She, her hands tucked underneath her armpits, looked back at him. Neither of them moved. It was as though the forces of attraction and repulsion between them were equally strong. After five or six seconds, however, Michael felt the balance of power begin to shift. Immediately, he repeated, "It's true. I called your old man a Nazi. Do you think I was wrong?"

As he spoke, he extended the box of cigarettes still closer to Olivia.

"But why *him?*" said Olivia. "I mean, I hate the way he earns his living as much as anyone, but he isn't the only guy doing it. There are others. So why pick on him particularly? I mean, I got the impression you'd sort of singled him out."

Michael said, "You thought I'd—? Oh, come on, no. No, I've nothing against *him,* personally. Just his job. Just his trade. I mean, I've seen the end result of it, the people his guns have killed."

"But how did you know . . . I mean, his name? You knew his name and where to find him."

"Chance, that's all. I'd seen his picture in the papers once and remembered it on account of what he does, I suppose. And there he was, there you both were, last night, on the platform. He's got the sort of face you remember, see. He's a good-looking man, your dad."

"What papers?" asked the girl.

Michael said nothing. He had a plausible answer to this question, but was hoping that Olivia would supply her own. Waiting for her to do so, he was nervous, but not frightened.

"Oh," she said, "I remember. That thing in the *Sunday Times*. It must've been that."

"I don't think so."

"It must've been. A couple of months ago."

"Maybe. I can't remember."

"Yes, it was," she said and, as she did so, her right hand jerked in a reflex gesture from its hiding place, spread out, and took the proffered cigarette.

Michael ran the tip of his tongue along the inside of his lower lip. It was cracked and tasted of blood.

When both he and the girl were smoking, he said, "Anyway, that's all I wanted to tell you: how as I was sorry for having upset you. And to explain. I know it must've seemed nasty, what I did, heavy and—pointless, anyway, but I just saw red. You know, seeing him there, unexpected like that. Oh, look, I know you don't really understand what I'm saying. You couldn't. But thanks for hearing me out, all the same. It was kind. Not everyone'd've done it."

"No! I mean, for Christ's sake don't *thank* me."

"Why not? Most people'd've told me to fuck off. And you couldn't blame them, not really."

"*I* could. *I* could blame them very much."

Olivia's face, Michael noticed, although solid and wooden in repose like that of a carved cherub, with the flow of thought or speech became like rippling silk. The notes of her voice were limited and controlled, as was usual in members of her class—her public-school education—but not so the muscles of her face. These moved without inhibition, and although he found this quality—this childish, unwitting transparency—pathetic, it did make his job easier.

"As a matter of fact, I'm pretty glad I did hear your side of the story," she said. "You don't know how much the whole thing . . . Oh, it doesn't matter, but . . . Look, it wasn't really an accident, you bumping into me here, was it?"

"How do you mean?"

"You know what I mean."

"Don't you believe in fate, then?"

"Okay," she said; then, smiling, she tossed her hair to one side and blew smoke in a vertical column in front of her eyes.

The two nuns walked toward them and past them, whispering still in their girlish, excitable manner.

"How were they, then?" she said. "The . . . what was it? On the second floor?"

"Manuscripts," said Michael. "They were all right."

He, too, smiled.

"You really are different, you know," he said.

"Please, drop it. I may be my father's daughter, but what did you expect? That *I* was going to lay into you, too? I'm from a different generation to him, you know."

"That's got nothing to do with it."

"Well . . ."

There was a silence. Together, they flicked ash away from themselves onto the parquet. Olivia glanced over her shoulder, then back again, and said, "Are we supposed to be smoking in here?"

"No. We'll probably get chucked into nick if they see us."

"Worse than that. Hanged. Arson in Her Majesty's museum."

"*I* may be hanged. *You'd* be beheaded. Hanging's only for the proles, you know."

"Oh, look . . . What's your name?"

"Michael."

"Michael, I don't know what you think I am, but . . . All right, this is going to sound corny, but, really, most of my friends at university were 'working class.' I'm just not a snob.

69

In fact, often *they* were more snobby than *I* was."

"You're bloody naïve, though, aren't you? 'At university'! There are people don't get as far as 'O' levels, let alone university. Sods like me, for instance. Ignorant bastards who can hardly even write their names . . ."

"You're being melodramatic. You're not ignorant."

"I haven't had much encouragement not to be."

"But you've managed."

"Oh, aye! I've taught myself a thing or two. But it doesn't stop your lot looking down on me, or pretending to be deaf if I dare to stutter out some opinion or other. Take my word for it."

Inhaling a last rough drag of smoke, Michael threw his still-lit cigarette end to the ground. He watched as Olivia's eyes followed the movement, saw her dislike of its careless-ness, her resolution not to criticize.

"It's all right having nice liberal ideas about the disintegra-tion of the class system," he said, "but it's funny how often those ideas themselves disintegrate when brought face to face with reality."

"Maybe you're right."

"I am. But, like I said, you are different. Just a bit young, that's all. No, I'm glad we got to talk to each other. Hey, look . . . No, it doesn't matter."

"What?"

"It's all right. You'll think I'm taking advantage of the situation. Besides, for whatever reasons, I *was* pretty heavy with your old man last night."

"I've told you, I understand about that. I feel just the same way as you do about what he does."

"All the same . . ."

"Look, it's true. I wouldn't just say it."

"Still, you wouldn't want to see me again, would you?"

He was looking beyond her, at a caseful of ivory figures in the adjoining gallery, but, because he was expecting it, heard the hiatus in her breathing before she answered him, before she said, "Yes. Why not?"

"Tonight?"

"Tonight? Oh, I can't. I mean, I really can't. I've promised to go to a party."

"I see. Posh party, is it? Evening suit and all that?"

"Christ, no."

"I mean, you have to have an invitation?"

"Well . . . no. No."

"Then perhaps I could go along, too, could I? Or would it be embarrassing? I mean, your friends might—"

"It's not that. Only, I'm going with somebody already."

"Oh, I didn't mean . . . I just meant, perhaps I could drop in, if you was to tell me where it was. I'd like to talk to you again. You know. If you don't mind, that is. Your boyfriend wouldn't object, would he, if I just dropped in?"

"No. Why should he?" said Olivia.

On the steps of the museum, she gave him the address. Her handwriting was large and circular, with the "e"s formed in the Greek fashion.

As soon as he had disappeared, as soon as his powerful body had drilled its way into the swarm of people moving along the pavement toward it, Olivia turned and ran in the opposite direction.

She ran until she reached Hyde Park.

There, on the summer-parched grass beside the Serpentine, she collapsed. She rolled onto her back and swallowed with her eyes the wash of light blue, cloud-floating sky above her.

She did not know what, if anything, it was that had happened in the museum. She did not attempt to work it out. She assumed that, for some reason, the man Michael wanted to make her, but other than this she understood nothing from the encounter.

Nonetheless (and in spite of the dozen other problems still unresolved within her), for the first time that day Olivia felt clean. It was as though a breeze had forced its way through a crack in her oppression. Mindless of its source, its composition, she gulped it in.

15

For a moment, Michael stood motionless in the telephone kiosk, his eyes narrowed, the tip of his tongue flicking along the rough underside of his mustache. Then he grabbed the receiver, lifted it, and began to dial.

The numbers that his fingers chose were multiples of three. Having been forbidden to do so, he had never written them down, but he was not worried that he might have forgotten them. He didn't make a habit of forgetting important facts.

"Good morning."

Michael inserted the relevant coin into its slot.

"It's O'Keefe," he said.

"O'Keefe?"

"Yes. We met in that pub on Saturday night. We were introduced by . . ."

"Of course I remember you. How are you, my dear boy?"

16

"I wish you could stay."

"Yes, of course. But you know it's impossible."

"Is it?"

"Now, Sally, don't be ridiculous. You know it is. I haven't been in the office all day. I was with the accountant before you."

"Yes. It's ironical, isn't it, *you* having to rush back to *my* husband? I still find that funny. Don't you? Don't you find that funny?"

The woman began to laugh, with a dry, choking laughter that caught at the back of her nose. She was sitting on a velvet-covered stool at a dressing table, and when she spoke, it was not to the man himself, but to his looking-glass reflection.

"Please don't get hysterical," said Edward, jerking the knot of his tie from side to side, his chin thrust in the air. "It's been a pleasant hour or so. Let's not spoil it, shall we?"

"Bastard," said the woman quietly, and her tired brown eyes slid from his face to her own. She was forty-five or -six. Her mouse-colored hair was sprinkled with gray and, for a week at least, had been neglected by the hairdresser. She had a wide mouth and a turned-up nose: generous, exhausted features.

"It wasn't easy for me to come at all today. There's a problem cropped up which I'd like to get sorted out quickly."

"So I gather. It's not often you ring us in the middle of the night."

"No. Well, it's nothing insoluble, nothing we can't cope with."

"It's all right. I know better than to ask you for details."

Edward decided not to hear the implicit recrimination. He liked Sally Hastings. She was a soft and intelligent woman, whose virtues passed as unnoticed by her husband as would the changing keys of a symphony by a tone-deaf listener. She was not, however, above the faults of her sex. Sentimentality and irrationality and, on occasions, bitchiness smothered her soul no less than the hideous quilted dressing gown she wore now smothered her brittle body.

She had been Edward's mistress for five years. One night, when Dick had been abroad on business, he had taken her out to dinner and, having escorted her home, had made love to her. That very evening, he had made it clear that there neither was nor ever could be any question of their affair becoming more important than her marriage.

"Than your business partnership, you mean," she had replied.

"No," he had said, that was not what he meant. Of course he would be sorry to lose Dick as an associate (and, of course, that was what would happen, should Dick learn of his wife's infidelity), but what he had, in fact, been trying to say was that whatever happened, he had no intention of marrying again. Did Sally understand?

She had said that she did.

Since then, they had seen each other, had had sex together, approximately once a month. When Sally was feeling confident and happy, Edward enjoyed these occasions. Her giving body and her light, sharp mind refreshed him. When she was tearful, however, or bitter, he wondered whether he might not be better off seeing a whore.

He put on his jacket. Sally was painting her lips red. A band of brilliant midday sunlight sliced across her face, making her look both very hard and very vulnerable.

"Do I look old?" she asked.

"What a ridiculous question."

"I feel it. It's autumn coming, I suppose. And winter. I hate winter."

"What winter? It's sixty-five degrees today."

"But not for long. Tomorrow, the day after, you'll wake up and find that the air's got a thin coat of iron on it."

"You sound like Cassandra," said Edward.

Fastening the middle button of his jacket, he walked toward the dressing table and stood behind the woman. There he bent down, so that his face and hers were framed together, and kissed her on the forehead. She reached across her breast to clutch his arm.

"I'll see you soon," he said.

74

"Let me show you out."

"I can manage."

"No, please."

Halfway down the stairs, she said, "How's Olivia?"

Edward knew that she was speaking to postpone his departure.

"Quite well," he answered.

"Good. She's a nice child. A bit mixed up, I suppose, like they all seem to be at that age, but thoughtful. And caring. I'd've liked a daughter."

They had reached the hall. The reds and greens of a stained-glass fanlight floated like liquid jewels on hatstand and table and picture frames. From beyond the front door came the sounds of a Fulham afternoon.

"Well," said Edward.

"Has she found a job yet?"

"Who? Olivia? No, not yet. She turned down that thing in publishing, you know. But she will. As you say, she's going through a difficult stage."

"And, of course, you couldn't expect her to do something like be a secretary. You know, just waiting for a husband. She's too intelligent for that. You must be quite proud of her, really."

"Yes, yes, I'm sure she'll turn out all right. Though, God knows, she can be pretty bloody impossible at times. Still, it's just a question of keeping one's temper, keeping one's patience, until she realizes that the world *wasn't* made for her and her alone."

"What do you mean?"

"It doesn't matter. She's just a bit spoiled, that's all. I suppose it was inevitable. Now, I really have to go, Sally."

He kissed her cheek and turned the knob of the lock. Before he pulled the door toward himself, however, he said, "You were beautiful. You always are. Look after yourself, darling."

Then he left.

In the taxi, he had to roll down a window to dispel the plastic stuffiness therein. A light breeze touched his face.

"Winter!" he said to himself.

Stretching backward and closing his eyes, he smiled.

"Women!"

17

"It's the bossman back again," Malcolm said, letting fall the net curtain whose hem he had been holding.

"Already?" said Barbara.

"Yeah. No sense of timing, has he?"

Barbara scrambled out of the double bed she had been lying in, and squatted on the floor, gathering around herself her scattered clothes.

"What d'you think's happened?" she asked.

"How should I know? His little plan probably didn't work out, that's all."

"Well, don't just stand there. Get dressed, for God's sake, can't you?"

"Barbara! Malcolm!"

"Coming!"

"Where the hell are you? Oh, up here. I might've bloody guessed. All right, stay as you are. You've neither of you got much worth covering."

Michael had entered the room like a conqueror. His face above the darkness of his beard was bright with an emotion more like lust than satisfaction. As though it were a no longer useful stage costume, he pulled off his denim jacket and flung it onto the bed.

"What happened?" said Malcolm.

"She's ours," he said.

"D'you mean—?"

"I mean, she's ours. Mine. I've stolen her from Mannion's pack. Now . . ."

He looked around, as though searching the plywood furniture and drab gray fittings of the room for something he had lost. Malcolm, having pulled up his pants, took cigarettes from the dressing table and handed him one.

"Thanks. Now . . . Now, all we've got to do, my darlings, is work out how best we can use her."

Without changing the depth of his focus, he accepted a light, inhaled, and said, "Yes. That's it. I've got it. The list. That list of Pieter's, of firms trading with South Africa. Get it, Barbara."

"But . . ."

"But nothing, my sweetheart. Get it. Then I'll tell you what I propose to do."

18

Simon Shaw enjoyed parties.

When challenged with this predilection, he would deny it, would ask how such taste could be possible when the drink was always unpalatable, the company always predictable, the conversation always inane, and the music either too loud or too soft. And he believed in these deficiencies.

In spite of them, however, Simon did enjoy parties. He liked the dressing up, no matter how informal, the entering into a roomful of apparently haphazard human groups, the gradual emergence of classifications and subclassifications within these groups, the hum of unspecific sexuality, the ephemeral intimacies, the breakdowns in convention that alcohol (and here the quality of the alcohol was unimportant) contrived. He liked to make new conquests and to hear new secrets. He liked to forget, for a night, that living might be anything other than the participation in an amusing, intriguing, bathetic, irresponsible carnival.

Climbing the unlit staircase that led to Teddy Royce's studio flat, a bottle of Burgundy in his hand, Olivia Mannion at his heels (hearing the muffled thud of drums and bass guitars, the babble of talk, the eruptions of laughter), Simon was more than usually tense with anticipation.

The journey thither had not been pleasant. He had anticipated some reserve in Olivia's behavior toward him that evening, but none as great, none as impregnable, as that with which, since their meeting at nine o'clock, she had treated him.

"Liv, for goodness' sake, talk to me," he had said as they had stood together by the bus stop. "You haven't uttered a word in the last five minutes."

"Haven't I? I'm sorry."

"Look, it doesn't matter," he had said, "but if you're still upset about last night, about me not getting in touch with you and so on, it'd really be much better if we talked about it. Wouldn't it?"

"It's not that. It isn't anything."

"Come on! I've known you for . . . nearly two years now. Long enough to know when there's something worrying you, anyway."

"All right. But just—just take my word for it, talking about it is *not* the answer, this time."

"How can't it be? Talking always helps."

"I know that's your philosophy."

"It's not my 'philosophy.' It's a fact."

Simon had flung his hands wide, in a gesture of frustration. Olivia had closed her eyes, then opened them and looked beyond him to search the approaching traffic for a bus.

"Look, Liv, would you rather we didn't go to the party?"

"No. No, of course not."

"We don't have to. Liv?"

"Please, Simon, forget it."

"How can I? For God's sake, I love you."

Even as he had spoken the last three words, Simon had known that he should not have done so. They had not amounted to a lie. They had not been the opposite of the truth. They had, however, been uttered without regard to truth: as a ploy, as a dramatic device. It had given him no satisfaction when they had achieved the intended result.

Olivia had focused on him again, had brushed his hand with a movement of her hand, had creased and uncreased her face with a succession of incompatible emotions.

"What do you mean by that?" she had asked, her words extending a way of escape to him, her voice denying one.

"You know what I mean. It's nothing new," he had answered.

"Oh, but it is, Simon. You've never said that before. Never."

"Well, okay."

"So what does it mean? Does it mean you're fond of me and you like screwing me and you feel you've got certain rights over me? Or does it mean— Does it mean that you care for me? Enough so that when something hurts me, it hurts you, too? It doesn't matter how stupid it seems, whatever's done it, whatever's made the hurt, but the very *fact* of my suffering makes *you* suffer. Does it mean that? Does it mean that you're prepared to give and give and go on giving because you've got the faith to know that it'll all come back to you? Does it—?"

"Okay! Livvy!"

"What?"

"Well, don't get so pedantic."

"You're the one who likes definitions."

"All right. But let's get something straight. You're making it sound as though 'loving' someone means 'becoming' them. That's not right. You know that. I mean, we've talked about it, about individuality and self and so on. I can't *be* you. I wouldn't want to and, for God's sake, surely you wouldn't want it either? We're two people. Two different, distinct people, who happen to have a lot in common."

"Yes. Yes, you're right, that's just what we are. And I'm not even sure I can remember what it is we *do* have in common."

"Oh, for God's sake! We both like Swiss breakfast cereal, for a start."

But she had stepped beyond the reach of his humor, had done so words ago, he suspected. That the bus had arrived at that moment, that circumstances had compelled them to change the topic of conversation from love to money, had been irrelevant.

"Simon! Olivia! Come in! Teddy's in the kitchen preparing some ghastly concoction to poison us all with. How are you? You look so brown."

"Hi, Frank."

"Come in. Umm, Olivia, you smell lovely. Come in."

"Hello, Frank."

"Through here. Now, let's see, who do you know? Everybody, I expect. Rosie! Here's Simon and Olivia! Let me get you something to drink. Red? White? Oh, some Nuits-Saint-Georges. How smart. Thank you, darlings."

"Simon!"

"Rosie!"

"Olivia!"

"Hello, Rosie."

As in a church service, the questions and responses swung from speaker's lips to listener's ear, from speaker's lips to listener's ear, with the force of autopropulsion. Each was the inevitable result of its precedent. Each was the inevitable cause of its successor. Each was unthought, unquestioned, reassuring. Simon longed to fall beneath their spell. Only the restrained and, therefore, restraining presence of Olivia prevented him.

80

"Look," he said to her, "we needn't stay."

"We've only just got here."

"I know, but it doesn't matter. Nobody'd mind. Would you rather we left?"

"We? *You* can go, if you want to. *I'm* not."

"Oh, look here!"

He reached out to touch her, to pull her toward him and away from the encircling confusion; then, ashamed of the violence within himself, he drew back his hand and thrust it in the pocket of his cardigan.

"I'm sorry," he said, "but you are being unreasonable."

"Am I?"

"You know you are."

Righteous indignation tightened his heart, counteracting —to some extent justifying—his resentment at Olivia's self-absorption. Not enough, however. He had to make *certain* that he was in the right.

"Please," he said, "can't we just slip along to the kitchen or somewhere? It's ridiculous trying to talk here."

"Teddy's in the kitchen. Anyway, we've agreed, there's nothing to talk about."

"You're not helping, you know."

"Well, what, then? What is there to talk about? Our future? Where we're going? Or where you're going and where I'm going: 'two different, distinct' things? We don't need to be together for that."

"I don't see what you're getting at. I mean, why this sudden rush to get things charted out? Fixed? You never used to want that. I mean, you don't want me to propose to you or something, do you? Surely you don't want a little ring on your finger, so that everything's pretty and formal?"

The last part of this question had been intended as a joke, as a humorous hyperbole. Olivia spat her response to it.

"Cunt!" she said. "You smirking, pompous cunt!"

Accepting his first paper cup of wine, exchanging his first piece of gossip, Simon Shaw believed himself exonerated.

19

By half past eleven, the party had achieved that the state that lies halfway between enthusiasm and lethargy, smartness and dishevelment, sobriety and maudlin drunkenness. At one end of the studio, against the backdrop of a high, curtained window, a dozen or so couples jerked and swiveled in time to the music from a tape recorder. Between these and the door of the room, other men and women, in clusters or in pairs, talked and laughed and blew streams of smoke into the already clouded atmosphere. Beyond the door, in the entrance hall and kitchen, still other guests held fervent arguments, or kissed, or delved among plates of cheese and bowls of salad. Nor were these groups static. The particles of one were constantly changing for the particles of another, as dancers retired to refresh themselves, lovers decided to dance.

Olivia, however, had been in the same position for over an hour. Seated on a mattress, inside and to the right of the studio entrance, her feet tucked under opposite knees, her back against a wall, she watched through slitted eyes the otherwise kaleidoscopic activity. Her stillness was catlike. Those on the mattress with her (two men and a woman discussing their summer holidays) had long ago dismissed her as asleep or stoned.

"But, my dear, can you imagine, three weeks without so much as a drop of hot water?"

"It sounds really great."

"Well, to you, maybe. But we're not such hardy souls. And the food! If I *see* another stuffed tomato, I swear I'll vomit."

"Well, Gus and I had a really great time. Really great."

Olivia heard the words, but was unaffected by them. Nor did the sight of Simon, his arm hung limp over Rosie Baker's shoulder, his smiling mouth up close to Rosie's ear, affect her. It was as though her emotions were suspended, waiting.

All afternoon she had wandered in such a state, moving from park to coffee shop to department store, delaying her return to Chelsea until the last moment, pumping her senses with energy in order to enfeeble her thoughts.

After the tumult of the preceding weeks, the conflict, the fear, the despair, and the desperate hope, it was good to be thus empty. It was good to know that she need do nothing, that an undeflectable force was moving towards her, was seeking her out, would fill her.

On a mattress draped with Indian cotton, in a pose of meditation, she waited for the man who seemed to be this force's messenger.

20

"Look, mate, if I want to crash a party, I don't pick one at the top of fifty bloody pitch-black flights of steps! Olivia— Olivia Mannion—asked me to meet her here. Is that all right? Can I go in now? Or would you like her to come and identify me first?"

"Okay, man, there's no need to get heavy."

The long-haired boy half turned, his movement restricted by the crowd behind him, and nodded toward a doorway on the far side of the hall in which he stood.

"She's probably through there somewhere," he said.

"Thanks. And next time I'll remember to bring my visiting card."

Removing his hands from his pockets, Michael began to shoulder his way toward the place that the boy had indicated. A woman staggered against him.

"You don't know where Terry's buggered off to, do you, sweetheart?" she asked.

"Tallish sort of guy?"

"That's him."

"Ah! Well, in that case, I just passed him on the stairs with a Chinese chick," said Michael.

When he had reached his destination, he stopped. He wanted, if possible, to see Olivia before she saw him, to assess from the outside her involvement with the people around her, her relationship to her boyfriend. Pressing against and merging into the door lintel, he scanned the scene before him. It was one with which he was not unfamiliar.

Five years ago it would have been unfamiliar. Five years ago such a gathering, of black and white, of homosexual and heterosexual, of aristocrat and plebeian, of artisan and intellectual, would have bewildered him. He would have searched in vain for a common denominator. Passing from elderly poet to student, from earl's daughter to hairdresser's assistant, from established middle-aged film producer to junkie with holes in her arms, he would have become angry and bemused.

Five years ago, however, was before he had discovered his escape route: the route that had led him around and into and through these people, with such thoroughness that bewilderment had soon degenerated into contempt. He knew now what it was, the common denominator that united them, time after time, in pubs and cafés and each other's houses. His name for it was "fossilized adolescence" and by this he meant a disregard of reality, a facile fluency on subjects not experienced, a naïveté disguised as idealism, an ignorance disguised as tolerance, a complacent belief in one's moral supremacy.

Now he could laugh, remembering his first uncertain steps among them (these ridiculous children masquerading as adults), remembering the nervousness he'd felt at the first of their parties he'd attended. Nervous! Of what? Of being denounced for a fraud? How could he have been when, for them, there were no standards of genuineness? Everyone and everything was acceptable to them, since, even when they were physically involved with them, everything and everyone existed not as facts but as concepts, or aspects of concepts.

The invulnerability implicit in this quality did, from time to time, anger Michael. More often, however, he was grateful for the license that it gave him—grateful, but no less contemptuous for all that.

He saw Olivia.

She, apparently at one with the party, squatting in a mock-yoga position, her eyelids lowered, became the focal point for his distaste. He licked his mustache and patted the pocket of his jeans.

Then he became aware that *she* was watching *him,* that her eyes, although closed, were not locked.

At once, he shuffled his feet and coughed and said, "Hello."

Nor was the embarrassment completely false. It was annoying to him to be caught off his guard by an amateur.

"Hello."

"I found you, then."

He took a step toward her, searching her face for signs of awareness.

"Would you like some wine?" she asked.

"Okay," he answered, the tone of his voice as uncommitted as the word.

She lurched to her feet.

"I'll get you some," she said.

"Look, it doesn't matter. It'll take half an hour to get through that lot out there. I'll share yours, if that's all right."

"Yeah, fine."

She bent down, picked up her cup, then returned to the standing position.

"Have it all," she said. "It's pretty revolting."

"Ta."

Michael drank. The girl had seen nothing untoward in his expression during the seconds he had thought himself unnoticed. He was sure of this; sure, also, that she had been waiting for him to come, was waiting for him now to make a first move.

"Where's your boyfriend, then?" he asked, extracting from his jacket a box of cigarettes.

"Simon? Oh, somewhere around. I never said he was my boyfriend, though."

"That was the impression."

"Yes. Well . . ."

She shrugged and Michael did not feel it necessary to pursue the subject.

Instead, he said, "Would you like a smoke? I mean, not tobacco. Or might your friends get a bit huffy?"

"No, of course not. Yeah, go ahead. Would you like to sit down?"

"There doesn't seem to be much room."

"Oh, of course there is. Frank, could you move up a bit?"

They sat together on the mattress. Then Michael unpeeled a couple of cigarettes, rerolled the tobacco (together with some strands of marijuana) into fresh paper, lit the joint, and passed it to Olivia.

"Thanks," she said.

"These your friends, then?" he said. "From university?"

"Some of them. Not all."

"But you like them?"

"Yes . . . Well, some of them are okay. Why?"

"Oh, I suppose . . . I don't know. I mean, the guy who let me in, he seemed like a real daft idiot. All 'Hey, man,' you know, in that phony American accent."

"Well . . ."

86

"No. I mean, I'm sure he's really nice. I'm just not used to this sort of thing, that's all. The people I know seem to be . . . more serious. Boring, I suppose you'd call them. Only, you see, they've never had the chance to think of life as some sort of game. But then, *you* don't look as though *you* do, either. . . ."

"I don't. And nor do they. People always . . ."

"What?"

"Come on. You're being difficult on purpose. You know what I mean. At parties . . ."

"I'm sorry. I come barging in here, uninvited, and start criticizing your friends. You must think I'm the most loud-mouthed bastard going. And I'm probably just jealous, anyway."

"Jealous? What of?"

"Well, you know, the charm, the self-confidence, the being able to use words the way they want to."

"Oh, fuck charm!" said Olivia.

Michael said nothing.

"Damn it and fuck it!"

Her look slid across the room, to where a slim boy, with baby hair and grasshopper legs, was dancing.

Michael said, "Well, I don't know. It can be useful."

"You're too bloody right it can. And I'm sorry, you were right about what you said before, too. People do treat life like a game. Or, at least, not all of them, but some."

She sank back against the wall and Michael handed her a second joint, which he had been rolling in preparation.

Through the haze in front of her eyes and the haze behind her eyes, Olivia studied the man who sat beside her. The crudeness of his appearance both attracted and repelled her. His skin was dark and rough and pitted by the scars of either chicken pox or acne. His hair, particularly that around the mouth, was coarse and almost black. His lips were moist and when he smiled one saw that his well-spaced teeth were pointed.

Although he was neither tall nor stocky, there was about him an impression of hard strength. Only his eyes seemed nimble, seemed to dart and flit, like rats inside the carcass of a bear.

Superimposing upon him a picture of Simon (Simon, with his soft, deliberately unfocused eyes, his pearl-pale, pearl-hard lips, his downy face, his gangling, downy body), she thought, He's not very good-looking, and was surprised by a feeling not of pity, not of scorn, but of alarm. If what little she knew of this man appealed to none of the usual senses within her, to what *did* they appeal? What part of her *was* it to which he was so attractive?

She searched the studio again. Simon was dancing with Rosie still, but now he was facing Olivia, and for a moment their eyes met.

Please, she thought; do something. Rescue me.

She knew the entreaty to be absurd, knew that Simon would not hear it were she to shout it in his ear, was no longer even certain that she wanted him to, but it seemed essential to give him the chance. If only to create one specific moment that would remind her, should reminder ever be necessary, that it was *he* who had abandoned *her* first.

"What did you do with yourself this afternoon, after you left me?"

The voice that drew her away from Simon was gentler than she had heard it before, more confident and relaxed. Looking at the speaker, seeing his gold-brown eyes, his red lips, his wide black nostrils, the alarm and the attraction clashed once more within her.

"This afternoon?" she asked, as though she might have misheard him.

"Yeah. Did you go back home?"

"No. No . . ."

"Look, Olivia, do you want me to go? I mean, if you wish you hadn't asked me to come here . . ."

"No, of course not."

Olivia swallowed spittle. Over the last quarter of an hour, her tongue and lips had become like rubber, her eyelids like iron. Her head hummed with the friction of battle within it.

"You know, I really like you, Olivia."

"No, I didn't know."

She wrinkled her forehead. Even speech, even facile conversation, seemed difficult now. She would have preferred to have said nothing, to have thought nothing, to have done nothing. She wanted to be passive. She was ready to be acted upon.

"Well, I do. Does it annoy you, me saying that?"

"Why should it?"

"It shouldn't. A compliment should never be swatted away, like a fly. But there are people who do that, all the same. People who are frightened of getting stung, or dirty."

His voice was like a soft and powerful bird. She curled herself up on its back, waiting for it to carry her away.

"Are you feeling all right?"

"Yes."

"You look to me like you could do with a bit of fresh air. Come on. I'm going to take you outside."

He eased her upright. With his fingers round her elbow, he guided her toward the door, through the doorway, through the hall, and out onto the landing.

"You haven't left anything back there, have you? A coat or somet'?"

"No. Nothing."

"Good."

He supported her down the wide, worn carpeted staircase, past dark door recesses and scuttling drafts. Thus close to him, she could smell his sweet-sour perspiration, his hair, his seasoned breath, and, unable to escape from these odors without escaping from him, allowed them to overwhelm her.

"Olivia?"

"Yes?"

They had reached the street. Along the pavement's edge, a line of silent cars was parked, and Olivia thought, What's wrong with them? Then she realized. The windscreen of each was blinded by a cataract of frost. Exhaling, she saw her breath curl visibly across the night.

"That's odd," she said.

The man said, "Well, it had to happen, didn't it? Summer had to finish sometime. Anyroad, I'm not sure I don't prefer winter."

"Yes. It's cleaner, isn't it? Less . . . putrid."

"That's right. That's quite right. I'd never thought of it like that. Olivia . . ."

He turned her toward him and she thought that he might be going to kiss her. Instead, he raised one hand to her face, then stroked its nail-bitten fingers across the mound of her lips.

"You are coming home with me, aren't you?" he asked.

"If that's what you want."

"Of course it's what I want. Come on, I'll find us a taxi. You're not cold, are you?"

"No. No, I'm not cold at all."

21

The sound of the bell had not yet faded into silence when Edward Mannion reached the front door of his house and let Dick Hastings in.

"Sorry about the hour, old chap," said Dick.

It was quarter past twelve at night.

"That's quite all right. Come in."

90

The two men passed into the drawing room. From its place on a circular lucite tray, Edward lifted a decanter of whisky, poured some into the glass from which he had been drinking, and waved the rest at Dick.

"No, thanks, old chap."

"Gin?"

"Well, all right. Just a drop."

When the drinks had been poured and their consumption started, when the men had seated themselves in black leather armchairs, Edward said, "I'm afraid I couldn't understand one word you were trying to tell me on the phone."

"No, well, you know, I didn't want to be *too* specific. It was a public call box, in a pub."

"Of course. So, anyway . . ."

"Well," said Dick; he deposited his glass upon a side table, wiped his mustache, and rubbed his thighs. "Well, I'd gone there to meet this chappy I told you about this afternoon, the one who'd said he might have something for us. Way up in North Finchley, it was. That's where he lives. And *that's* why it's taken me such a deuce of a long time to get round here. Anyway, I'd only sounded him out on the off chance. More mentioned it casually, in passing, this morning. You know, given him the description and asked him if it rang a bell. . . ."

"And did it?"

"Well . . ."

With conscious solemnity, Dick reached into the inner pocket of his worn tweed jacket and produced a folded sheet of newspaper. Having smoothed an imaginary crease from it, he passed it to Edward, who unfolded it. And there, flanked by three equally smudged and dehumanized photographs, was the solid, pitted, bearded face of the man in the underground station.

"That the fellow?" asked Dick, anxiety and eagerness struggling to suppress themselves within his voice.

"That's him," said Edward.

"Read the article."

"I am, I am."

The story that accompanied the pictures, which was dated several months previously, was an earlier chapter from the one that Edward had read twenty-eight hours before in the *Evening Standard,* in a taxi between Chelsea and Piccadilly. It told of the arrest of four young people for offenses connected with an explosion at a Midlands factory in which one man had died: of Pieter van der Walt, aged twenty-five; of Barbara van der Walt, his wife, aged thirty-two; of Malcolm Davis, aged twenty-four; of Michael O'Keefe, aged thirty.

"Michael O'Keefe," said Edward. "So that's where he got his information. Well, I've got him now, the bastard. How did your friend come to have this?"

"Oh, he collects things like that. Bits and pieces of information that could be useful to him, or to others. He's a bit of a —well, not exactly an informer, but, you know, he keeps his eyes and ears open."

"I know," said Edward. Smiling, he folded the sheet of paper.

"I'm afraid I'll have to give it back to him," said Dick.

"Of course. Take it. I've got everything I need. I was pretty sure there'd be a vulnerable spot if only we could find it."

"But, I mean, presumably they couldn't pin it on him—this what's-it, this explosion. If he's still wandering about and so on."

"No, they dropped the charges against all of them except van der Walt. But I bet they didn't like having to do it, all the same. And one little word from me about O'Keefe's proposed 'bargain' the other night—"

"But you couldn't do that, Edward."

"What?"

"Go to the police."

"Well, of course, I don't *want* to. Of course I don't *want* this oaf singing his nasty, little songs all over the place. The publicity could be disastrous. But that's all, Dick. That's all that could happen. For him—for O'Keefe, though—it'd be a different story, wouldn't it? You see?"

Edward paused, a schoolmaster insuring his class's comprehension; then, apparently satisfied, he said, "So that's *that* problem disposed of," and smacked his hands together.

A few minutes later, Dick, having refused, then accepted, a final tumblerful of gin, stepped out into the night. Edward watched him go. When the tacking, rolling figure of his junior partner had veered from sight around the corner of the street, he drew into his lungs a satisfied draught of air. Now he knew for certain that O'Keefe was nothing more than an amateur anarchist, a delinquent, a left-wing loser with a festering chip on his shoulder; not a threat, no threat.

He would have stayed for a long time on the doorstep, inhaling and exhaling his satisfaction, had not a shiver interrupted the swing of his concentration. His physical senses, previously focused on a point close to where Dick had left his field of vision, snapped back. His eyebrows tightened.

"God, it's cold," he said.

He rubbed his forearms. He turned back in to the house, where, along the entrance hall and down the narrow staircase, a rush of silence poured to meet him.

He wondered where Olivia was.

Then he remembered that she had gone to a party with her boyfriend. He looked at his watch and decided that she must be spending the night with him. He supposed that one or the other of them used a contraceptive.

Dick would be spending the night with Sally.

Edward closed the front door of his house. He extinguished the hall light. He thought once more of the news that he had been brought and, climbing the dark stairs to bed, smiled.

22

Never had anyone made love to her like that. Never had she thought that she would want them to. And yet, although her intellect had been appalled by the brutality and gracelessness of his attacks, her body, less deceitful, had devoured them. Even now, half an hour after he had fallen asleep beside her, his hair-matted back not covered by sheets, his tarantula arms flung heavy, she was galvinized by recurring spasms of pleasure, as though fine strands of electric wire had been threaded across the top and inside of her thighs and were now being charged and recharged with the memory of his power.

They no longer touched each other as they lay (he on his stomach, she on her back) side by side in the untidy double bed, but she could feel his hold upon her still, through finger-bruised skin and aching muscles.

On the far side of the room from them, a window, its glass besmeared by orange streetlight, its curtains colorless and limp and pushed apart, rattled against its frame. Next to it stood a dressing table and, farther round the room, on the right-hand wall in relation to the bed, were a mantelpiece and fireplace and a chest of drawers. These were common items of furniture, both in themselves and in their design, yet it occurred to Olivia that there was something strange about them. Then she realized: there was nothing on them. On none was there an ornament or a photograph; on none was there a brush or a comb or a book or a crumpled paper handkerchief. Each was as sterile and anonymous as the furnishings of a hotel.

Where is this place? she thought.

Having slept on the journey there, she knew only that she was at some distance from the center of the city, in an area of red-brick semi-detached houses, with waist-high gates and cemented paths leading to glass-paneled doors.

Is this where he lives?

She tried to sit up, as though sitting would enable her to think. A weight of tiredness and of the still-felt presence of the man along her body prevented her.

She closed her eyes and sleep rushed through her.

23

"Hey, Simon, it's way past three o'clock, you know."

"Is it?"

"Look, would you like to spend the night here? We could put some blankets on the sofa, if you want."

"What? Oh, sorry, Teddy. No. No, I'm going."

Simon lifted himself from the floor and looked around him, as though searching for a hat or coat. Teddy Royce's studio, now empty of everybody but its owner, Frank, and Simon, had the sordid, exposed appearance of a theatre when the play is over, the audience gone home. Tables and windowsills and floors were littered with paper cups and wine bottles, with ashtrays spilled over; plates of uneaten food stared out from previously shadowed hiding places; chill, smoke-stale air hung in the vacuum made by the guests' departure.

Simon thought, God, how horrible. Is this what it was all in aid of?

As a rule, he did not stay at parties until their end. As a rule, Olivia and he would . . .

"I couldn't have some coffee, could I?" he asked.

"Of course," said Teddy. "Come into the kitchen."

"Look. I mean, do *you* know who that guy was?"

"Which one?" Teddy was pouring beans into an electric grinder. "The one Olivia—?"

"Yes."

"No. No, I gather he . . . I think Olivia invited him, actually."

"How do you know that?"

"One of Frank's friends let him in. Isn't that right, Frank? He said—he gave the *impression*—Olivia'd asked him to meet her here. I can't say I took to him, from what little one saw."

"No," said Simon, "he wasn't exactly charming. So what—?"

His fists, a second before half raised in impotent questioning, now smashed through the air to hit the drainboard in front of which he stood, and in the moment that flesh and stainless steel made contact, a flare of white pain erupted within his head, a pure, crystal agony of loss and loneliness, of hatred and of love. But it passed. No sooner had it arrived than it passed. In the time it took for him to accept a cigarette from Frank, Simon was able to speak again.

"So what," he said, "is that stupid girl doing with him? I mean, who is he? Where did she meet him? Okay, okay, so quite obviously they're having a thing together. I mean, you'd have to be mentally deficient not to realize that. They weren't exactly ambiguous about it, were they? But why couldn't she just have told me? Why couldn't she just have said, 'Look, while you've been away I've met this other guy and'—well—'I like him better than you,' or something? I mean, for God's sake, wouldn't that've been the civilized thing to do?

"I'd've accepted it, after all. There wouldn't have been much point doing anything else. It's ridiculous, clinging on to a relationship that doesn't exist any more. Well, of course I wouldn't've just said, 'Oh, it's finished, is it? Fine. Well, see you around sometime.' I'd've wanted to know why. What went wrong. But I wouldn't have thrown a scene or anything and she bloody well knew that."

"Milk, Simon?" Teddy asked.

Frank held a bottle at arm's length, a look of tactful inquiry on his face.

"Oh, no, thanks."

Simon was grateful for the neutrality of his audience. Knowing that its members had neither sympathy for nor empathy toward his problem, knowing also that they were strong enough together to have no need to feed upon the weaknesses of others, he felt able to use them as a sounding board without the risk of distortion.

He swallowed a mouthful of coffee. Its rich, bitter taste seemed to be the taste of the morning: the taste of overfull ashtrays and of pre-dawn silence.

"Am I being unreasonable?" he asked. "No, I'm bloody well not. I'm not saying that she 'owed it to me' to tell me, or anything. Our relationship wasn't like that. We didn't have some contract of behavior. . . .

"Perhaps that's what she wanted. That *is* what she wanted. But why? She never used to. Couldn't we just've gone on the way we were, trusting each other? I don't know. Accepting each other? Respecting each other? Why did she have to try and pin me down, and then, just because she couldn't, go fucking off with someone else? Some fat, lecherous, middle-aged opportunist? I mean . . ."

Simon paused. Teddy Royce had thrown himself into a rocking chair, from where, his legs outstretched, his head tossed back, he watched the kitchen ceiling. Frank, at the table, studied the rim of his coffee cup.

"Oh, bugger. It's all so stupid. We were about to break up anyway. In Canada I realized we were. I didn't sleep with anyone else, but . . .

"But perhaps if we'd *talked* about it . . . I don't know. It just seems like such a waste, such an ugly, messy . . . Still, if this is what she wants . . . I'm not going to cry about it, anyway. That's for certain. And I'm not going to go making ghastly scenes all over the place, either. That'd be the last straw. It'd mean that everything *I'd* said was as meaningless and hypocritical as everything she'd . . . Oh, fuck, fuck, fuck."

Simon crushed his eyes with the heels of his hands. When his brain was filled with a soft purple fog, he lifted his face again.

"Still," he said, "it's over. That's . . . I mean, in a way I'm not . . ."

He sighed. He rubbed his long-extinguished cigarette against the bottom of a saucer. He drained the tepid coffee from his cup. He stood up.

"You're sure you wouldn't like to sleep on the sofa?" Teddy asked.

"Quite sure. Thanks. I'm fine."

"Okay. Well, go carefully."

"I shall. And thanks for listening to me. You must be half dead."

"Not at all. None of us has got to get up for work tomorrow, in any case."

"Yes, that's something."

Simon left them. He walked slowly down the staircase and out into the street, waiting for a return of pain now that he was alone. None came. Instead, as his feet began to slap faster along the pavement, as his body straightened to receive the night air, he was filled with a sense of escape, of freedom, with a hysterical desire to sing.

24

Michael's back felt cold. Twisting his arm from the shoulder, he groped behind him for the blanket and pulled it up to lie across his neck. Then he burrowed with his face into the flat gray pillow and waited for sleep to repossess him.

He had been dreaming. About what he could not remember, but the echoes that remained were strong and confident and strangely joyful. He would have liked to have heard the original note again. This, however, proved to be impossible. Shut his eyes as tightly as he would, he could not prevent his own awareness from wedging itself with growing persistence between his body and the dream. Fifteen seconds later, he abandoned the struggle. He raised his head and torso and opened his eyes.

Daylight startled him.

He turned his wrist to expose the face of his watch. It was twenty past ten. It was twenty past ten and it was Wednesday and there were still a dozen things to fix. He mumbled his annoyance out loud.

Then a movement in the bed beside him grabbed at his breath. It was not that he had forgotten the girl, rather that he had counted on a minute or two alone in which to assess the last stage in his progress with her.

Their making love had been no more than he had planned and, as such, did not need analyzing. What did require some careful evaluation was the character of the lovemaking, the unpremeditated depth and ferocity it had acquired.

Still watching the circle of time around the inside of his wrist, Michael listened. The creaking of bedsprings had stopped. The other person's breathing was slow and regular.

He eased his weight onto one elbow.

Olivia lay on her back, but her face was tipped toward him, so that he could see how flushed her skin was, how swollen and raw her lips, how bruised the thick white ligaments of her neck. As he watched, a flame shot up from Michael's penis to sear the muscles of his lower stomach. He clenched his teeth and tapped at the air with his fist. With a drawn-out shudder, the passion passed away.

His annoyance with himself, however, increased. It wasn't convenient that she should excite him, either at this or any other moment.

Nor could he understand why she did so. The women with whom he enjoyed his sex as a rule were coarser and less serious, were (in attitude, if not profession) scrubbers. It had never occurred to him that Olivia would be capable of giving him the pleasure that she had last night, still less that she would have been able to receive *his* lust so eagerly.

He told himself that it must have been the marijuana that had liberated her, and this answer, although plausible, did nothing to placate his growing irritation. The suspicion that, were he to touch her now, she might push him away and insist on going home was not easy to bear. Yet he dared not put it to the test, since failure would be more disastrous than uncertainty.

He let his focus slide away from the girl's face and out onto the faded flower-patterned paper of the room. He narrowed his eyes and tucked his upper lip behind the lower.

No, the girl must *not* leave; not yet—not until he was sure that she would return. He forced himself to concentrate.

Item by item, he ran through the plan in his mind, through the things he had already done and the things he had yet to achieve. It wasn't a simple plan. Even Malcolm and Barbara were unaware of its complexity. Yet this complexity, this need for the dexterous manipulation of people and circumstances, was as enjoyable to Michael as the prospect of his ultimate reward. With it, he could at least begin to assuage the bottomless hunger that gnawed, day in, day out, at his gut: the hunger for control, for status, for revenge.

This morning, his first move would be to introduce Olivia to her fellow pawns.

It wouldn't have been suitable for her to meet them before. Yesterday evening, she would have seen them as a threat, as conspirators against her rather than with her. (It was for this reason that he had instructed Barbara and Malcolm to make themselves scarce when he should turn up with the girl.) Today, however (when, by letting him make love to her, she had already taken the first voluntary step toward commitment), the presence of the others would act as a reassurance, as a confirmation that what she had done was more than a personal act of rebellion, was an acceptable, group-approved gesture.

Then he would pack her off home to think things over, while *he* got on with the practical arrangements.

With this thought, his glance traveled back across the room to rest once more upon Olivia's face. Annoyance against her relaxed into an amused pity. She was, after all, nothing more than a sheep, as so many people were. Coming from the class she did and having the education she had, he had feared that this might not be so, that she might have been, like himself, a dog. She wasn't, however. His fears had been groundless. He would drive her wherever he wanted: against her fellows, over cliffs, anywhere that was convenient. In spite of her money and freedom and opportunities (or perhaps because of them; he supposed that this was possible), she wanted nothing more than a herd to belong to and a dog to guide her heels.

Michael smiled. The smile spread into a grin. The more sheep in the world, after all, the more fun for the dogs.

Then he stopped smiling, stretched out his hand, and trickled his fingers over Olivia's face. Her muscles jerked. Her eyes slid open.

"Morning, Olivia," he said.

"Oh, hi—?"

"Michael."

"Michael. I'm sorry."

He was pleased to see her blush, aware that it wasn't only his name that she was remembering.

25

Breakfast consisted of instant coffee and toasted white bread spread with butter and rindless marmalade, yet Olivia ate and drank as though she had done neither for a week. The kitchen to which Michael had escorted her and where she now sat was flooded with a hard, clear light, through whose center an oblique and dancing beam of dust was plunged. Beyond French windows, sparrows hopped across a rectangle of motley grass, and these, or other birds, called to each other, shrill above the softer, baser hum of traffic.

She was amazed at the feeling of safety and peace that surrounded her, the sense of all danger having been locked outside.

On waking, she had not felt safe. On opening her eyes to see, enormous above her, the full, dark, red-lipped face of the man, on regaining consciousness to the pungent smell of his sweat, she had had the impression of standing with her back to a pit. Fear, remorse, and disbelief had frozen her. Thoughts of her father and of Simon had arisen to catch in her throat.

Then Michael had called her by name, had linked *her* name to *his* name and, like a tidal wave, the force of her commitment to him, the totality with which she had offered herself to him, had struck her. She had lifted her hand and laid it within the cup of his.

"How are you feeling?" he had asked.

"Fine," she had answered.

"You're lovely."

He had helped her from the bed and, when they were both dressed, had led her downstairs. Hearing voices from within the kitchen, it hadn't occurred to her to be surprised.

"Barbara, Malcolm, this is Olivia. Olivia, that's Barbara and that's Malcolm. So how about some breakfast, then?"

The woman was approximately ten years older than Olivia, with a sagging, scraggy body and a face strung out between aggression and apology. The youth, who was more her own age, wore sexuality like a gun and intelligence like a flick-knife.

Olivia saw these things, saw also the chipped, circle-marked varnish of the kitchen table, the greasy orange of the kitchen walls, the last year's calendar, the soot-gray curtains, the paper shopping bags spilling over with sodden garbage. She saw them, but as a crude and hastily painted gauze, behind which other, more important things were taking place. It was as though the tidal wave of commitment, having swept her off her balance, had retreated to leave her afloat in a scum-covered sea, beneath whose stagnant and apparently motionless surface, however, she could sense the drag and pull of fresh, cleansing currents.

The conversation that took place across the breakfast table was, in its banality, a part of the surface calm.

Barbara said, "I see. So you've just left university, have you? That's nice."

Olivia said, "Oh, I don't know if it is."

"Why's that, love?"

"Well, I don't know if being there in the *first* place was *so* wonderful, and having left—well, I seem to have come to some sort of giant full stop."

"What were you reading?" Malcolm asked.

"History."

He laughed. "I know," he said. "I did a year at art school. But what's the point? *I* end up teaching forty kids that blue and yellow make green and *you* end up teaching forty kids that the battle of Hastings happened in 1066. Shit!"

"Yes, there's that. But I wasn't just talking about that, about job prospects and so on. It's more . . . Oh, how can I explain it? A loss of identity, I suppose. I mean, at the beginning of June I was a student, and at the end of June . . . nothing. Nobody. So I've got to start all over again, redefining myself, in a way. And I don't mean as a 'teacher,' or a 'housewife,' or whatever. No, I don't mean that. But as a person, with . . . oh, a direction, a shape."

"But that's already there, inside you," said Barbara. "Isn't it?"

"Yes, of course. Well, the basic things, anyway. The basic character. The basic inclinations. But I'm not *aware* of them. Not aware enough, I mean. What I've got to do is decide my priorities—what's important to me and what isn't, what's got to be discarded in favor of what. At the moment, everything's so . . . muddled."

"Cigarette, Olivia?" Michael asked.

Malcolm said, "You shouldn't think so much. While you're thinking, someone else is treading you into the ground. Just do. And think about it afterwards, if you've got to."

Barbara said, "He's right, love. We can tell you that. Can't we, Michael? I mean, I don't know exactly what priorities you're talking about, but if there's something you think you ought to do, then you go out and do it. And bugger the consequences."

The conversation was not extraordinary. Having only just thought them, Olivia had never before said the things that now she said, but the words she used, the assumptions she operated from, and the concepts she framed her ideas within were no different from what they would have been had she been speaking with Simon, or with any other of her friends. Nor were the interjections of Barbara and Malcolm alien to her.

What *was* exciting (what made her notice the sunlight in the kitchen rather than the furniture, the view beyond the kitchen window rather than the dirty windowpanes) was the force that flowed in countermotion to the conversation, the force that revealed itself in Barbara's hectic nervousness, in

104

Malcolm's bitterness, the force that was of a different element from the enervating restlessness with which Simon was sometimes charged. Feeling it—or, more exactly, feeling the effect of its outermost ripples—Olivia's senses tingled. She yearned to be swept away by its central power. She knew also that this was not a hopeless wish; that, having come so far, the final immersion was possible.

"Olivia's not averse to action," said Michael. "Those ideas of hers don't stay stuck in her mouth, like they do with some middle-class intellectuals."

"What ideas are those?" Malcolm asked.

"Well, she's a great believer in justice, for a start. In fairness. And in truth."

"Is that right?" Malcolm asked.

"Well, yes," said Olivia. "Yes, of course. But then, so are most people."

She could see that the men were treading in ever-decreasing circles around her. She could feel the wide noose of a lasso tightening. And she didn't mind, because the energy behind this inward momentum was the same single-minded energy that lit up the house and caused its inhabitants to hum with the high, clear note of a common purpose.

Barbara said, "Oh, come on, love. Most people don't believe in anything. As long as *they're* all right, that's that. Pull up the drawbridge and let the other fuckers drown. That's what most people believe in."

"Well, maybe. I don't know."

"*I* do. *We* do, don't we, Michael? We know what selfish, don't-give-a-damn bastards people can be."

"Why? What happened?" Olivia asked.

She spoke in the same passive tone as before, but within her throat a pulse of apprehension thudded. What they were about to say, what (with such lack of subtlety) they had been preparing her for, *had* to be important. It had to be big enough and powerful enough to carry her. An anticlimax, a petty grudge, an obvious lie would sink beneath the weight of her longing.

"I mean, what makes you say that? In particular? About people being bastards?" Olivia asked.

"Do you ever read the papers?" said Malcolm.

"Yes. Of course."

"Did you read about the guy who just got fifteen fucking years for planting a handful of explosives in a factory?"

"A factory that made over *twenty percent* of its profits out of trade deals with South Africa?" Barbara's hair had broken loose from its elastic band. Her fingers tapped the ash from a cigarette. "Selling machinery to slaveowners?" she said. "Growing fat on the misery of slaves?"

"Yes, I think I read about it," said Olivia. "But wasn't someone killed in the explosion? I don't know, a night watchman or something?"

"Ah, yes. The night watchman."

Michael pushed back the chair on which he had been sitting and stood up. He walked away from the table. Turning round again, thrusting his hands in the waistband of his jeans, he said, "The night watchman."

Three pairs of eyes made him the focal point of their attention.

"The poor, innocent old man who 'died as a result of the explosion.' The poor, innocent old man whose heart was so dicky it might've given out at *any* moment, for *any* bloody reason. A kid creeping up behind him and going 'boo!' A cat eating his favorite budgie. Anything."

"I didn't know he died of a heart attack," said Olivia.

"Whether you knew it or not, that's what happened."

"But the papers didn't say anything about it."

"No, I know bloody well what the papers said. 'Died as a result of . . .' But you weren't in court for the trial, were you?"

"No."

"Right. Well, at the trial it was established, beyond any

question of doubt, that the man not only died of a heart attack, but had a history of coronary weakness going back years. The prosecution and, of course, the judge took it upon themselves to dismiss these facts as unimportant. The press, too, evidently."

"Well, in a way they were right," said Olivia. "I mean, perhaps not legally, perhaps not in relation to the sentence the guy got, but morally they were. Okay, so the night watchman might've died at any time, for any reason, but *that* night it was the explosion that killed him. And anyway it was only by chance that it didn't literally kill him. I mean, blow him to pieces. The fellow—what's his name? Van der Walt?—doesn't seem to have given a damn one way or the other."

"Van der Walt," said Barbara, "is my husband."

For a long while, Olivia said nothing. Nor was she aware of thinking anything. If a conflict was taking place within her head, its pitch was too high, its speed too fast for her to be aware of it. She only knew that the force whose ripples had tantalized her consciousness all morning had risen up at last to slap her in the chest.

"Van der Walt is my husband. He has been imprisoned for fifteen years for what must surely be an understandable political protest." These facts were not like the lights thrown off the dancing rivulets of Simon Shaw's intelligence. Nor were they like the debris spewed ashore by her father's disdainful and oceanic tide. They were the splinters from a torrent in full flood: a torrent of caring and of hatred, of truth and of destruction.

"I'm sorry," she said, at last. "I didn't know. Michael never—"

"That's okay. How could you've? It's not your fault."

"But still . . ." She touched the side of a marmalade pot, picked up a slice of cold toast. "I mean, didn't he know that the night watchman was going to be there?"

"Well . . ."

"Yes," said Michael, "he knew. He also knew, down to the nearest second, at what time the guy was likely to be in what part of the building. He spent days watching him, working his routine out. So it wasn't exactly chance that the fellow wasn't—how did you put it?—'blown to pieces.' It was more like careful, bloody planning."

"I see. I'm sorry," said Olivia. "I didn't know. I'm sorry."

Barbara said, "If you knew what it was like, living in South Africa. Being black or colored, I mean. Not just the working conditions, but the living conditions: the petty, bloody degradations; the prying; the red tape keeping you down at every turn; husbands and wives not seeing each other for months on end because she's a servant in one town and he's a miner in another; old men being shouted at—'Come here, boy!'— children dying of malnutrition while the whites drink gin and tonic round the swimming pool. . . .

"And everyone you tell here says, 'Oh, how terrible.' Even the bloody British government says it. But we don't do anything about it, do we? We still go on trading with them.

"God knows how many letters Pieter wrote to the papers about it, and to M.P.s. God knows how many talks he gave and how many demonstrations he organized. But still nobody listened. So in the end there was nothing for it, *but*—well, an explosion. Something big. Something to fucking well *make* people sit up and listen. And what do they do to him? They put him in bloody prison for fifteen years. Fifteen! He'll be forty-four—*forty-four*—when he gets out."

She was speaking through tears now. Her eyes and the rim of her nostrils glistened.

"Fifteen years for just trying to *tell* people, for just trying to make them *see.*"

"It is an incredibly long sentence," said Olivia. "Isn't there some chance of appealing against it?"

"What do you think?" Malcolm asked.

Michael said, "It's all right if you're a professional gangster.

You just get yourself the best solicitor going and the chances are you'll never see the inside of a prison cell at all. Even though you've murdered thousands of people. But it's not quite the same if you're a penniless idealist. Legal Aid's a bit —how shall I put it?—haphazard. No, God, if we had the money . . . Still, enough of all that. It's not your problem. We'll find some way of coping with it."

He moved toward Olivia and pressed the back of his hand to her face.

"Come on," he said, "I'll see you to the tube station."

"Oh, all right. Well, what time is it?"

"Getting on for twelve."

He threw his cigarette into an ashtray.

"See you two later," he said. "All right, Olivia?"

"Yes, fine. Well, it was good meeting you both. And, you know, if ever—I mean, if there's anything I can do . . ."

Michael left the kitchen and went to the front door of the house. He opened the door and, his back toward Olivia, waited for her in the doorway. Beyond him, a woman pushed a wicker basketful of shopping home. Its wheels rattled over the uneven pavement.

"Anyway," said Olivia, "I'll probably see you again soon. I hope so."

"Yeah, I hope so, too," said Malcolm.

"We'll have to see what happens," said Barbara.

All three were aware, the one as the others, of Michael's authority over the situation, and Olivia, although unwilling at that moment to leave the house, although nervous of returning alone into the world from which Michael had lifted her, recognized the fellowship to which submission admitted her; recognized it and rejoiced in it.

As though to illustrate it with a physical gesture, she shook both Barbara's and Malcolm's hand.

"Bye," she said.

"Look after yourself, love."

"See you."

She left them.

Hearing the fond goodbyes from his position on the doorstep, Michael smiled. He felt like saying, "Don't worry, Olivia. Just so long as everything goes the way it should, you'll be seeing your little friends again very soon. *Very* soon. I promise you." Then her footsteps came toward him along the hallway and the harmony of her subservience to him sang through his body like a contented yawn. That the contentment might, before long, deteriorate into boredom was not improbable, but by the time that happened, it would no longer matter. He didn't wait for her to reach his side before stepping out of the house and onto the sloping, weed-cracked path.

The morning had exceeded his expectations. Unrehearsed, Barbara had provided the very notes of passion and pathos that he had known were indispensable to Olivia's conversion, yet had been unable himself to produce. As he had watched the child's face progress from regret, through hope, to fulfillment, he had swelled with satisfaction. Even the three occasions on which it had been necessary for him to reassert his directorship over the scene had caused him no irritation. Rather they had increased his satisfaction, lifted it from the level of complacency to that of exhilaration.

Now, reaching Wimbledon High Street, Olivia still a pace or two behind him, he asked, "Where are you? Look, that's the tube station over there. It's on the District Line, so it shouldn't take you too long to get home."

Then he paused, turned round, and stretched out to touch her face.

"Am I being very abrupt?" he asked.

"I don't know. Are you?"

"If I am, it's . . . You were okay last night. You know that, don't you? I'm not pushing you off; only, van der Walt, Barbara's husband, was a friend of mine and I'm trying . . . Well, it doesn't matter, but there's things I've got to do today. That's what I mean."

"That's okay. But, Michael?"

"Yes?"

With his free fingers, he lifted a fall of hair from Olivia's eyes and held it against the side of her head. Olivia, forehead puckered, plump lips swollen apart, thrust back at him the intensity of his gaze.

He let the hair fall.

"What?" he asked.

"About Barbara's husband. Just because, at first, I was—"

"Oh, it doesn't matter. You weren't to know."

"No, I know. That's not what I meant. I meant, if . . . Well, if there's anything . . ."

"Look, for Christ's sake, you do realize you mustn't say anything to *anyone* about all this? Not anyone. Even if they ask you. You know—that you've *met* us, Barbara and Malcolm and me, and where we are. You do realize that, don't you? Okay, I'm sorry, of course you do. Only, in some ways, you're such a kid and—"

"Thank you!"

"I'm not insulting you. You're a lot more . . . aware than most kids of your age and education. But you can't escape your upbringing altogether, you know, and you are—how shall I put it?—still 'clean.' Clean in a way Barbara, for instance, has never been."

"But Barbara's not . . . I mean . . ."

"No, all right, she doesn't come from the slums. But all the same, everything she's learned, she's learned the hard way. Not like you. And it does make a difference."

"My life hasn't been entirely free from bloody problems, you know, whatever you may think. And I have been looking after myself quite well, without your help, up till now. Getting by, anyway."

There was a silence. As they faced each other, a· thin breeze ruffled their clothes.

"Okay," said Michael, at last. "Okay, Olivia. Only, will you *promise* not to try and get in touch with me till I ring you?"

"You're going to ring me?"

"Would you rather I didn't?"

"You know not."

"Oh, shit!"

Michael tugged a cigarette from the packet in his jeans, lit it, and threw the match to the pavement.

"Look," he said, "perhaps it'd be better if we *didn't* . . ."

Olivia snatched her eyes from his face and stared at a point beyond his shoulder.

He said, "It's more involved than you *know,* sweetheart. But, okay, okay."

He took her chin between his fingers and brought her gaze back to his. The anger that mixed with the tears in her eyes both surprised and, for a moment, impressed him.

He said, "Hey, Olivia . . ."

She said, "I'm sorry."

He said, "Forget it. It's all right. Understand? Now, go on. Go and get your train."

When she had gone, he walked to the bus stop to wait for a bus going west.

The parting had worked even better than he had envisaged, yet he found that he was willing himself to forget it, was forcing himself to move on to the next operation.

26

Simon awoke at noon. Having eased himself into a sitting position (in such a manner as not to jolt against the fragile shell of his skull the hangover suspended like a demolition worker's ball within it), he climbed from his bed and wan-

dered through the flat to the bathroom. There he ran himself
a tubful of steaming pine-scented water, then lowered himself into it and lay for twenty minutes on his back.

Afterward he made himself breakfast. While drinking orange juice and thick black coffee, while eating scrambled
eggs and toast and greengage jam, he listened to the outpour-
ings of a local radio station:

"Thank you very much, Janice Spurling. And now, for you
and for your daughter Karen, who's going to be married on
Saturday, here's Cilla Black with a song I'm sure you'll both
enjoy. . . ."

When he had finished breakfast, he exchanged his towel-
ing wrap for a cotton shirt and a pair of jeans and returned
along the hallway to the kitchen. By this time, it was quarter
past one.

Half an hour later, at quarter to two, he had cleared the
formica-topped table of cups and plates, had filled a fountain
pen with ink, had opened a notebook to a clean page, had
poured some wine into a glass, had lit a cigarette, had studied
his face in the looking glass above the sink, and was ready to
begin writing.

Now, he thought.

It was about his liberation from Olivia that he wanted
to write, about the weightlessness of relief upon which,
the night before, he had flown from Teddy Royce's flat.

> *The sticky winter bud has split,*
> *The snake has shed his skin . . .*

His pen, having formed these words, withdrew from the
paper. Two seconds later it returned, to annihilate them with
a fat and spluttering line.

> *How painful and sweet, the first breath,*
> *Free from the foetid womb . . .*

At twenty-five past two, Simon had covered half a dozen pages with such phrases, with such crossings-out. The ashtray beside him was full of cigarette butts. His head ached and his stomach felt as though it were lined with dust.

"It's no good. It's no bloody, fucking good. I can't even begin to put it into words."

He stood up and walked to the window. A long way below him, cars nosed around searching for parking spaces and a woman with a Yorkshire terrier hesitated by a lamppost.

He lifted his eyes and looked beyond this small activity, looked out as far as the enclosing rooftops and office blocks would allow him, southeast toward Chelsea.

She was still there. He had thought that he had lost her, had rid himself of her, but she was still there: a magnetic point pulling at his attention. This, then, was why he had been unable to capture his feelings, why every poem had flagged, impotent, after the first few lines. He could not write in praise of freedom because he was not yet free.

Simon frowned. He shivered and went to the bedroom where he put on a sweater. He returned to the kitchen and lit a cigarette.

He had to go and see her.

During the two years of his relationship with Olivia, he had given as little thought to the possibility of their parting as he had to the fact of their being together, but what thought he *had* given had always been based on the assumption that the event would take place at university, that the man for whom she left him (if that was how it happened) would be another student, someone they both knew, that the breakup would be civilized, analyzed and discussed. It had never occurred to him that it might happen like this. How *could* she have left him in such a way and for such a person? He had to know. He had to understand.

However much he might *wish* (like a spoiled child stamping his foot and crying "Unfair") that things had happened the way he had pictured them, he could not, now that the false euphoria of the previous evening had passed, *pretend* that they had. It was as though the shock of Olivia's brutality had frozen—for the moment, at least—the usually fluid texture of his thoughts, as though the preposterousness of her behavior had called forth some new quality in him.

And this newness frightened Simon. Not just the newness of the situation, of Olivia's having cut herself off from him, of the appearance of the strange, bearded, and threatening man, but the newness within himself: of the newly felt uncertainty and vulnerability that were straining his confidence, eroding the strength of his faith.

He had to go and see her, speak with her. He had to make her say something that he could understand.

He extinguished his cigarette and took his keys from the top of the refrigerator, checked that there was money in his pockets. Then he left the flat, descended the main staircase, and, walking fast, set out along the Kensington back streets.

As he walked, Simon thought about summer, about the slow, hot, wandering days in which there had always been time not only to work, to revise for the coming finals, but to talk, to make love, to drive out to the country with friends, to drink beer on the grass outside a pub, to lie beside a river (Olivia's head upon the pillow of his abdomen, her body sprawled, her long cotton skirt dragged back above brown, scarred knees) and discuss the world as though it were an old, loved book.

Yet even as he invoked them, there pushed through these gentle memories others, less soothing. A month before finals, a boy, whom they both knew, had killed himself. He had jumped from a suspension bridge into a river gorge. When Olivia had heard about this, she hadn't cried but had shouted, "For Christ's sake, doesn't anyone think there's something wrong about that? That a kid should kill himself because he's frightened of failing an exam? Don't you think there might be something about this 'privilege' of further education that we haven't realized?"

Nor was this the only occasion on which she had expressed such bewildered despair. Several times he had had to stroke her to sleep, had had to calm some nightmare about the futility not just of university but of life.

Now, as he turned in to the quiet, tree-dotted street in which Olivia lived, he wondered whether he might not have been overhasty in his patronage of these fears. Perhaps, had he listened to them with more care, had he attempted to understand them, their source, had he explained them away instead of soothing them below the surface, might this breakup never have happened, or happened sooner? Either would have been preferable to the present situation.

He had reached the door. He climbed the steps and rang the chromium-plated doorbell. As he did so, he had the simultaneous impressions that something was slipping between his fingers and that something was rolling down a mountainside to crush him.

"Be in," he whispered. "Please be in."

He heard the footsteps, the clattering of a lock being turned.

"Please, Olivia. Please."

"Simon."

"Hi."

"Well, you'd better come in."

"Thanks."

"Would you like some coffee?"

"Yeah, fine."

"We'd better go down to the kitchen, then."

She was pleased for the excuse to turn her back on him as they moved in single file along the hallway, past the glass door that led onto a gray and sterile courtyard, and down the steep, cramped stairway to the basement. When they had reached their destination, she said, "Sit down"; then, still without looking at him, she filled the electric kettle at the tap.

She had hoped that he wouldn't come. Knowing how he felt about "creating scenes," about making a positive move to alter the course of events, she had hoped that he would wait for *her* to go to *him*, and that, having grown bored with waiting, he would have dismissed her from his life with the callousness of which, also, she knew him to be capable. That he had not done these things could only mean, she supposed, that he had decided to ignore not only the happenings of the previous night but the whole atmosphere of their encounters since his return from Canada.

If this were so, then it was no less typical of him than his staying away would have been. That would have meant he had decided that by *not* turning up today he would be making more of a statement, would be taking more of a stand, than by *turning* up.

Olivia tightened her face and tapped at the side of the kettle, waiting for it to boil. Having reminded herself, however, of how much she disliked the moral fence-sitter in Simon, she felt less nervous than she had done. If (when, as it had to, this meeting turned into a trial) she could see Simon not as an ex-lover, or an ex-friend, or a boy with soft eyes and long, restless limbs, but as the representative of all those who, directly or indirectly, had sentenced Barbara van der Walt's husband to fifteen years' imprisonment, she knew that she would emerge from the ordeal intact.

"You have it with milk, don't you?" she asked.

"You know that, Livvy."

Her back always to him, she took the jar of coffee from its place on the work surface, tipped a mound into each of two mugs, covered them with water, added milk, then turned around.

"Here," she said and found, to her annoyance, that still she could not look into his face.

"Thanks."

He rose from his seat and came toward her. She smelled the gentle, lemony fragrance of his eau de Cologne, felt the brush of cool fingers as he lifted the mug from her hand.

"Aren't you going to come and sit down?"

"Sure," said Olivia. "Would you like a biscuit, or something, with it?"

"No, thank you."

"I think I would."

She took a couple of digestive biscuits from the tin that, as a rule, was opened only by Mrs. Clifford. Having broken a crescent from one of these, she placed it in her mouth. It adhered to her palate like a communion wafer.

"Livvy," said Simon. "What's up? What is it?"

"What do you mean?"

"Oh, come on. I mean, you needn't get worried I'm going to throw a scene or anything. . . ."

"No! Of course not!"

"Well, would you rather I did, then?"

Olivia forced the now sodden lump of whole wheat, fat, and sugar down her throat.

"There's nothing to tell you," she said. "If you didn't understand last night . . . I mean, there's no point me saying the same things over and over again if all you're prepared to hear is a few nice comforting noises, is there?"

"But that's just the point. You haven't said anything. Oh, I'm not so bloody stupid I haven't sensed all the vibrations you've been sending out, but I just don't know what they mean. Okay, so maybe I should. Maybe I'm thick and selfish and immature. But, in that case, couldn't you just help me, Livvy?"

"Oh, for God's sake! Can't you see how grotesque you look, pretending to crawl and—and grovel, like some underaged

Uriah Heep, when all the time your smug, complacent face is registering nothing but contempt for me?"

"That's not true."

"Yes, it is. Don't think I'm stupid, either, Simon. *I* know the only reason you're here is to try and make me feel awful for behaving the way I did at Teddy's party. I know you've only come to confirm for yourself what Teddy and Frank and Rosie bloody Baker have already told you, that you're better off without me. Well, confirm it, confirm it. And then go."

"Olivia, what you're saying—it absolutely isn't true."

"Isn't it? All right, tell me, then. Tell me what you thought about the way I behaved last night."

"You mean, that guy?"

"You know what I mean."

Olivia pulled a chair toward herself and sat on it. She wedged her feet against a crossbar of the kitchen table and stretched across to the adjacent windowsill for her tobacco tin. Simon made a circular movement with the heel of one hand against his forehead. Above them, from the level of the street, came the approaching cry of a newspaper boy. The wordless call echoed from housefront to housefront, stopped (while, presumably, an evening paper was bought), then carried on from the same note as it had left off.

"Okay," said Simon. He pushed his mug of coffee away from him. "Okay, well, let's think. First of all, I suppose, I was pretty fed up with you anyway. You weren't exactly being your easiest, you know."

"What do you mean by that?"

"I mean that you'd retreated, for reasons best known to yourself, into that hiding place from logic you're occasionally so fond of."

"I see."

"Well, it's true. You know you were always saying—what was it?—that arguments could sometimes do more to obscure the truth than reveal it. Weren't you? Anyway, whether I was justified or not, I *was* feeling pretty fed up. And then, I don't know, that guy . . . Look, what I'm about to say, it's not a judgment. I never even spoke to him and, for all I know, he's terrific. It's just what I felt. The impression I got."

"Yes?"

"You're not helping, Livvy. You asked me a question and I'm doing my best to give you an honest, unmelodramatic answer. I got the impression that he was laughing at us, at both of us, at you as well as me. I got the impression that he thought the whole party was stupid and infantile, and that he was only there to have a bloody good sneer at it. Well, okay, maybe he was right about the party, but in any case, I hardly think he was in a position to criticize. I mean, he hadn't exactly been invited, had he?"

"I invited him."

"But it wasn't your party."

"Oh, for Christ's sake! You're not actually trying to accuse me of bad manners, are you? Surely you couldn't be that crass? You know as well as I do that nobody cares who you ask to that sort of do."

"All right, all right, point taken. But you must admit that there was something—how can I put it?—deliberately offensive about the way you never introduced him to anybody, or—"

"Didn't 'circulate'? Is that what you mean?"

"All right."

Simon closed his eyes. Having taken a couple of slow breaths, he opened them again, shook his head, and plowed his untidied hair with his fingers.

"I'm sorry," he said. "You're right. I'm avoiding the issue. I suppose what it really is isn't that *nobody else* knew who he was but that *I* didn't. I mean, you might've told me. You might've warned me. Wouldn't that have been fairer, don't you think?"

"Warned you of what? That I'd asked some guy, if he

wanted, to drop in to a party?"

"You know that's not what I'm talking about."

"What, then? There wasn't anything else, if you'd only bothered to . . . Oh, never mind, never mind. Go on."

"I don't know what you—"

"Go on with what you thought. Go on with your 'impressions.' "

"Well, the other thing was that I couldn't help getting the feeling you were—I don't know—making some kind of gesture, I suppose. I mean, the guy wasn't exactly . . ."

"What?"

"Oh, I don't care if this sounds ghastly. It's what I thought, so it's all that matters. He isn't exactly lovely to look at, is he?"

"No. It's true. You're a lot more beautiful than he is, Simon."

"Fuck 'beautiful'! What I meant . . ."

"I know what you meant."

"Well, as I said, I didn't speak to him. He's probably incredibly witty and intelligent."

"As a compensation?" asked Olivia.

She stood up. She dropped her cigarette into her coffee, so that it sizzled and turned on its side to float upon the puckered surface of the milk.

If a part of her had hoped that Simon would not behave as he had done, another part, nearer to the surface now, was happy to accept the consolation prize of having been sure that he would. She had known that only his pride would be hurt, that only his sense of propriety would be outraged, and she had been right. He was a self-opinionated, shallow, egocentric bastard and her behavior toward him had been not only justified but just.

"Olivia?"

"You'd better go, Simon."

"But it's me who's done all the talking."

"That's not unusual. If a mirror could grunt 'yes' and 'quite right' from time to time, you wouldn't need friends at all. Now, please. I obviously can't *chuck* you out."

"Okay."

He, too, stood up. His face was pinched white and his teeth glistened behind the slit of parted lips, yet, like eyes behind the holes in a mask, an emotion that might have been relief shone.

"I hope you and whatever-his-name-is can make each other very happy," he said.

"His name's Michael," said Olivia, "and I don't suppose he'll make me happy at all. But somehow that doesn't seem to be the most important thing in the world any more. Though I dare say you think that sounds too 'melodramatic' for words."

"You're right. I do," said Simon.

He left the kitchen and Olivia listened to the tread of his feet on the staircase, along the hall. She heard the front-door lock being pushed aside and the door closing.

"Goodbye," she said.

Then, like a fragile house that has received the final and destructive onslaught from a hurricane, her body shuddered and collapsed onto the floor. Nor, once there, did it lie still, but tossed and jerked in irregular, violent spasms as she beat at the rush matting with her fists and rolled her face from side to side, hot tears running.

For an hour she cried thus. Even after the tears had evaporated on her burning skin, her lungs continued their frantic fight for air and the muscles of her face contorted themselves into hideous, desperate grimaces.

It was five o'clock and dusk had already begun its silent infiltration of the room, when, head throbbing, strength exhausted, Olivia fell asleep upon the floor where she had dropped.

27

It was Edward who found her. Having returned home to change before meeting Dick and a couple of clients for pre-dinner drinks at the Connaught, he had decided to pour himself a glass of milk and, for this purpose, had gone down to the kitchen.

For a second, as he stood in the half-light and stared at the body hunched like a rag on the floor, he thought that it was not his daughter but his wife at whom he was looking. It was an absurd idea. Caroline had died nine years before, and her body, when at last they had allowed him to see it, had been flat and neat, beneath white bedding and the glare of hospital lights.

"Olivia," he said.

The horror that he had felt released itself in notes of irritation.

"Olivia."

He could not imagine what the child's motive might be for choosing to sleep at such a time and in such a place. The decision, however, was not atypical of the inelegance and laziness that had appeared to govern most of her behavior since her arrival in his house.

"Olivia, what are you . . ."

A noise halfway between a sigh and a moan emerged from the bundle on the carpet. Frowning, Edward stepped forward. Then, lifting his trousers at the thigh, he knelt beside the girl in such a position that he was able to see her face.

"Well, well, well," he said, at last. "Who would've believed it? She's been and cried herself to sleep."

His expression softened, and he stretched out his hand and removed a string of damp hair from his daughter's cheek.

"Poor old thing."

The first explanation to offer itself, which he accepted, was that she had had a row with her boyfriend. This did not seem improbable. Edward had met the boy twice and on both occasions had found him immature. While Olivia, it appeared, had probably been overpossessive of late.

Now, asleep, with her fists clenched on either side of her head and her skin inflated and pink, she had become a child once more. Remembering the afternoons when he had taken her, by bus, to play in Kensington Gardens, and the mornings when, hand in hand, they had crept from the house to buy a box of chocolates or a bunch of flowers for the still-night-gowned Caroline, Edward smiled.

"Poor thing," he said again.

He wondered whether she might want to talk about it, and decided to leave her a note saying that he would not be late coming home. Easing himself upright, he walked to the hanging paper pad where Mrs. Clifford wrote her shopping lists. When he had covered one sheet of it with words of promise and apology, he placed it in the center of the kitchen table and went upstairs to dress.

28

To begin with, the telephone bell was a part of her dreams; was not, in fact, a bell at all, but the sound of a human voice that was calling her, "Livvy, Livvy . . ." After a while, however, by the strength of its persistence, it succeeded in wrenching itself away from her head and becoming an outside entity over which she had no control.

"Brr, brr. Brr, brr. Brr, brr."

Still she didn't understand what it was that was making this noise. It occurred to her that Simon might be ringing the doorbell.

124

"Brr, brr. Brr, brr."

It was the telephone. She staggered to her feet and across the kitchen, uncertain where she was going, uncertain where the machine lived. There were several extensions in the house, none of them, however, in the basement.

"Brr, brr."

Then she remembered. There was one in the entrance hall.

Even as she climbed the stairs, swaying from wall to banister rail and back again, it didn't occur to her that the ringing might stop until it had received its answer. She imagined that it could visualize her progress toward it, that its pitch was one of annoyance at her lack of speed.

"I'm coming," she said. Then, after reaching the single-legged table on which the machine was enshrined, steadying herself against it, and lifting the receiver from its cradle, she said, "Hello? Who is it? Can I help you?"

A series of rapid "pips" answered her, followed by the dropping of a coin and a voice saying, "Olivia?"

"Michael!"

"Thank God for that. I thought maybe you'd gone out or something."

"No, I've been here all afternoon. Ever since I got back. I just fell asleep, that's all. You haven't been ringing for ages, have you?"

"No, it's all right, not long. Are you alone?"

"Yes. Or, at least, I think so. Hang on."

She turned and listened at the stairs. No sound greeted her.

"Daddy?" she called.

"It's okay," she said. "There's no one else here."

"Great. Now, look, I haven't got any more twopenny pieces, so listen carefully. I've got to see you, Olivia."

"Of course. When?"

"As soon as you can make it. I'm in this pub just up the road from you. The one by the tube station. Do you know it?"

"Yes, I think so. The large one?"

"That's right. Now, can you come at once? It's . . . Well, never mind. I'll tell you when you get here."

"Okay. I'll be as quick as I can."

"Fine. I'll be in the saloon bar."

Then he rang off.

More slowly than he, Olivia replaced her receiver. Having done so, she didn't immediately move, but stood where she was for a minute or two, limbs heavy, as though to allow the scattered pieces of her emotions and thoughts a stillness in which to reassemble themselves into recognizable shapes.

"He rang," she said.

And, if he had done so, she knew that it was not through kindness or politeness. It must, she knew, be because he needed her. For some reason (it was immaterial what) he needed her.

No sooner had this thought finished shaping itself than Olivia thawed, turned, ran upstairs to collect her bag and a pullover, and, face split by a smile she could not have controlled had she wanted to, escaped from her father's house.

29

Michael had taken his glass of beer to a table by one of the pub windows. From this position, he had a command of the street along which Olivia must come, and as he waited for her to do so, he amused himself with observation of the passers-by. It was early evening. The majority of those who strode or scurried or sauntered unaware beneath his scrutiny were people returning from work.

Watching them, Michael was pleased to despise them. The secretaries, the accountants, the shop assistants, and the managing directors: they were none of them any better than his father, with his fifty years of trudging to and from the

126

factory. They were all members of that mindless army of Yo-Yos that spins from home to work to home again throughout the potent years of its life, numbing the quick between childhood and senility, ignoring the purpose of its labor, ignoring that there ever was a purpose.

Here Michael filled his mouth with beer and smiled. In the seven hours since he had parted from Olivia, he had achieved, in terms of both job satisfaction and potential financial gain, more than most of the gray-faced commuters who now filed before him could hope to achieve in a year.

Yet (and this it was that he could never forget, could never forgive in himself) there *had* been a time, not five or six years ago, when he had been prepared to deny not only his pride but his intelligence, if only they would accept him into their fold.

The picture of an interview flashed across his memory. He saw the schedule-papered staff room of a technical college, the line of tables stretched across one end of it, the line of men and women seated behind the tables. He heard the voices:

"Now, Mr. O'Keefe, could you give us some idea as to why you'd like to join our sociology course?"

"I see here that you left school at fifteen and that the only 'O' level you have is in biology."

"You don't seem to have had much luck with your jobs to date, Mr. O'Keefe. A few months here, a few months there . . . Do you find difficulty in applying yourself?"

"How would you fucking well apply yourself to dipping zip fasteners into a vat of purple dye eight hours a day? Or turning the same bolt, with the same spanner, on a never-ending line of identical cars? Or freezing on top of some scaffolding at eight o'clock on a February morning? Or pushing wheelbarrows full of wet cement across the plowed-up surface of a building site? How many fucking months would you lot stick it out?"

127

This was not, of course, the answer he had given them: the elderly man with the spectacles and the faded tweed jacket, the woman chain-smoking untipped cigarettes, the long-haired boy, the irascible Indian, the girl with the cold and the large red nose, at which she dabbed from time to time with paper handkerchiefs.

That had been what he had thought, but what he had said was "About the 'O' levels: I am studying in night school, as I think I put down on that form, and I do hope to have all the necessary exams for this course by the summer. I realize, of course, that you get lots of people applying and that most of them'll be academically better qualified than me, but I am very serious about wanting to do sociology. I've been reading a great many books on the subject."

Remembering the tone of his voice as he had said these things, remembering how he had sat with his hands clasped on his thighs and his shoulders inclined in a pose of humility, Michael wanted to vomit.

Thank God, he thought. Thank God they didn't have me. Thank God that even then I was too far gone for them to take me and mold me and churn me out, a worthwhile member of society's middle class. Thank God.

"Michael?"

"Olivia!"

"I'm sorry. I didn't mean to startle you."

"No. You didn't. Look, sit down. What would you like to drink?"

"I don't mind. Some beer. Shall I get it?"

"No, you sit here. A half or a pint?"

"A half, please."

"Right."

He went to the bar, glad for the opportunity to recompose himself, furious at the carelessness that had made such an action necessary. The hand he had to play that evening was too important for him to jeopardize by inattention.

"A pint and a half of best bitter."

"Right you are, sir."

Glancing over his shoulder, Michael saw that Olivia was watching him. He didn't greet her, but turned back to the bar.

There were times when it seemed as though she were using him as much as, if not more than, *he* was using *her;* when the trust in her wide, strong face became perverted to insatiable greed. On these occasions, too, Michael sensed in the bright blue eyes a ruthlessness all the stronger for being tempered not by indifference but by despair.

Now he told himself that this was a delusion, that he must not let the accident of their lovemaking upset him, that she was more complicated than he had accounted for, perhaps, but, for all that, a gullible, overeducated, underexperienced middle-class fool.

"Thanks," he said to the barman and took the proffered glasses in exchange for a handful of coins.

Then he returned to the table, deposited both beers, and sat down and drank for a minute or two in silence. After which, he lit a cigarette.

"Do you mind if I have one?" asked Olivia. "I left my tin at home."

"Help yourself."

Next to them, a quartet of middle-aged and red-faced businessmen told each other jokes about the Irish. Around them, the buzz of pub talk and the jangle of canned music pulsated in waves across a thickening atmosphere. A poodle begged for peanuts. A woman laughed and accused a man of having pinched her bottom.

"I'm sorry it had to be here," said Michael. "Only, I'd got to see you quick like."

Olivia said, "It doesn't matter."

"No, but I don't much go for this type of place as a rule. More like a nightclub than a pub, with all that wrought iron and soft lighting. Still, they're all the same down here. Not like back home."

"What was it you wanted to tell me?" Olivia asked.

"Yeah, well, I don't quite know how to begin. Look . . ."

As though in an involuntary gesture, his hand shot out across the tabletop, rested a second by hers, and then withdrew.

"Oh, bugger, I don't know how to say it. It's just that I'm not going to be able to see you again, after all," he said.

"I don't understand."

She spoke as though her lips were numb, as though he had hit her across the face and made her mouth swell.

He said, "There's no other way I can put it."

"But it can't be true. I mean, why did you ring me, then? Why? I mean, I thought . . ."

"Look, I'm sorry. Only, it seemed fairer to tell you to your face, that's all. I reckoned you'd at least deserved that much."

For a moment, Olivia floundered. Her face became contorted, her lips drew back, her breathing became audible.

"Please, Olivia, you're only making it worse. It's not what I wanted, either, you know. You've just got to believe that the reasons for my decision are bloody important. More important than us, even. You've just got to take my word for it."

"I am trying. Honestly I am, Michael. But can't you just . . . I mean, these reasons—can't you just tell them to me?"

"You know what they are, Olivia."

Sliding his hand across the tabletop once more, he allowed it, this time, to remain by hers, so that the sides of their little fingers touched.

"You know," he repeated.

"Yes, of course; it's Barbara's husband, isn't it?"

"Pieter? Yes, it's to do with him."

"Well, what?" she asked. "I mean, you appeared to trust me this morning. Or doesn't that count any more?"

"Of course it counts."

130

Lifting his glass to his lips but not drinking from it, Michael scanned the other occupants of the bar. None of them appeared to be listening to him, or even to be aware of his presence amongst them.

"Okay," he said. "It's like this. You remember what you said this morning, about wasn't it possible for us to appeal against Pieter's sentence? And about how I said we could if we had the money? Well, I've worked out a plan to *get* the money. And not just that, but to draw people's attention to the whole fucking business again. To jolt their memories. To kick up the sand they've buried their bloody heads in ever since the trial finished. Or even before that, most of them. Only, it's not . . . I mean, obviously it's not going to be easy. Well, straightforward. A question of selling the family shares and taking a full-page spread in the *Times,* if you get me."

"Yes, of course," said Olivia. "I'm not simple. So, what? I mean, what've you decided to do?"

"The details aren't important."

"You mean, you *don't* trust me. When it comes down to it, you don't. For God's sake, Michael, what have I got to do to convince you? Surely you can see I'm on your side. Can't you?"

"This isn't just some students' demonstration I'm talking about. Some sit-in, with banners, and everyone chanting 'We Shall Overcome' at the top of their bloody voices."

"I know *that.*"

"Okay. Keep your voice down."

"Well, how am I supposed to get through to you?"

Olivia took a second cigarette from Michael's packet. Michael reached toward her and ignited a match. From behind the flame, Olivia said, "Look, I'm not trying to tell you I share your views on South Africa. You know that. You probably knew it the moment you first clapped eyes on me, for all your talk about how 'different' I was. It must've been obvious. Just as it must've been obvious I'd smoke pot and . . . and disapprove of my father's job. I wear the uniform, after all.

"No, it's not that. What I'm trying to make you understand is that what you said this morning, about me not being averse to action . . . I know you didn't really mean it, I know you were only trying to goad me, but . . . Look, over the last few weeks, and this has got nothing to do with meeting you— well, not everything—I've come to realize more and more not just how futile but how *evil* words on their own can be. How they can twist things and hide things and . . . I don't know . . .

"I mean, at university we spent most of our time talking, analyzing ourselves and the world and how things were or should be. Analyzing, and then putting back together into convenient little blocks of thought, into arguments that could be trotted out for review every so often, just to make sure they were always up to date. And I'm sure that most of what we said was quite right. Okay! You probably wouldn't agree. But it was. Right in the sense that it was mostly toler- ant and liberal and humane. But it wasn't *true*. It wasn't true because it pretended to be self-supporting. I mean, *we* pre- tended. That it was enough to recognize wrongs without doing anything about them, that ideas were an end in them- selves, that to think without acting on our thoughts was a complete and fulfilled human gesture.

"And now, you see, what I'm trying to say is that I've realized not only how such an attitude can be *used* for evil, by rationalizing about it and covering it up, but how such an attitude *is* evil, in itself. Like . . . like a vampire, if you want. Apparently harmless and elegant, and even a bit romantic, but really life-sucking, really dependent on other people, on their violence and passion and suffering, in order to maintain its own pure intellectual existence at all. Do you see what I mean, Michael? Do you?"

Michael released a breath that he hadn't noticed he was holding. He felt like a violinist who, having begun to improvise a melody upon his instrument, finds that the bow has assumed its own control and is playing the very tune that his brain had imagined; not simply playing it, either, but adding to the basic theme embellishments that the musician had not yet begun to anticipate.

"You do understand, don't you?" Olivia asked.

"Yeah," said Michael. "Yeah, I understand. You don't have to say anything else, sweetheart."

He had been wrong. The nature of the girl's receptiveness *did* admit of aggression. Her vulnerability *could* be shaped, not just as a shield, but as a sword. With an outrider like her, a man could get almost anywhere, could . . .

Reluctantly, Michael lifted his foot from the accelerator of his enthusiasm. Such speculations were not, for the moment, useful.

"Look," he said, "if we're really going to talk, I think we'd better get out of this place, for a start."

Olivia rose from her seat. Through the now overcrowded bar, Michael followed the path that she made toward the door.

30

"It's like this," he said. "Pieter—you know, Barbara's husband—had got a list together of all the firms he could find who did any sort of business with South Africa. I mean, at first, you know, he'd only intended publishing their names, but then . . . Well, Barbara explained all that—why he decided that he'd have to do something bigger . . . Anyway, this list, I've got it. And on it there's a company in West London who send all sorts of office machinery out there. Now, the point is I've done a bit of nosing around down there and tomorrow's their payday. You know, from about eleven o'clock onward, all the non-salaried staff start trickling down to the cashiers for their weekly pay-packets. . . . Anyway, one way and another, there'll be quite a bit of small change lying about."

"And that's how you . . . I mean, that's where you're thinking of getting the money from? For the appeal?"

They were walking without concern for where they went, past restaurants that had not yet started business and antique shops that had long since ceased to do so. It was the dead hour, the neutral hour, the hour that hangs like a lowered curtain between the acts of "London by Day" and "London by Night."

"I warned you it wasn't just a question of selling Auntie's shares," said Michael.

"No, I know," said Olivia. "But . . . I mean . . . Do you mean a holdup?"

"That's right."

"Oh! I . . ."

She stopped and he stopped, too. The street in which they were, although a main one, was, at that moment, empty of traffic and she heard the echo of their footsteps carrying on without them.

"I suppose . . ." she said.

"Look, I don't have to tell you any more if you'd rather. I know that what I'm talking about isn't just shoplifting, or jamming parking meters. It's a serious criminal offense. I know that. And, what's more, it's going to be pretty bloody dangerous."

"No, please. I'm sorry. I was just being . . . I mean, what else did I expect? I was just a bit . . . startled, I suppose. Well, you know, it's not exactly—"

"It's not exactly the sort of thing you're used to. Is that it?"

He mimicked her accent as he said this.

"That's not fair," said Olivia. "For God's sake, that's not fair."

"No, okay. Hey, come here."

He held the tops of her arms and drew her to him.

"I'm sorry," he said. "You're right, that was cheap. Unjustified, too. But what I said before, about this thing being dangerous, I did mean that. And if I don't want you getting more mixed up in it than you have to, it's not because I don't trust you, or don't think you're up to it, or anything, but because I . . . I just don't want you to get hurt. You're too nice a kid for that, Olivia."

"I'm no more a kid than Malcolm." Her throat was tight with various contradictory pains. "Nor am I a piece of Sèvres china to be wrapped up in tissue paper and cotton wool. Whatever you've planned, I don't just want to *know* about it, I want to be *in* on it."

"Do you know what you're saying?"

"I'm not senile, either."

"No, okay . . ."

"Or romantic. I'm quite aware what'll happen if I'm—if any of us is caught. I know someone who's been inside, for drugs. I'm under no illusions about prison. I know it's not just a holiday camp without the swimming pools."

"Okay, Olivia."

"But I don't just want you to take me along for the ride. That's important. I mean, if I'm going to be in the way . . . I just want to come if I can be useful. Nothing else. Nothing else."

"Of course you'll be useful," said Michael.

Then he leaned toward her and brushed her eyelids with his lips, which were soft and hot. She would have liked the softness and the heat to have enveloped her whole body.

"Come on," he said.

They set off again, his arm across her shoulders now.

"You see," he said, "it's not just the money. That'd be justified, I know, but it's more than that. What we've also got to do is make sure they bloody well realize *who's* gone and taken it from them, and *why*. We've got to make sure the whole bloody country realizes."

"So what are we going to do?"

"I'll tell you all that later, when we get back. But, look, first hadn't we better drop in at your place? It's only just up the road from here, isn't it? In the telephone directory, I . . ."

"Yes. But why?"

"Well, you must have some things you want to collect, even if it's only a pair of knickers and a toothbrush."

"I suppose so."

Until this moment, Olivia's mind had been attuned to the abstract, the theoretical implications of her commitment to Michael. Now the sudden descent to practical details shocked her. While appreciating the absurdity of this in the light of what she had just been saying, she could not shake off the sudden feeling of degradation—of having been tricked—with which the man's words had shadowed her previously clear exhilaration. It was as though, in the middle of lovemaking, he had said, "You're putting on weight, you know."

Neither could she understand how, in the full flight of her self-dedication to him, he could have had the thoughts to spare for its practical implementation. Or, rather, like so many things about Michael, she did not want to *have* to understand. The unanswered questions, the discrepancies, the occasional glimpses of a hostile mind were unimportant flaws in the perfection of his strength, in the totality of his power to encompass her. She couldn't pretend that they did not exist, but with his help she knew that she could disregard them.

It was in those moments when he seemed to withdraw his help that she became frightened, in those moments when *his* faith in what he was doing appeared to falter.

She said, "When . . . I mean, it was tomorrow you said, wasn't it? The . . ."

"I've told you, we'll discuss all the details when we get back to Wimbledon."

"Yes. Of course."

"Now, look, you'd better go in first, just to make sure the old man's still out, and call me when you have? Okay? If he isn't . . ."

"Oh, he will be. I'm sure he's supposed to be going out somewhere for dinner tonight."

"Right. But best make sure."

They had reached the end of the street where she lived.

"On you go," said Michael.

It was an order. More than that, it was an order that had foreseen disobedience and defied it. Strong in his strength once more, Olivia went.

As soon as she reappeared in the front doorway, Michael sprinted to her.

"Okay," he said. "Have you got your things?"

"Not yet. I'll just . . ."

"Look, before you do, hadn't you better write a note or something? You know, like you're going to stay with friends for a day or two. Just so's the old man doesn't go getting the police in."

"All right. There's a pad downstairs in the kitchen."

"And something to write with."

"I don't know. I think I've got a pen in my bag."

She began to search. Michael said, "I'll get the paper."

A minute later, he returned and handed Olivia the clean white pad, only slightly indented from the last message that had been written there.

"What shall I put?" she asked. "A couple of days?"

"Yeah, anything."

"But, I mean, it won't be much longer, anyway, will it?"

"No," said Michael.

He didn't know whether the girl really believed that it was possible to be a part-time outlaw, or whether it was just that she preferred to believe it for the moment. In either case, it was not in his interest to disillusion her. In two days' time, he hoped that Olivia's opinion of his trustworthiness would be as unimportant as it had been two days previously.

"Is that all right?" Olivia asked.

"Daddy," she had written, "I shan't be home for a couple of days as I'm going to stay with some friends in the country. Sorry I couldn't see you to tell you, but I'm getting a lift down and couldn't wait."

Michael said, "That's fine. Absolutely fine. Now you go and get whatever you need and I'll wait for you down here. Hey! Have you got some jeans and a sweater and a scarf? Dark ones? And some dark glasses? Right. Well, put them in, too."

When she had left him, he took from his jacket a pen of his own, removed the cap, hesitated, then added some twenty or so words to Olivia's letter. Having done this, he folded the sheet of paper into four, kissed it, and pushed it behind the dial of the telephone.

"Sweet dreams, Edward Mannion," he whispered.

31

In the darkness of a cinema off Notting Hill Gate, Simon Shaw allowed himself to be seduced by Greta Garbo. The film was *Queen Christina,* and the star—part male, part female, part monarch, and part principal boy—absorbed him into herself to the obliteration of the smoke-hung atmosphere and ice-cream-cartoned floor that were reality.

When the last frame had faded into nothingness, Simon rose from his seat and left the cinema with the abstracted carefulness of a sleepwalker. At a late-night news and tobacconist's shop, he bought himself a paperback copy of *One*

Flew Over the Cuckoo's Nest, by Ken Kesey, and took it with him to a hamburger bar, where, having ordered a half-carafe of wine and some food, he began immediately to read, stepping from the film director's world to the novelist's without once putting foot upon his own.

32

Barbara said, "And then, when we've got the money, we'll each use one of these spray cans to paint our slogans on the walls and counters and things. You know, 'No to Apartheid,' or . . . Well, it doesn't matter what, as long as it's obvious *who* we are and *why* we're doing it."

"I'd think of something beforehand if I were you," said Malcolm. "Inspiration might be even less forthcoming tomorrow."

Michael said, "Yeah, but not too long, if you don't mind. It wouldn't do for the fuzz to come walking in and you still not finished chapter three."

Olivia drank from the glass of whisky they had given her.

The kitchen where she sat with them (the kitchen which, that morning, had shone with the sharp definition of novelty and fresh beginnings) enclosed her now with a gentler warmth. It and the objects it contained had become blurred with associations.

So, too, was Michael's plan becoming more and more familiar, more and more soluble in the matter of her mind. As Barbara and Malcolm reiterated it in their several ways, as phrases they used reminded her of phrases she had heard from student leaders organizing sit-ins, she found herself accepting it with ease. If it had been exciting to hear Michael say "This isn't just some student demonstration I'm talking about," then it was also reassuring to discover that it was not something altogether different.

Barbara said, "The slogans are important, though. Pieter'd hate it if he thought we were abusing his ideals."

"Sure, sure," said Michael. "Only, it's not going to help anyone if we're caught, is it?"

Malcolm said, "I don't know. You'd probably enjoy it inside. All those opportunities for hustling? And thinking up ingenious escape plans? Just your cup of tea, I'd've thought."

He winked at Olivia and Olivia laughed—not at the humor of the remark, nor the truth of it, but at the tremor of nervous pleasure that it sent through her. It was not far removed from sexual arousal, this feeling of being involved, of being accepted by a group of her peers. She would have liked to hug them all: the sallow-skinned, scrawny Barbara; the thick-muscled Malcolm; Michael. She looked at her watch. It was twenty past ten. Soon someone might suggest that they go to bed.

"What happens," she asked, "if the cashiers just refuse to hand the money over? I mean, I don't know—perhaps I'm being stupid. But it's a possibility, isn't it?"

She had asked the question in a light tone, not with the intention of creating a polemic, but in order to add her voice to the multipartite, yet harmonious, chorus of which she was so recent a member. The change in key that followed her speech, therefore, astonished her.

"Well," she said, "isn't it possible? I mean, mightn't they decide just not to take us seriously?"

"I don't see why they should," said Barbara, but she spoke in a hesitant, staccato fashion and looked from one of the men to the other, as though in need of a prompt. Malcolm acknowledged the entreaty, but returned it with a mock-help-less smile. Michael did not appear to have received it.

"No, okay," said Olivia. "I don't see why they should either."

Her voice came out louder than she had intended, over-compensating for the general lowering in pitch.

"But supposing. Supposing one of them decides it's his duty to protect his employers' money."

"We're going to have a gun," said Michael.

A phonograph record that had been running down for some seconds now stopped. Non-human sounds reasserted themselves: the fluttering of a draft-blown curtain, the spray of rain in the wind. Olivia became aware of the life flowing in and out of her, of her rib-cage rising and sinking, of the counterbeat of her heart.

"A gun?" she asked.

"Yeah," said Michael.

"No," said Olivia.

Malcolm swung down from his seat on the drainboard and went to fill his glass with whisky. The glugging of the liquid through the tight neck of its bottle became important.

Michael said, "What does that mean, 'no'?"

"It means no. It means . . . It means you're wrong. You can't . . . *Nothing* justifies that!"

"Justifies what, Olivia?"

"Violence, Michael. The hurting of people. The taking of people's lives. I'm sorry, but if your only idea of action is that, then I'd rather . . ."

"What? . . . Look, darling, you're making me angry. Whether *anything* does or doesn't justify killing is a highly interesting question, but hardly relevant at the moment. For God's sake, what do you think we are? Either a bunch of cretins or gangsters, by the sound of it. Of course we're not going to kill anyone. Or hurt them . . ."

"The night watchman. I suppose you didn't hurt him."

There was a pause. Barbara picked at a scab of grease on the kitchen table. Malcolm ran the rim of his glass across his lower lip.

"Thanks," said Michael, at last. "Thanks, yes, we'd forgotten about that. But, you know, when you've knocked off as many old-age pensioners as we have, you start losing count."

141

"I didn't mean that. I just meant that if you've *got* a gun . . ."

"An unloaded gun?"

"What?"

"A gun that isn't loaded?"

"I don't understand."

"Oh, come on, you've been to university. A gun without any bullets in it."

"But then, I mean, why bother?"

"Because, my sweetheart . . ."

He leaned across to her and took her hands from the tabletop.

"Like you said, if we was to go in there with a peashooter, or nothing, the chances are they'd just sit back on their arses and laugh at us. Even Robin Hood used to wave his bow and arrow around from time to time, you know. Just so's people'd realize he was serious."

"I see. I'm . . ."

"All right. For God's sake, don't say you're sorry. Life's too short for all that. Just finish your whisky and let's go to bed, eh?"

Olivia inhaled, held the breath, then eased it out. Her body juddered into relaxation. Thought and logic drifted away, and in their place came a roaring wash of relief.

As though through a thick glove, her hand answered the grip of Michael's fingers.

"Eh, Olivia?"

"Yes," she said.

"Come on."

They stood up together.

"Good night," said Barbara and Malcolm.

33

Making love to Olivia for a second time had never been an integral part of Michael's plans, and more recently it had become even less than that, had become an eventuality to be avoided. It had upset him, therefore, to realize, as he had done in the kitchen, that Olivia wanted to reconfirm the sexual side of their relationship; puzzled him, too, as he had been sure that her involvement in the morrow's conspiracy would have been more than enough to satisfy her.

Yet now she lay on her back on the bed, her hips tipped toward him, one arm curved above her head, the other flung wide, and he was surprised by a feeling of shock, as though she were his daughter.

It occurred to him that the boyfriend, Simon, could not have been much of a lover for her to be so hungry for *his* egotistic attacks.

Nor, when faced with the fact of her body (the fact of her hard brown thighs, of her white breasts surmounted by urgent nipples), could he withhold them. If his instinct told him that the safest course of action would be to ignore the girl's unspoken invitation, his crotch said, "To hell with safety," and his brain, an accomplished and obedient servant, added, "After all, it wouldn't exactly be 'safe' to risk upsetting her pride, would it? You've nearly lost her once this evening already. And what a balls-up that nearly was. What are you frightened of, anyway? A screw's just a screw, isn't it?"

He finished undressing and walked across the carpet to the bed. Then, as he placed one knee on the mattress and prepared to lower his body across the girl's, she lifted a hand to his chest and restrained him.

"What is it?" he asked, angry at the frustration, angrier still at the complexity of emotions that had replaced desire on the screen of Olivia's face.

"Oh, nothing."

She bent her arm and he, as though supported by it, followed the progress downward.

He did not ask her again what she had meant. He preferred not to know. It was better to see nothing but the arched and glistening neck, to hear no sounds but the quickening of breath and the catch of pleasure at the back of the half-open mouth.

34

"I'll break him! I'll break him if it's the last thing I ever do!"

Edward hurled the screwed-up sheet of paper across the hallway, watched it hit the wall, then drop without noise or impression onto the pile of the carpet.

"I'll kill him," he said.

"Is there anything the matter, Mr. Mannion?"

"No, it's all right, Mrs. Clifford."

"Thought I heard you say something."

"It's all right."

Impervious, however, the cleaning woman was climbing the basement stairs toward him. He heard the noise of her feet and the inexorable gasp of her bronchitis. Kneeling to retrieve the piece of paper, he felt his anger harden with humiliation.

"Thought I heard you say something."

Mrs. Clifford stood at the far end of the passage. Her body —head cocked to one side, hands rubbing themselves dry in the folds of an apron—was a featureless silhouette against the glass courtyard door.

"I told you, nothing," said Edward.

"That's all right."

She came toward him, and as she did so, he saw that her eyes had located the note that his fist did not hide.

But all she said was "You off now, then, sir?"

"No. No," he answered, "I think I'll work at home this morning."

"Oh, I see. So you won't be going out, after all."

"No, I've just remembered I've some things to do here. But you just carry on."

"Yes. Well, I will. Only, you know, I like to know."

"Of course," he said. "I'm sorry. And your husband's around the house all day, too, isn't he, at the moment? With that leg of his? You must be fed up with us men under your feet."

He waited until he had seen her thoughts veer off along the false trail he had laid for them; then he patted the banister rail and began to climb the stairs.

It was infuriating, at such a moment, to have to channel energy and time into evaporating his cleaning woman's curiosity, into repairing the bonds of her allegiance to him. Edward felt as though the tentacles of O'Keefe's subversion had reached inside the very structure of his establishment, and as he came to the first-floor landing and stopped in front of Olivia's bedroom door, he cursed him once again.

There was, however, little point in swearing. A new game had been started. A new and more threatening challenge had been slapped across his face. Thrusting the note responsible for this development into his jacket pocket, Edward listened; then, having ascertained that Mrs. Clifford was pushing her vacuum cleaner around the drawing-room floor, he reached out and turned the handle of the door in front of him.

His daughter's possessions, as he had guessed they would be, were scattered around her room with more regard to the laws of circumstance than those of design. Clothes lay where they had been discarded, books where last they had been read. On the dressing table, bottles of eau de Cologne and shampoo were interspersed with ashtrays, letters, coins, bus tickets, articles of underwear, and photographs. On the floor were shoes and bulging suitcases, essays scrawled on sheets of foolscap paper, and magazines and toys.

It took Edward several minutes to locate the thing for which he had come: the address book he was certain his daughter must own and in which it was possible she had written a number, or a name, that would assist him.

When he did find it (in a drawer with socks and ball-point pens and a paperback history of modern Greece), he turned at once to the page headed "O."

Having read through this, he turned back to "M"; then to "K." But none of them gave him the information he wanted. He closed the faded leather book and tapped its spine against the palm of his left hand. There had to be a key, an opening, a doorway of some sort through which he could step out onto his journey of retaliation.

Flipping for a second time through the curled and indented pages, he saw it: the letter "S"; the name Simon; the telephone number (amongst a medley of telephone numbers and addresses) that bore the prefix 937, for the High Street Kensington area.

The boyfriend from university. If anyone knew or could guess where O'Keefe and Olivia had gone, it must be he.

Edward closed the drawer, slipped the book into his jacket pocket, listened once more for the covering sound of the vacuum cleaner, then left Olivia's room and climbed the remaining flight of stairs to his own.

35

"Look, it's really none of my business any more, sir. I mean, perhaps she didn't tell you, but it's all over between us. Her decision, not mine. So you see . . ."

"Yes, yes."

The voice on the other end of the line was businesslike and impatient. It snapped with what Simon's housemaster would have called "the quality of leadership."

"I do realize all that," it said. "In fact, it's part of what I want to talk to you about. Now, where can I meet you?"

"Meet me?"

"Yes. We really can't discuss it on the telephone. Perhaps I could come round to *you?* I've got the address. It is flat five, isn't it?"

"Yes," said Simon. "Yes, it is. But look—honestly, Mr. Mannion, I'd rather you didn't. I mean, you can come round, of course—"

He stopped, cut short by the absurdity of what he was saying. It was hardly likely that Olivia's father would want to visit him for the simple pleasures of a chat and a glass of wine.

"What I mean is, wouldn't it be better for you to say what you want to say to Livvy herself? It does seem to me that that'd be far more sensible."

"I've no doubt it does, but then you don't know the situation yet, do you?"

"Well, tell me."

"I'll be with you in ten minutes."

"For God's sake," said Simon, into the dead receiver.

He did not, however, leave the flat. Instead, he began to move from room to room, tidying things, rearranging things, checking up on his appearance in the looking glass.

Since Olivia's dismissal of him the previous afternoon, Si-

147

mon had been in a state of trance. He had put himself into it, as though this time to give the euphoria of freedom a chance to solidify and develop. That Edward Mannion with his telephone call had awakened him should have made him angry.

Instead, he had the impression of having come to in some strange chrysalis state, some blind and powerless condition, with blanketed walls muffling both past and future. The fear that he had felt the previous morning (upon realizing that Olivia had left him and that *he* could not yet leave *her*) *had* risen up again, had become reactivated by this second intrusion on his serenity, but this time it had acquired a gray, insidious, formless quality, less easy to feel, less easy to react to.

He told himself, "You're mad. What's there to be frightened of? For God's sake, all he's coming to do is talk to you, ask you what's happened, I suppose. It's none of his bloody business, I know, but at the worst it'll only be embarrassing, for both of us. It's over. Everything with Olivia's over. She kicked me out of the house, didn't she? Well, nothing he says can change that."

All the same, as he emptied ashtrays into wastepaper baskets, as he combed his hair and tucked his shirt more tightly into the waistband of his jeans, as the bandaging ripped from his newly raw nerve ends, he felt a child's desire to cry and wish that he had not been wakened.

"He's got no business coming here. If he wants to interfere with his daughter's life, that's his concern, but I'm nothing to *do* with him. Why can't he just leave me alone?" he said as the doorbell sounded.

36

"Right," said Michael. "It's just about five to ten. Now, have you all got everything you need? Shades? Scarves? Paint cans? Gun, Malcolm? Okay. Now, in a minute or two, me and Olivia are going to leave for the bus stop, and I want *you* two to wait a few minutes longer before following us, to the underground station. And you know what to do when you get to the other end, don't you? The café'll be twenty yards or so to your right, on the same side of the road as you'll come out on. It's a small place with a large glass window, so it'll be easy enough to see if we're in there or not. If we are, stay looking at the display menu long enough to make sure we've seen you, then walk on. And if we're not, you go in and we'll do the other bit. Right? Now, I'm just going to go over the getaway once again and then we're off. So if any of you've got any questions . . . And don't worry. So long as you keep cool and do everything just the way I told you, we'll be home and dry in time for a champagne lunch."

37

"Thank you," said Edward. "A cup of coffee'd be very nice."

The boy said, "Fine. Oh, please sit down," and indicated a sagging, chintz-covered armchair.

He was a good-looking lad, in the current effeminate style. He wore his hair long, but clean, and his clothes (a fine green-and-white striped shirt and a pair of jeans) were not eccentric. It would be but a small step, Edward reckoned, for him to revert to the suit and tie of his fathers.

"I really must apologize, Simon," he said, "if I sounded

149

abrupt on the telephone. You'll understand when I've explained, but I'm afraid there are several extensions in my house and my cleaning woman puts M.I.5 to shame when it comes to listening in to conversations. I don't know how she does it, but I never even hear a click when she lifts the receiver up. Just a certain hollowness that wasn't there before."

He smiled and the boy returned the smile. It was probably only politeness that made him do so, but politeness seemed an easier launching pad than open hostility.

"Well, I'll just go and put the kettle on, then."

"Certainly," said Edward.

When the coffee had been made and Simon, by perching himself on one of the arms of the sofa, had indicated that he was ready to listen, Edward said, "I think I'm going to have to tell you straightaway, that Olivia's disappeared."

As he began this sentence, he was looking at the cup between his hands, but on the last word he raised his eyes, to be sure of catching uncensored the boy's reaction.

Which was one of bewilderment.

"I don't understand."

"Oh, come on, you must've had *some* idea. You and she had a row yesterday, didn't you?"

"Yes, but . . . Look, how do you mean, 'disappeared'?"

"Just that. Run away from home, if you like."

"It doesn't make sense."

The boy stood up and walked to the mantelpiece.

"It was her who wanted to finish it, not me," he said. Then, "Oh, of course!"

"What?"

"She's—"

Simon stopped. He turned to look at Edward. His forehead contracted and his eyes became narrow, as though he were peering at something, some shadow in the dusk.

"What?" asked Edward. "She's what?"

"Nothing. I just . . . Oh, listen, sir, don't you think this is all a bit stupid? You talk about 'running away from home' as though Livvy were eight or something. She's twenty-one. She can do what she wants. I mean, if you feel she should have told you where she was going—well, that's a question of manners and I agree. But otherwise it isn't any of our business. Certainly not mine, anyway. I'd be furious if anyone came chasing after me just because I'd decided to bum off somewhere for a bit."

"You call me stupid?"

Edward, too, had got to his feet, and if the anger in his voice was calculated, it was nonetheless real for all that.

"What would you call yourself?" he asked. "You know as well as I do that it's not just a question of 'bumming off somewhere.' What you're perhaps *not* aware of is that your successor, this Michael O'Keefe, is a professional terrorist. A killer, my smart young man. Here, look at this."

He thrust Olivia's note (with O'Keefe's postscript) across the room at the boy, who started toward it, then stopped.

"A terrorist?" he asked. "What do you mean?"

"Oh, for goodness' sake. You know even less than I thought."

"What am I *supposed* to know?"

"I'm sorry."

Edward felt behind him for the sofa and sat down again. The time for anger was over.

"I'm sorry, Simon," he said. "It's not your fault. You've been hoodwinked as much as any of us."

It had become obvious that the boy would be able to tell him little, if anything, that he did not already know. Now the only use that Edward could hope to make of his time with him was to win him to his side. In the impending showdown between himself and O'Keefe, an ally, however incompetent, could make all the difference between victory and defeat.

151

He said, "I've got no right to get angry with you for this mess-up. If it's anybody's fault, it's mine. I should have seen the danger days ago and done something about it."

"I don't know what you're talking about," said the boy.

Edward gave him the note. Simon read it.

When he had finished, he said, "What does it mean? 'In actual fact, your daughter's coming to stay with me for a while. See tomorrow's evening papers for details of what we get up to. M. O'K.' He hasn't . . . I mean, he can't have kidnaped her, can he?"

"No, nothing as straightforward as that. There wouldn't be the two messages if she hadn't gone of her own accord. He must've added the last bit without her knowing."

"So?"

"So obviously he's persuaded her to join up with him and his merry band of bombers. He's not alone, you know. There's a couple of other people in it with him. They exploded a factory in the Midlands not so long ago, killing somebody. Anyway, I can't imagine it took much doing, converting Olivia to the cause. . . ."

"What cause? And why go to all the trouble of making sure you knew about it, anyway?"

"Because they want something from me. Explosives, to be precise. I expect Olivia told you I was in the arms and ammunition trade. O'Keefe approached me three nights ago asking me to supply him with some and, of course, I refused; so now he's decided to use my daughter as bargaining power."

"You mean, they're going to do something today, blow up something, perhaps, and Livvy's going to be involved?"

"I should say that was the situation, yes."

There was a silence. Edward waited for the outcome.

"Well, fuck them! How dare they? How dare they use her like that? *Whatever* the cause, they've no *right* to manipulate people, *pervert* their ideals. What sort of cynics are they?

152

God, the poor kid. And she's got no idea they're just trying to get at you?"

"None," said Edward, his face a mask of sympathetic concern. "She was with me when O'Keefe approached me, too, but I sent her away and afterwards told her some story. That he was just a hoodlum who wanted to pick a fight with me."

"For goodness' sake, why?"

"Well, I don't know if you'll understand this, but it was really a question of inverted pride. You see, Simon, Olivia's so determined to believe that just because I sell guns I must also be devoid of morals and humanity, it would've seemed like a plea for sympathy for me to have told her that I'd just turned down a very favorable deal simply because I *won't* condone the murder of innocent civilians. It would have been as though I were begging for her understanding, and I couldn't do that. Am I making any sort of sense to you?"

He hoped he was. To himself, he sounded surprisingly convincing.

And when Simon said "Yes, and I know what you mean about Livvy, too; she does tend to see things in black and white a bit," Edward knew that even if he had failed to get the information he had come for, his subsequent aim, at least, had been realized.

Placing his coffee cup on the floor, he stood up and prepared to leave.

"Anyway, you've no idea at all where they might have taken her?" he asked.

"No, none," said the boy. "If I knew anything . . . Yes, if I knew anything I *would* tell you. Only, it must be too late by now, mustn't it? 'The evening papers.' That must mean that whatever they've planned, they've planned it for this morning."

"I'm very much afraid so. Yes, all we can do now is wait for their next move. But thank you. Thank you, all the same, for being so reasonable. I was a bit frightened you might find the whole thing rather amusing."

"Amusing?"

"Exactly. But I'm sure there are people of your age who would. Or justified, anyway. You know, the dramatic irony of it all! Forgetting that the people terrorists kill don't just get up and walk away when the drama's over. Still, I'm sorry; I shouldn't have insulted your intelligence. It was wrong of me. Well, goodbye for the moment and, as I said before, thank you."

Edward shook the boy's hand between both of his, in a gesture of restrained but unmistakable emotion.

When he had left the flat, he hailed a taxi to take him to Fulham. Sinking into the padded seat and watching through glass the backward passage of houses and shops and scattered autumnal trees, he wasn't dissatisfied. If it was true that there was nothing he could do to prevent whatever act of defiance O'Keefe had prepared to throw at him, then it was also true that, in the passage of time since his initial fury, he had come to realize the advantages of its *not* being prevented.

Stroking his breast pocket to reassure himself of the presence therein of O'Keefe's message, with O'Keefe's initials, he closed his eyes and allowed himself a sigh of satisfaction.

38

There had been one moment of panic when, on preparing to alight with Michael from the bus, she had seen Malcolm and Barbara, not six yards away, emerging from the mouth of the underground station.

"It's gone wrong already," she had said to herself. "We're all going to arrive at the café at the same time," and the contents of her mind, already confused (the excitement, the doubt, the pride, and the shame), had risen up in a fear-blown storm to blind her.

"Please, Michael," she had said, groping for contact with him, "let's call it off. It's just not going to work."

"Calm yourself, for God's sake. It's all fine."

His fingers had gripped at her elbow and jerked her toward him, so that they had stepped from the bus platform together. The pain of this movement had acted like a shock of cold water on her stupefied reasoning.

She had said, "I'm sorry."

"Let's go into this tobacconist. I want to buy some fags."

"I'm sorry, Michael."

"There's no need. . . . Morning. I'll have twenty Players, please, and a packet of chewing gum."

Two minutes later, when they reached the café, Malcolm and Barbara were seated just as it had always been planned that they would be, in profile, one on either side of a table, drinking tea from thick china cups.

From that point onward, there was no uncertainty. On the contrary, as though by his mastery of the unpredictable Michael had lifted a fog from in front of her vision, Olivia now saw everything with intoxicating clarity. The display menu that hung in the café window and in front of which she and Michael had stopped, the widening and narrowing of Malcolm's eyes as he became aware of their presence there, the quiet midmorning pavements along which she and Michael then walked (and along which, shortly afterward, the others followed)—all appeared possessed of an unusual presence. Their shadows seemed blacker, their lights brighter, their details clearer, and their dimensions deeper and taller and wider than anything that normality could have bestowed.

Olivia had the ecstatic, angry impression of having discovered the use of another sense, a sense of whose existence she had been deliberately kept in ignorance by jealous custodians.

And the factory gates, when soon they reached them, shone with this same supernatural quality, this quality of a play in which the important scenery, props, and actors have been spotlighted in order that there should be no irrelevant questions or distractions.

"Put your arm over my shoulder," said Michael as they passed between the brilliant, red-brick gateposts, with their signs about speed restrictions and their notices of staff vacancies; and Olivia raised her arm thoughtlessly to the command.

Ahead of her, again just as he had always said there would be, stretched a compound lined with rank upon rank of workers' cars, through the middle of which ran a path straight from the gates by which they had entered to the buildings on the compound's farther side.

These buildings were, for the most part, low gray factory sheds, stretching away for fifty yards or so to Olivia's left. To the right of the sheds, however, and separated from them by a narrow concrete alley, was a taller, two-storied building, with plate-glass windows and double plate-glass doors: the office block. This stood immediately at the end of the path along which Olivia and Michael walked, arms slung over each other, heads tipped toward each other.

Seeing it, Olivia also saw (as though with X-ray eyes) the strip-lit corridor that it contained, the doors that opened off from either side of the corridor, the particular door (the second on the left) that led into the cashiers' office. For a moment, she had the impression that she had stopped walking and that the building and everything inside it was gliding toward her on gigantic, silent rollers.

Then Michael's voice, so clear that it appeared to have by-passed the distortion of hearing, asked, "Okay, Olivia? Got everything? The scarf? The paint can?"

His hand slipped down to touch the metal cylinder that was held by the wasitband of her jeans and was hidden beneath the loose black folds of her sweater.

"Yes," she said.

"Good girl. Now, over there, to the right of the offices, see? That's the wall we go out by."

She looked and saw a brick wall of the very height that he had promised, no more than five feet tall and unadorned by broken glass or wire: a demarkation line between factory and adjoining side street, not a barrier.

"Yes, I can see it," she said, and began to return her focus to the ever-approaching offices, when, with a sudden shaft of light that brought the world to a halt, the doors of the office block swung open and a group of women in head scarves and overalls emerged.

"Don't stop. For God's sake, don't stop."

Michael's lips were against her ears and he was laughing as though he were telling her that she was sexy.

"Just keep going."

She did so and the women, having glanced up from their pay-packets and, evidently, seen nothing to astonish them in the presence of four young people wearing sunglasses, moved off. They skirted the wall of the offices and disappeared along the alleyway that separated the offices from the sheds.

"All right."

It was Michael's voice again, sounding like an automatic pilot within Olivia's brain. They had reached the single step that fronted the entrance doors and, like a horse before a jump, she had been checked. Not just her, either. Behind her, the double footsteps of Barbara and Malcolm had also stopped. Michael was riding them all, was driving them all. They and he were one body and one mind.

"All right. Now, from here on, there's no stopping."

He did not turn round to insure that they were listening,

nor did he raise his voice above that volume with which he had spoken to Olivia alone. He said, "When I give you the word, just move and don't look back. Are you ready? All of you? Then it's 'go.'"

Olivia had been prepared for the suddenness of the signal, yet was nonetheless surprised at the dexterity with which her fingers extracted the scarf from her pocket and tied it around her mouth; or at the certainty with which her feet waited for the others to pass her, then followed them up the steps, through the double glass doors, along the linoleum-covered corridor to the cashiers' office; or at the firmness with which her body remained on guard at the door of the office while Michael and Barbara ran with their sacks toward the two tills on the far side of the room and Malcolm, gun in hand, shouted, "Okay! Nobody move or you'll get hurt! Just fill up those bags and do it quickly! And, you lot, turn round and put your hands up on the wall! Now, get cracking!"

It was the dream of perfection: the dream in which one drives a racing car at a hundred and twenty miles an hour, slicing corners on two wheels without skidding, or plays a virtuoso piece on the piano to orgiastic applause.

There had been three men in the office when they entered, two at one till and one at the other. Now, as though held by a violent wind, they were flattened against a wall, backs turned and bowed, arms raised, fingers spread in helpless supplication. At right angles to this paper-cutout line of unmanned overalls was the counter, behind which sat the two cashiers: a red-haired girl and a plump matron. And in front and to one side of each of these women stood the masked and anonymous form of either Michael or Barbara, holding at arm's length an open-mouthed sack into which the cashiers pushed bundles of crackling white envelopes.

Malcolm stood in the middle of the room, his attention swinging from the faceless line-up to the activity at the tills. His knees were flexed, his arms were thrust in a rigid line from his body. Between both hands, he held a square black automatic pistol.

Olivia felt a thrill of power charge through her. It occurred to her that fate was being held captive between the pincer arms of Michael's plan and Malcolm's gun and that she was on the side of the captors.

At that moment (with her intuition stripped of its reasoning, her confidence uninsulated by self-awareness), she saw something that, the day before, she would either not have seen at all or, having seen, would not have known how to react to. The elder of the two cashiers (a motherly woman with plump arms pinched by the short, tight sleeves of a cotton dress, her mottled neck encircled by plastic beads), although still plunging envelopes into Michael's open bag, had altered the line of her concentration, had switched it away from her hands and into her right leg.

This change was not expressed by any modification in the woman's outline (or, at least, not in that of the upper half of her body, which was all that Olivia could see). It was no more than a shift of muscular emphasis, of ocular energy, a shift so insignificant that it caused no ripple to pass across the taut skin of the surrounding atmosphere. Yet Olivia saw it, felt it, heard it, and as though the words were a part of her senses rather than a result of them, she called out, "That woman! She's pressing an alarm bell!"

Michael swung round and away from the till. A second later, there was a crack, then a scream, then an intake of air, followed by the curious sight of the middle-aged cashier rising, as though stung by a comic-strip bee, in a vertical line from her seat. Her mouth had become an "O" of surprise. The plastic beads leaped from her mottled neck, to ping and bounce on the counter top, and in their place appeared what at first seemed to be a delicate garnet flower, but was quick to spread into something darker and wetter and less attractive.

Then, as the anger and fear in the room began to collect themselves into vocal sound, Michael's voice commanded, "Be quiet, all of you. And back against the wall. I'm warning you! Now, you lot, collect your stuff and get going."

"The slogans!"

"Well, for Christ's sake, be quick."

The air became full of the smell of paint, the sound of spraying. From across her desk, the middle-aged cashier dripped blood into a pool on the linoleum.

RELEASE PIETER VAN DER WALT.

NO TRADE WITH SOUTH AFRICA.

ABOLISH APARTHEID.

Then, as though it had been there all along but had not been turned up until then, came the sound of several pairs of footsteps running along the concrete path outside.

"That's enough! Get going, can't you."

Paint cans thudded and clattered to the floor. The footsteps outside grew fainter, then much clearer, approaching along the corridor now.

"Beat it!"

Olivia reached for the door behind her, pressed against it, and tumbled backward into the passageway. Having recovered her balance, she looked for the oblong of daylight that was the glass exit door, then ran toward it. Although aware that there were people between her goal and herself (men —three or four men, heavy and dressed in overalls), she felt no resistance from their bodies as she passed, no pain from their outstretched fingers. Nor did their injunctions "Stop, you! Come here!" make any impression upon her.

The only authority her brain admitted was that of Michael's plan. She had learned its words by heart, and now, like the impulses of remote control, they directed her out of the office building; then left, between parked cars, to the wall; then up the wall, bricks grazing skin through thin wool; then onto the wall and over the wall; then along the pavement, and finally, with the momentum of an athlete crossing the finish line, underneath the first high-bodied car she came to in the line of cars parked on either side of the residential side street.

It was only when she had reached this point, this place, this cool but constricting cave between metal and tarmac, that the waves of Michael's power began to withdraw. Lying face down on the rough stone chips, her head on her forearms, her chin raw from scraping along gravel, her diaphragm swelling and shrinking as much as the restrictions of her hiding place allowed, Olivia felt their force drain out of her with a slow, convulsive retreat. Her muscles trembled. The sweat that coated her body began to evaporate, to chill. The blood in her sinuses and at the surface of her skin where it was torn thudded its slackening of pace.

". . . When you get under your car, just wait there. Don't move, don't do anything, whatever happens. Just wait till I come and tell you it's okay. All right? Whatever happens. That's important. They'll be expecting us to run, see. Or drive away, most likely. Not hang around, in any case. But that's what we've got to do. . . ."

Oh, God, she thought. Oh, God.

This prayer had not had time to specify itself, however, when the sound that had just died in her ears, of shouting voices and hurrying feet, rose up again, tightening her nerves into a pain all the more acute for having, for a moment, been allowed to subside.

"Where did the girl go?"

"I don't know. Look! There are the others."

"Where?"

"There. Quick!"

"We'll go down this way and cut them off."

"Watch out. One of them's got an iron on him."

"I know that, don't I?"

"Where are the cops?"

"They're coming. Dave rang them."

"Quick, boys! Over here!"

Sometimes the voices were above her. Sometimes she could see the feet an inch or two from her face. She imagined them kicking, those heavy, angry workmen's boots, and the desire to run, to join in the running, was great.

". . . whatever happens. Just wait till I come and tell you it's okay."

It was faith, not logic, that kept Olivia clamped against the ground, that kept her pushing farther and farther against rust and the camber of the road. It was faith that held her hot face against the damp wool of her sweater, that allowed the base of her spine to tolerate the pressure of a down-hanging exhaust pipe, while around her the chase encroached and retreated with torturing irregularity.

Silence came, to be troubled by the humming of car engines, to be shattered by the blast of sirens started and stopped in mid-note. Conversations drifted toward and away from her as though carried by unpredictable breezes. What had seemed like one person became a crowd. What had been a crowd became, abruptly, nobody.

Direction ceased to exist.

Time was a series of infinities.

39

"Oh, lovely, lovely Sally."

"What's happening, Edward?"

"What do you mean, 'what's happening'? Nothing's happening. You and me are happening, that's all."

"Twice in one week?"

The woman heaved herself into a sitting position against

the bedstead, causing the man to roll off her, onto his side.

"That's unusual enough, for a start," she said. "Twice in three days, actually, isn't it?"

"Are you complaining?"

"I suppose not. It's just not the *best* thing in the world for a person's morale, to feel she's being used as a pep pill."

"What the hell are you talking about now?"

Edward reached for Sally's shoulders and pulled her back to his level.

"Careful," she said. "You're rough sometimes."

"No, I'm serious. What *do* you mean? Usually you complain because you don't see enough of me. Now, all of a sudden, it's too much. What's happened? Don't tell me you've gone and fallen in love with Dick again. Don't tell me that you've seen through that beer gut to the heart of gold beneath. Or is it just that you've grown too old for illicit affairs?"

There was a pause. Sally Hastings worked her lips as though she were about to spit, then said, "Sometimes you're like a child pulling the wings off a butterfly. Not just cruel, but grotesque."

"I see."

"There's no use looking martyrish and despising. It's true. And it's also true that you're at your nastiest when there's something worrying you. Still, I suppose that's not unusual. I suppose we all are."

She had let her head sink back into the pillow and her brown, faded eyes gazed at the ceiling as though they were seeing everything, or nothing. This combination of anger and sadness in Sally always troubled Edward. It gave him an uneasy feeling of inferiority, as though there were fields of emotion and knowledge to which she had access, but not he.

He said, "Thank you for that revealing piece of analysis. I'll leave my fee on the dressing table. And if there ever really is anything worrying me, I'll know just where to come for sympathy and understanding, won't I?"

He pushed the sheets away from him and climbed from the bed. Walking across the room to the stool where he had laïd his clothes, he was pleased that his body was tight and almost flawless, that his legs were not disfigured by veins, nor his skin wrinkled and white.

"Edward, come back. Oh, for goodness' sake, what do you want me to do? Crawl? You know I would if you asked me to."

He continued his dressing, shaking the creases from a blue cotton shirt.

"The fight's over, Edward. I've given in."

That Edward had known Sally would apologize did not detract from the satisfaction of hearing her do so. That she had previously placed him in awe of herself added to it. If he stayed with his back to her, legs apart, pushing buttons into buttonholes, it was partly in order to prolong this satisfaction to its most fulfilling climax and partly because it was already noon and he had not yet been to the office.

"Okay, if you're determined not to take any notice, then don't. But you do know that whatever I say about you, even when I mean it, it's only hypothetical. It's all canceled out by the fact that I love you."

"Isn't that a bit perverse? Aren't people supposed to love each other because of their virtues, not *in spite* of their *vices?*"

He heard the soft, relieved flow of her laughter.

"If that was true, there wouldn't be many people loved, would there? Of course it's not. Come on, there must've been one person you've loved without liking them. Or without liking lots of things about them, anyway."

Edward deflected the suggestion from his consciousness, as though unwilling that even he should know its answer.

"It's romantic novels that ought to be banned, not pornography," he said. "Some enchanted evening, across a crowded

164

room! His eyes met mine and I knew he was the only one for me! What nonsense! If you ask me, romance, in that sense, was just another Victorian euphemism for lust."

There was a thud and Sally's feet had landed on the carpet. Then her arms were around his waist, the hands reaching up to hold his chest.

"Oh, Edward, Edward."

She spoke with her face pressed tight into his back. He could feel its rocking motion against his spine and ribs.

"You talk such rubbish sometimes, darling. But I suppose you can't help it. It's all part of being male. You know—never crying or getting emotional. And doing all those practical science subjects at school."

He didn't bother to contradict her. It would have been a shame to have dammed up the easy course of her adoration. Besides, although a believer in cerebral judgment where his own decisions were concerned, like most judges, he preferred the judicial process not to be reversed. He eased himself from her hold, to kiss her, and the telephone rang.

"Oh, blast."

"Don't answer it."

"I'll have to. It might be Dick."

"Why? Does he often ring you in the middle of the day?"

"No, but he does sometimes. And if I don't answer, it'll involve all sorts of petty lying, which I'm hopeless at."

He released her and sat down to put on his shoes.

When the telephone conversation, to which he had paid little attention, was over, he said, "So it was him. He's not getting jealous and checking up on you, is he?"

"No, but it was pretty unnerving. He wanted me to give you a message, just in case you should ring here."

"What the hell's he playing at? Why *should* I ring here?"

"Because he's going out of the office. And he's not telling . . . What's her name? Your secretary?"

"Margaret."

"Margaret, where's he's going. Anyway, let me tell you before I forget. He's gone to North Finchley to see his 'friend,' who's got some more information about the 'same matter as before.' Does that make sense? I must say, it sounds like something out of *Boys' Own* to me."

"No," said Edward. "No, that makes sense all right. Thank you, Sally."

"Pleased to have been of help. You're not really leaving, are you?"

"I must."

Edward couldn't imagine what further light Dick's informed and informative acquaintance was about to throw on the problem of Michael O'Keefe (whether it would be that he had discovered the location of the gang's hiding place, or that he knew the nature of their morning's coup, or, more likely, that he had unearthed some past crime attributable to them), but whatever it was, its existence had reignited the flame of battle within him. A waiting game, even with a strong hand, was not one he enjoyed. Nor, if there were two to be had, was one advantage enough for him.

"Wouldn't you even like something to eat?"

"No, nothing, really."

"Just a drink, then? A glass of wine?"

"If anything were going to tempt me to stay, it wouldn't be food or drink. But I really must go, Sally. And I'll let myself out. You can't come down with nothing on, anyway."

40

"Olivia! For God's sake!"

"Don't say anything. Just let me in and shut the door. Please."

"Of course."

Simon stepped back, farther back than was necessary to let

the disheveled, alien figure past him, and, when he had closed the door, stayed for a moment staring at the white-painted, paneled-wood surface, as though it were bars that he had been tricked into pulling around him.

"There's nobody else here, is there?"

"No. No, of course not. Olivia . . ."

"Can I just go and wash myself? I'm a bit dirty."

"Yes, but for God's sake, what happened?"

He followed her into the bathroom, where, feet planted wide on the linoleum, she proceeded to remove her clothes with the defiant lack of eroticism of a prostitute or an art-school model. The gray-white planes of her body, the yellow-gray mounds of her once suntanned thighs, were mottled with superficial cuts and bruises. When she turned toward the basin, he saw that at the point where her spine curved out to become her buttocks, there was a damp red sore.

He said, "Aren't you going to tell me what happened?"

"I don't know. Yes. Look, please, can I just get washed?"

"You're going to need some disinfectant on those cuts."

"I'll manage."

"Well, it's in the medicine cupboard if you want it. And plasters and things. I'll go and put on some tea."

Simon couldn't connect this Olivia with the one he had known the day before, nor with the one her father had spoken of five hours previously. The girl for whom he performed the mundane rituals of teamaking was not a stranger (for a stranger would have aroused his intellect rather than his emotions) but an acquaintance magnified, glorified, into something all the more awe-inspiring for having been once familiar.

At his public school, there had been a Roman Catholic boy named Falkener with whom he had shared a room for a couple of terms. One day, intrigued by the esoteric mystery with which this boy's religion was surrounded, he had asked to see the leather-bound missal that lived beneath Falkener's pillow, and between the pages of it he had discovered, as bookmarks, a quantity of those miniature reproductions of "Christ Crowned with Thorns" of which the Roman Catholics are often fond.

The Christ face, so baroque, so Oriental with its dark-rimmed eyes, so grotesque in its blood-trickling agony—in all, so different from the gentle, pastel Jesus of his own illustrated childhood Bible—had appalled him more than any doctrinaire heresy could have done.

"Goodness, Falkener, these are pretty morbid, aren't they?" he had said and afterward, with his friends, had enhanced his reputation as a wit by dubbing Roman Catholicism "that sadomasochistic orgy."

It had been from that time, however, that his previously unquestioned acceptance of Protestantism had begun to waver. The baby in the manger, the forgiveness on the cross, the white, springtime resurrection had begun to seem like fairy stories hiding some uglier reality. By the time he had reached the sixth form, his doubts had resolved themselves into atheism, which itself was later modified, at university, into agnosticism.

Now, hearing the splatter of water from his bathroom, envisaging the bruised, blood-marked, and furious figure who was causing this sound, he was shocked by the same percussion blows of wonder, horror, amusement, and uneasiness that had assailed him upon opening Falkener's prayer book.

41

There had been no one point at which Olivia had understood that neither Michael nor anyone else was going to release her from her confinement beneath the car. Rather had there been a multitude of component awarenesses, which, like the dots of a pointillist painting, had for a long time meant nothing, then, suddenly, as though by a change in distance or focus, had united into an obvious, recognizable whole.

Into one of the many spaces of silence that had punctuated her endless afternoon had come a woman's footsteps, accompanied, as they grew louder, by the jingling of keys. Then a car door had opened, a car door had closed, an engine had started, and a car (a car parked next to the one that sheltered Olivia) had been driven away. It was this that had altered her depth of focus, had gathered into one idea her inchoate thoughts: Whatever he said, I can't wait any longer. If I don't get out of here now, I'm either going to be killed or caught. There's no alternative. Whatever he said.

She had lifted her face and begun to stretch one hand toward the rectangle of daylight that, darkening and flaring in pulses, had been her only view from time immemorial. The pain of the gesture, in muscles held too long in unnatural stillness, had caused her to withdraw it. Tears had burned across her eyelids. Her chest had swelled with an insufferable tiredness.

"Nobody's going to come," she had said to herself. "I've got to get out by myself."

Inch by inch, hurt by hurt, she had maneuvered herself from under the car and out onto the pavement where, for half a minute, she had stayed on her hands and knees incapable of rising. In front of her, two pigeons had circled and pecked around what might have been a bread crust. At the far end of the street, a woman had levered a stroller (piled high with shopping and a baby) off the pavement, onto the tarmac, across the tarmac, and up onto the pavement on the other side.

Olivia had watched her as though she were an engine performing mechanical actions. She had not conceived of her as a person capable of relating to herself, capable of calling out, "Hey! You! What are you doing down there?" Her brain had returned to life as slowly and painfully as her limbs.

I'm by myself, she had thought. The others aren't here. Whatever he said, they aren't here. Where are they? What happened to them? I've got to find out.

She had thought, I must get back to Wimbledon. They'll be drinking champagne.

Then she had remembered the police sirens and had thought, No. I mustn't go there. I must go somewhere else. Where?

The choice of Simon's flat as a destination had been not so much a decision as a procrastination.

"Tea's ready, Olivia!"
"Thank you."
"Do you want it in there or here?"
"I'm coming."

The inaptness of Simon's politeness did not annoy her. It was what she had anticipated from him, what she had come for. He, with his pale green shirt turned back at the neck and wrists, with his narrow, naked feet, with his smell of citrus fruit, was a neutral country in a continent at war. She neither envied him nor despised him. He was a condition, to be taken into account only when all other factors were equal.

As she entered the kitchen, he pulled a chair away from the table for her to sit on, then handed her a mug and offered her a cigarette.

"Did you find the disinfectant?" he asked.

"Yes. Look, Simon, I'm very grateful to you for letting me in like this, after everything I said yesterday. . . ."

"What did you expect me to do? Slam down the ansaphone and leave you to bleed to death on the doorstep?"

"I was hardly bleeding to death."

"No, okay, but you were pretty shaken up."

"Yes—well, anyway, thank you."

Olivia wrinkled her forehead in an effort to shut him out, to concentrate. She had come to this place—to this familiar tile-walled kitchen, with its narrow window, its wooden hanging clotheshorse, and its air of half-hearted neglect—in order to gain time and space in which to collect her thoughts. She hadn't wanted help or inspiration, merely a nothingness wherein, uninfluenced, she might consider the events of the morning and, having considered, reach a decision about what her next move should be.

Yet this was proving harder than she had supposed. Every time she tried to force her mind back to the factory, the cashiers' office, the middle-aged woman slumped across her desk, every time she tried to see the bloodlike splashes of paint from an overturned can, or hear the scream of the sirens, the kitchen intervened.

Its normality, like an old, deaf nanny, denied the possibility of the other. Its lack of change would not admit that the other had occurred; or that, if it had, it had been anything more than a dream.

A new fear rose up inside Olivia. It occurred to her that it would be possible for everything that had happened to her that morning to be denied, not just by others but by herself. Her part in the events could, with little effort, be distorted into something quite different from what it had been: something small and unimportant and acceptable.

"Look, Simon," she said, "I'm going to have to tell you . . ."

And when he answered, "It's okay, Livvy, take it slowly; I know most of it, anyway—it must've been awful," her relief was as great as her surprise.

"How do you know? You haven't . . . Oh, you haven't heard from him, have you? From Michael? What did he say? Where is he?"

"No, of course I haven't heard from Michael."

"But you said . . ."

"Your father came to see me this morning. He showed me

the note you left him and on the bottom of it—"

"My father?"

Olivia rose to her feet. As she did so, her hand with its mugful of tea smashed down against the surface of the table. Hot liquid streamed through the air, then dropped with a smack on floor and skin and clothes.

A second later it was over, whatever emotion it was that had caused this reflex violence. All that remained was a burning sensation along her hand and forearm and a powerlessness, an exhaustion, that no longer minded where it came to rest.

She said, "I'm sorry, I don't know what happened. What did you say?"

"Your father came to see me this morning. And you know that note you left him. . . ."

Simon had collected a cloth from the sink and, with leaden tact, was wiping up the tea that she had spilled.

"Hey, did you scald yourself?" he asked. "It looks very red."

"It's all right. What *about* that note?"

So he told her, and as he did so (as he quoted the text of Michael's postscript; as he enumerated the evidences of Michael's guilt; as he extolled her father's virtues—his pride, his wisdom, his concern; as he questioned her and added her answers to his argument), Olivia waited for a reaction to take place within herself.

None came. She understood the words that Simon was speaking as he walked backward and forward behind the kitchen table, gesticulating with repetitive, jerky movements and tapping ash into a saucer each time he passed it. She understood the sentences, the reasoning, yet could not respond to them. They seemed like a story that she had heard too many times before, or one that, unaware, she had known always.

172

"You must understand that I'm trying to be perfectly objective about all this," the boy said. In his to-ing and fro-ing, he had arrived at that end of the kitchen where the window was, and the faded afternoon light made a negative halo around him. Olivia had the impression that he was in danger of slipping away from her, of disintegrating and drifting, in particles, back into the shadows, until he became a piece of them.

"Obviously it's not easy, but I think what I'm saying's as logical and unemotional as it can be. Now, okay, it's basically none of my business. But I just think you ought to know the facts, so that whatever decision you make's an informed one. That's reasonable, isn't it? Anyway, the facts are that this guy Michael's been using you to get explosives from your father. The whole robbery and your involvement in it was just a device to panic him into giving them to him. I mean, this story about raising funds for van der Walt's appeal—you must see that that can't be true. Even a lawyer wouldn't work for money the whole country knew to be stolen. Besides, seriously, Liv, it's all very well protesting about Britain's attitude towards apartheid. You know that I hate it as much as anyone. But, God! You say that a woman was *shot.* That's not funny. That's horrible.

"Okay, nobody's blaming you. If you were told that the gun wasn't going to be loaded . . . Only, the police won't see it like that. You're an accomplice to murder now. That's what that Michael of yours has made you into. He can't care about you, Livvy. He can't give a fuck about anything. Including the blacks in South Africa, I wouldn't be surprised. They're just an excuse for him to get his vicious little kicks.

"Please, you've got to go back to your father. He can help you. I'm not trying to say that he's perfect. I'm not trying to argue with you about that. He's from a different generation and he's got prejudices and attitudes I don't agree with. But at least he's . . . At least he's got the same basic human feelings as we have. Will you, Livvy? Will you let him help you?"

She shrugged her shoulders. The skin of her face felt tight, as though salt water had dried on it, and there was gravel behind her eyelids.

"I know it'll be annoying for your pride and so on, but it really is the only sensible solution. Whether the others— Michael and that lot—whether they've been caught or not, they're only going to drag you farther down with them. And what for? Not for an ideal. You must know that now. So please, let your father help you. He's the only one who can. I mean, even if you feel it's a compromise, surely it's better than going the whole way with something you don't—you *can't*—believe's right any more?"

"Okay," she said.

She stood up.

"You're going to? Livvy, that's—"

"Where is he?" she asked. "At home?"

"I don't know. Look, I'll ring him, shall I?"

"You mean to say he's not sitting there waiting for us?"

"No. Well, I don't know. Why should he be?"

"He asked you to send me to him, didn't he?"

"Of course not. He didn't know you were going to come here any more than I did. How could he've done?"

"Oh, I bet he did. Even if he didn't tell you, I bet he did."

She tossed her head and looked away. Although accepting that it was inevitable, she wanted to postpone until the latest possible moment her breakdown, for she had a premonition that it was to be her last. The elastic of her will to recover had been overstretched and she did not think that it would spring again to her assistance.

"Let's go, shall we?" she said.

"Right. I'll just get an umbrella. It looks as though it's about to rain."

174

42

On leaving Sally, Edward had gone straight to his office, where he had returned a telephone call from Amsterdam, signed a couple of letters, and, having decided that his mind was too preoccupied for further trivia, left a message with Margaret asking Dick to come to Chelsea as soon as he returned. Then he had gone home.

When he had got there, Mrs. Clifford had already left. He had registered the fact that she should not have done so for another ten minutes, but without emotion, as a closed-circuit camera records for possible future reference indiscriminate comings and goings.

In the kitchen, he had poured himself a glass of Riesling from an already opened bottle in the refrigerator and made himself a clumsy but tasty sandwich from potted shrimp and doorsteps of fresh white bread. While eating this, he had read the copies of the two evening papers he had bought on the way, but they had been early editions and he had not been surprised to find that they contained nothing of interest to him.

Now he sat at the desk in his study, watching without seeing as the sky darkened over into premature evening and the leaves on the hedge at the bottom of his garden tugged and rattled in a fretting wind. Beside his elbow lay a book he had attempted, for a while, to read: Galsworthy's *The Man of Property.*

Several times he thought, I'll go back to the office.

At least that would have been something to do. Then it occurred to him that Dick could already have gone there and even now be on his way to Chelsea. He pulled the telephone toward him and dialed the first three digits of the office number, meaning to ascertain from Margaret what the situation was. Instead, however, he withdrew his finger from the dial and relaid the receiver in its cradle.

This dependence on other people, this having to conduct his life at other people's rhythm, irked him as nothing else could have done. It sapped his energy—or, rather, transformed it into corrosive restlessness. It seemed so unfair that his proven, winning speed should be handicapped—by Sally's feelings, by Dick's pompous secrecy, by his daughter's gullibility and his daughter's boyfriend's pathetic unwillingness to fight for what was his. He had a feeling of envy toward O'Keefe.

Things were so much easier when one was young, when one was beginning. But the more one gained, the more weights one acquired: responsibility, respectability, knowledge. . . .

Edward felt sure that O'Keefe, in his position that morning, would have snatched the telephone from Sally's hands and said, "Okay, Dick, what is it this guy's got to tell you? Well, anyway, ring me as soon as you find out. It doesn't matter what I'm doing at your place. I'll tell you later." That was how *he* would have reacted twenty-five years ago.

He pushed back his chair, stood up, and left the study. The narrow passages and stairways of his house were gloomy with semi-darkness and restless, like himself.

"Come on, come on, come on."

It was terrible to be forced to wait in this limbo, where time could be heard creeping, where time moved so slowly that it bent back upon itself, causing the future and the present and the past to lie in one place.

Once, when Caroline had been alive, he had enjoyed this part of the day. Then they had taken their drinks to the sofa by the drawing-room windows, had listened to soft music, had discussed his work, their plans. When Caroline was alive.

As soon as the business with O'Keefe was over, Edward decided, he would book a flight to Cairo and stay there for a couple of weeks. It was about time he went there. And, after that, there was the new Holland deal to look into.

He had reached the living room. He filled himself a tumbler with whisky and water. He fiddled with the knobs of the stereo radio he had never been sure how to operate, until, from speakers on either side of the blocked-in fireplace, the sixth symphony of Tchaikovsky wailed forth. As long as he kept on planning, kept on moving, kept on doing, time would *have* to stream out behind him like a linear pennant, not coil around his brain with memories and malformed presages.

43

In front of her was the glossy olive-green door of the Chelsea house, with its chromium-plated knocker and its chromium-plated bellpush, on which (her keys being still in Wimbledon) Simon was putting his forefinger. And it seemed to her that her whole life had been spent like this: standing at the door to someone's house, waiting to be taken in. She saw herself as the parcel in the party game that is tossed from player to player for as long as the music continues, sometimes clutched at, sometimes snatched away, but always circling without will, until the maiden aunt at the piano (her back turned so as to avoid favoritism) lifts her fingers from the keyboard and decides its resting place.

"He's in," said Simon. "I can hear him coming."

"Dick, where the hell—? Simon! Olivia!"

"Can we come in, sir?"

"Yes, of course. For goodness' sake! Now, tell me everything. I want to know exactly what's happened."

"You tell him," Olivia said to Simon. She was not certain that her strength could tolerate this second narration.

"I don't care who tells me," said Edward, turning off the radio, "but one of you'd better hurry up."

"Well, okay," said Simon.

Olivia walked to one of the black leather armchairs and sat in it, her head slumped back, her eyes fixed on a print on the opposite wall.

"Yes, I see," said Edward once or twice, his voice as clipped and impatient as that of a general receiving bad news from the front, and then, "Oh, my . . . Oh, my God . . . Olivia, is that true? That a woman was killed?"

"I don't know."

"What do you mean? Simon's just said . . ."

"A woman was shot. And blood came out of her. So I suppose she must be dead, yes."

"All right. Carry on, Simon."

"Well, after that, apparently—"

"Hold on a second!"

Simon stopped talking. Edward held one hand rigid in the air as, from the street outside, two sounds crept into the room. The first was the patter of accelerating raindrops; the second the wordless but unmistakable cry of a newsboy.

"I'll go, sir," said Simon.

Olivia closed her eyes. Through the now open front door, the sounds of the dark afternoon were amplified: the clatter of rain on roofs and pavements and glass, the regular, bird-like call of the boy with the papers, the slap of Simon's feet, the hiatus, the resumption of the call, and Simon's slower return.

"Well?"

"Hang on a second. The pages are all sticking together."

"Here, give them to me."

They huddled like children around a caught tadpole. Her father's face had points of red on the cheekbones. Simon's hair hung like string before his eyes.

"You take that one and I'll take this one."

"Look under the 'Stop Press.' If it's anywhere, it'll be there."

"What page is that?"

"I don't know. The back. Careful, don't tear it."

"Look! Look here, sir!"

"Show me."

She did not watch her father reading. Instead, she stared at a spot on the mantelpiece, until it turned purple with her concentration.

"Well, thank goodness for that! We've still got a chance, then. Olivia, your friends appear to have got away, too. But how on earth—? Oh, my God, I don't believe it. 'From slogans painted on the walls of the office, it appears . . .' What the hell did you think you were playing at? Olivia! Well, never mind. The important thing is to act fast."

"But what are you going to do?" Simon asked.

"I'm going to go and see these people, that's what."

"Who? The . . . Michael what's-his-name and that lot?"

"Of course. Olivia, tell me where they'll be."

Simon said, "But the woman, the cashier. It says here—"

"I know, I know, but it can't be helped. Olivia? Oh, come on. Pull yourself together, girl. If you're going to play grown-up games, you can't expect to be mollycoddled like a child any more. Where is he? Where's O'Keefe hiding out? Look! This isn't bloody primary school. I'm not asking you to tell tales on your buddies. I've just got to know where the man is, so that I can talk to him. You've got yourself into very serious trouble, and if I'm going to get you out of it, I've got to get the others out, too.

"Don't think I want to. Don't think I wouldn't hang them all tomorrow if I had my way. It's just that if *they're* caught, *you're* as good as caught, too, my girl. And please, please, don't tell me that your friends'd never betray you, that there's honor among thieves. If you don't know how untrue *that* is by now, then you haven't learned anything. Besides, where's that bag of yours? That sordid-looking velvet pouch

179

you always carry around with you? Did you leave it here? Or there?"

When her father had begun to address *her* rather than Simon, Olivia had been forced to look at him, not because she felt that she ought to, nor because she had any idea of answering his questions, but because to have resisted the command of his voice would have required more energy than she now possessed.

She looked at him, but she heard him (as previously she had heard Simon) through distortive earphones. Only, this time the earphones did not eliminate her emotional responses, but twisted them in a manner that was, at first, startling.

For he had become a clown. Her father had become a clown, telling terrible jokes in a deadpan voice with a terrible deadpan face: "But the woman, the cashier . . ." "I know, but it can't be helped. . . . I'm not asking you to tell tales on your buddies. . . ."

It was very funny. Apart from anything else, he was having a dialogue with himself, providing *her* objections for *him* to overrule. And, back in his flat, Simon had done the same thing. At this realization, laughter beat in Olivia's stomach. They were *mad*, both of them. Or were they playing a joke on her? That must be the answer. They and Michael, too, had played a joke on her and she had fallen for it.

How stupid she had been, to think that all the intrigue, all the lies, all the greed and violence and acceptance of violence were real. It was a *very* good joke.

"Olivia, what's the matter with you? For goodness' sake, girl, there's nothing *funny*. How can you just sit there giggling like that?"

"She's had a bad shock, remember."

"I should bloody well hope she has. Olivia! Maybe she'll learn something from it."

Olivia gripped her ribs. The absurdity was painful.

"She's had a shock."

180

"Maybe she'll learn something from it."

They knew, they must know, that none of that made sense.

"Look, don't you think you should leave her alone for a bit? This third degree really can't be helping."

"I'm sorry about that, but I'm afraid we haven't got the time for niceties. Child, pull yourself together. Or do you want me to slap your face?"

"Mr. Mannion, please don't go on at her. It's too late to do anything, anyway. What's happened's happened. Even you can't change that."

"What do *you* want? For her to spend the next ten years of her life in prison? Be sensible, boy."

Edward lifted his hand, so that the cuff of his shirt slipped back to reveal an inch or two of narrow, suntanned wrist, and hit his daughter across the mouth.

She stopped laughing.

The rain, having found a chink between window and window frame, splatted onto the painted wooden sill.

"Where is he?" Edward asked.

Olivia said, "In Wimbledon. I don't know what the road's called, but it's on the other side of the High Street from the tube station and almost directly opposite. The house is on the left-hand side, painted . . . painted a sort of pale pink and a bit unkempt-looking. It's about halfway down."

44

"Oh, goodness me, what's happening now? I say, what's happening now?"

"We're changing drivers," said the bus conductor.

"But why?" Dick Hastings asked. "This is really too bad. It's already taken us half an hour to get to here from Oxford Street."

During this half-hour, Dick had tried, and failed, to imagine the reason for Mannion's impatience to hear his news. (Thinking the business closed, he had only gone after it as a conscientious gesture.) There was no denying, however, the urgency of Margaret's message: "You're to go there *as soon* as you get back."

He thought, I shouldn't have let that taxi go. You can never find them when it's raining. She may have been a woman, but all the same . . . And I wish I hadn't drunk so much. Oh, how I hate drinking at lunchtime.

He let his head drop forward onto the cool rail of the seat in front of him. The sleepiness in his skull held uneasy balance with the nausea in his stomach.

45

Michael's moment was coming. So sure of this was he, so tight with anticipation, that even the plaintive baaing sounds that Barbara was emitting at his elbow failed to irritate him.

"Who is he? Who is he, Michael? Oh, Christ, he's coming up the drive. They must've got her after all, then, mustn't they? But you said she wouldn't talk. You said you knew she wouldn't."

"Nor she would've, sweetheart, to the fuzz."

"Then this must be Daddy."

"Right first time, Malcolm, my old lad. No, hang round a bit! Let him knock. We don't want to seem too eager."

"Her father?" Barbara asked. "Mannion, you mean? What's he doing here? How did he know where to find us? For fuck's sake, Michael, supposing he's not alone?"

"You'll give yourself an ulcer if you carry on like that," said Michael. "Use your head, woman. D'you think he wants the fact that his daughter's a criminal splashed all over the newspapers? Not to mention that other little item. No, he's coming to us because the loser always comes to the winner. Didn't you know that?"

Through the gap in the net curtains, he watched with satisfaction as Mannion rat-a-tatted a second time upon the door. The man was wearing a raincoat, the plaid-lined collar turned up around his neck, but his hair was plastered to his head and a jet of water from a broken piece of guttering beat down onto his shoulder.

"Oh, nice, nice, nice," said Michael. "You know, the smarter a man's dressed, the more stupid he looks when he's sopping wet."

Nobody could say that he hadn't earned this moment. Thinking back over the previous weeks and, in particular, over the previous hours, Michael was astonished at how much he had achieved. Nor could anybody say that the odds had been with him. To have attempted an armed robbery for the first time with two women and one trigger-happy boy, to have expected from the robbery not just an immediate few thousand pounds but a secondary benefit of whose extent even his fellow conspirators were ignorant—these were not the steady, predictable steps of a favorite, but the reckless, neck-or-nothing leaps of a Grand National outsider with nothing to lose and everything to win.

There had been times, too, when losing had seemed not just probable but inevitable: when Malcolm had let fly that pointless, hysterical shot; when, on running from the office, they had seen that their way was cut off by a group of over-alled men, into whose midst Olivia was charging like a mad bull at a picador; when Malcolm and Barbara and he had turned down the corridor the other way, to their left, and found that the only possible exit was a locked and double-glazed window.

Yet there had been inspiration, too: "Upstairs," Michael had said, and the others had followed him to the upper floor and the predictable regulation fire escape. It had been a race, but no one had had the foresight to cut them off and desperation had won over unpreparedness.

And luck: the bus's passage intercepting theirs as they had reached the High Street, slow enough for them to jump aboard, fast enough to carry them away before their pursuers had rounded the final bend in the side street and seen them.

After that, there had been several changes of direction, several alterations in their method of transport, as well as, at an early stage, a separation, in which Michael and Barbara had walked arm in arm up Bayswater toward Marble Arch and Malcolm had taken the Circle Line of the underground system to Victoria. He had reached Wimbledon at quarter to two; the others at ten minutes past.

Then there had been the hours of uncertainty, the hours of jangling nerves and frustrated tiredness and reproach.

Malcolm had said, "We really shouldn't have just abandoned the girl like that."

"No? Well, what do you suggest we should've done? Hung around calling for her while those thugs put the boot in? People aren't so friendly when you've just shot one of their mates."

"Shove it, Michael. If I hadn't shot her . . ."

"What? She might've sounded the alarm and got us interrupted? Is that what you were going to say?"

Barbara had said, "We should've gone under the cars, like we planned. I'm sure that's what Olivia did."

"I'm sure you're right. And I'm sure we'd've done the same if we'd had half a second to do it in. Only, as you may have noticed, time was a bit pressing just about then and those louts may've been on the other side of the wall, but they weren't looking in the other direction."

"Okay, but what are we going to do now? We can't just hang around for the fuzz to pick us up. I mean, they might've got *her* and—"

"She wouldn't talk. You can take my word for that. Anyway, if she did get under a car like I told her, it'll only be a question of time before she turns up here. Unless . . ."

"Unless what?"

"It doesn't matter. Hey, Malky, where's the whisky?"

There had been no whisky. Instead, Barbara had made them some coffee and even this superficially innocuous event had added its tension to the already cracking afternoon.

Barbara had said, "For God's sake, just don't say anything about it not being strong enough."

Michael had said, "Okay, but it does seem incredible that you can't just put another teaspoon of the powder in."

"Then you fucking well make it."

"I will, I will. And cook the meals. And scrub the floors. Only, you'll have to arrange to get Pieter out of prison, because I don't think I'll have the time."

"You're not going to get him out, anyway."

"What d'you mean?"

"That story you spun Olivia . . ."

"My God, woman! You're not just a lousy coffee maker, you're stupid. Of course we're not going to mount an *appeal*. We never were, were we? I mean, that'd be about as much use as a sick headache. But what d'you think we're getting these explosives off Mannion for? What d'you think we've gone to all this trouble making sure he'll give them to us for? For Guy Fawkes night? No, you moron. It's so that we can *force* the government to let your darling husband out."

"He's not my 'darling' husband. You know bloody well it was only so he could stay in England."

"Well, your beloved leader, then. Anyway, *he's* what this is all about and what it always *has* been. It's just that little Miss Mannion's got some rather old-fashioned ideas about violence. You can't blame her. She's never had it practiced on her. And besides, it is her dad we're trying to use for our

185

evil plans. I don't know how far you think we'd've got if I'd told her *that.*"

"I still don't see it's going to work."

"You've got to have more faith, Barbara," Malcolm had said. "Michael may not have Pieter's crusading fervor, but you've got to admit he's efficient. And realistic, too. He knows it wouldn't be on to try and doublecross us. Don't you, Michael?"

The afternoon had been almost as full of dangers as the morning.

Now, however (as Mannion stamped on the doorstep and lifted his fist to the door for a third time; as the rain continued to fall as though tipped from a giant's slop pail), he knew that it had been worth it.

"Okay, Malcolm," he said. "We don't want him giving up and going away. Let the bastard in."

"Thank you. I was beginning to wonder how long it'd take before you'd decide I was wet enough. I suppose these status games are necessary, but they *are* rather time-consuming. I mean, suppose I'd decided not to come this afternoon, but to send Olivia back instead, so that *you'd* had to contact *me?* We'd still be at it this time next week, wouldn't we?"

The young man who had opened the door to him (a dark, well-built fellow with the vulgar good looks of a 1950's film star) remained impassive before this volley of sarcasm, but Edward was speaking more to relieve himself of venom than to create a particular effect and did not mind.

"Well, are you going to show me in to him? The great O'Keefe? Or should I take my shoes off first? Ah, this way. You must all be feeling very pleased with yourselves. What a blow against the establishment, eh?"

"He's here," said the young man.

They had entered a room to the left of the passageway: a long, narrow living room that stretched from the front of the house to the back and across whose middle a rectangular archway straddled (proclaiming an attempt at open-plan conversion, which, owing to a lack of windows and therefore light, had not come off). The room gave the impression of not being much used. It was still with dust and tidiness.

Before entering, Edward had noticed another, half-glass door at the end of the passage. He assumed that this led into the kitchen. He also assumed that upstairs there would be three corresponding rooms: two bedrooms and a bathroom. There had been a door beneath the staircase, too. That of a broom cupboard, he guessed. Now he glanced toward the window on his right, the window on the far side of the archway, which looked out over the garden. Through it, he saw neither sheds nor any other places for storage beneath the pounding rain.

"Good afternoon, Mr. Mannion. How kind of you to come."

"Mr. O'Keefe! And you must be Mrs. van der Walt."

"How do you know that?"

"Of course he knows that, Barbara. I shouldn't wonder if he hasn't been looking up our press cuttings."

"Well, you did ask me to. In that kind note you left me yesterday. Only, as you can see, there wasn't even any need. My daughter was able to give me far more details of this morning's fun and games than the *Standard* could. In fact, now I come to think of it, how can you have been so sure I'd recognize the particular article you meant? Oh, of course! How stupid of me! The slogans! I was wondering why you'd taken such an idiotic risk. No, I should've realized. Quite a clever idea. You weren't to guess that she'd get tired of your company so soon, after all. Though you should never underestimate the pull of the family, you know."

"Come off it, Mannion. I'll lay you ten to one it was that boyfriend of hers she went to, not you. You know bloody well she despises you."

Edward opened his mouth, then closed it. The offensiveness of O'Keefe's remark was no more than he had expected, but the perceptiveness of it was. It occurred to him that while the other two occupants of the room (the sullen youth and Mrs. van der Walt) were battering him with their hatred and suspicion and uncertainty, O'Keefe, like a more experienced and accomplished fighter, was holding reserves of emotion and thought in abeyance.

"If she despises *me*," he said, "what do you imagine she feels about *you*? She's not really used to seeing old women shot up in front of her eyes and I think it upset her a bit."

"Did she die? The cashier?" It was the young man by the door who spoke.

"It's not important, Malcolm," said O'Keefe.

"Oh, I don't think you can say that," said Edward. "They may have abolished capital punishment, but fourteen years' imprisonment isn't exactly fun. Is it, Malcolm?"

"You sod."

"Careful, Malcolm. You only get remission for *good* behavior, not swearing."

"The same applies to you, Mannion."

O'Keefe came forward from the window bay where, throughout the interview, he and the woman had been standing. His black-lined nostrils were stretched, and his teeth and scarlet lips glistened in the shadow of his beard. Mannion knew then that he had underestimated his opponent, that (by calling him a young man, by thinking of him as from the same nursery as Olivia and Simon) he had made a mistake. He also realized that his shoulders were drawn back as though in preparation for defense against a physical attack.

"I'm quite aware that the same applies to me," he said; "otherwise I shouldn't be here. In fact, don't you think we ought to start talking about that?"

"As soon as you want."

"Alone."

He was not surprised when O'Keefe accepted this condition.

46

On returning to the drawing room, Simon saw that Olivia was sitting in the same position as she had been when he had left her two minutes previously. Her body, always solid, was now as relaxed as granite and her face, too, was still, with a stillness that came not from patience or self-control or, indeed, from any other internal force, but was more like a death mask. Behind its cold impersonation of its wearer, decomposition might have been taking place.

He turned on the light. The battery of rain beyond the windows removed itself into another, less immediate dimension.

"That was some business partner of your father's," he said.

The Olivia statue did not answer him. Nor, with the exception of a few forced and abstracted monosyllables, had it since Mannion had left the house over half an hour before. Simon had the feeling that if something did not happen soon to change this state of affairs, the real Olivia, the one that the granite encased, would either disappear or become absorbed forever into its new and terrible skin. Yet he neither knew what it was that should happen nor dared to bring whatever it was about. Doubts hindered his actions as water hinders a running man's legs.

To begin with, he would have liked to have been appalled by the way Mr. Mannion had behaved toward Olivia: by his cynicism, by his lack of kindness, by the vengeful glee that he had seemed to take in her unhappiness. Yet each time he tried to condemn these things, he was frustrated by a sense of partnership in the guilt, of collaboration. Each time the anger rose in his mouth to be spat, it turned upon itself and caught like bile in his throat.

He tried to avert this process. He told himself that he had brought the girl there in good faith, that there had been nothing else for him to do, that if he had known how her father was going to act . . .

But then, like the cross-examination of a persistent and ruthless barrister, the questions intervened: "How else did you think he was going to act? You've heard her talking about him. You've even met him yourself. You had no reason to suppose that he was anything other than self-interested and given to expediency. Isn't it rather the case that you deliberately ignored all this, all the differences between you and him, all the things about him you don't approve of, because, for once, you and he had a common interest: the removal of Olivia from O'Keefe's influence? Because you were temporarily united in your aim, you allowed yourself to submit to the stronger man's methods of achieving this. Worse, you allowed yourself to believe that his methods would be yours, in spite of considerable evidence to the contrary."

Simon remembered the vague, insidious fear that had troubled him that morning on receiving Mannion's telephone call, the sensation of having been trapped that Olivia's subsequent appearance at his flat had provoked, and thought that he was beginning to understand their cause.

He looked at Olivia again. Apart from an occasional tightening of muscles around her eyes and mouth, she still did not move. It was only five o'clock, but Simon went to the drinks tray and poured himself a glassful of Martini, which was the nearest thing to wine that he could find.

"That guy," he said. "The one who was at the door just then; he was pretty put out. Apparently your father'd asked him to come here urgently. I said that he'd had to go off and would he like to leave a message, but he wouldn't. Just said he was going home and your father could ring him there. He was sopping, poor guy. You can't blame him for being angry."

These were the only things he dared to speak about: unimportant facts and events. Ideas about himself, or Olivia, had become so frightening that even to have said "Look, don't you think you ought to snap out of this a bit? Don't you think it'd be better to discuss the situation than for you just to sit there, stupefied?" would have been to take a risk of which his conscience was not, at that moment, capable.

47

They were in the kitchen. Before he had sat down, Mannion had brushed the seat of his chair with his fingertips and, even now, although apparently relaxed, his body was held in such a way as to come into minimum contact with its surroundings.

Michael, too, felt a physical disgust at the dirt and grease of Barbara's housekeeping. To have admitted as much to Mannion, however, if only by implication, would have been to lose the advantage of holding this meeting on his own home territory.

"I hope you'll forgive me, not having offered you a drink," he said; "only the glasses mightn't've met with your standards of hygiene. Besides, now I come to think of it, the Dimple Haig's finished. I couldn't tempt you with some instant coffee, could I?"

"No, thank you."

"No? Well, I quite understand. It doesn't have much in the way of 'tone,' does it? Though I believe there are those who drink it every day without any *visible* bad effects."

"All right, O'Keefe, you're a very funny man. And quite a clever one, too. But let's get down to business, shall we? The squeal of police cars outside the front gate would be rather embarrassing to both of us."

"Don't try and intimidate me. The fuzz's got no more idea where we are than the Queen has. I bet you even checked to make sure you weren't being followed, didn't you?"

"All the same, even professionals get caught."

"Exactly! And because they *are* professionals. Because they follow the same old code of conduct, which the fuzz knows inside out."

"You could be right. I'm not going to argue. You seem to have been right about most things, so far. I will give you that."

"I don't want your congratulations, Mannion."

All the same, there had been a short leap of pleasure on hearing himself described as clever by the man who, three days before, had told him to go and piss off. No sooner had it arisen than he repressed it, but it had been there.

"Just give me a delivery date for the goods," he said.

"The explosives?"

"I'm not talking about cream doughnuts."

"I'm afraid I can't remember exactly how much it was you said you wanted."

"Five hundred pounds weight," said Michael, and Mannion's expression confirmed his suspicion that forgetfulness was *not* one of his opponent's weaknesses. He added, "It's gone up."

Mannion said, "So I see. Can you tell me why?"

"Inflation, I think they call it. But then, being a businessman, you probably know more about that than I do."

"Possibly. All the same, it does seem like an awful lot. What could anyone want so much for?"

"That sort of information isn't part of the deal."

"Am I allowed to guess? I mean, you're not by any chance thinking of terrorizing Her Majesty's government into releasing your poor imprisoned friend? By blowing bits of the country up until they do, perhaps? No, that can't be right. A man with your intelligence couldn't think that'd work, could he?"

"Like I said just now, it's none of your concern. I mean that, Mannion. Save your jokes for the Army and Navy Club."

"I'm sorry. As you so rightly pointed out, I'm a businessman. I couldn't be expected to understand the finer points of idealism."

Michael clenched, then unfolded, his right hand. The pleasure it would give him to shatter the polished showcase behind which Mannion sat would be no compensation for the smile of superiority with which Mannion would, beyond doubt, retaliate. Besides, the bastard's insinuations, although annoying, were irrelevant to the matter in hand.

"Just tell me how soon you can deliver," he said.

"How soon? I wasn't aware we'd even agreed on how much."

"We've agreed."

"Or even on whether there was going to be a delivery at all."

Michael rose to his feet.

"Now what are you playing at?" he asked.

He glanced toward the kitchen door. For a moment, it seemed possible that Mannion's power was limitless: that a squadron of policemen would burst in and take him, laughing at his attempts to implicate Olivia in his crimes, deaf to his accusations against her father. Then reason returned, accompanied by anger at the ease with which Mannion had shaken him. Even if others were fooled, *he* should have been able to distinguish the bark from the bite.

"Please sit down," said Mannion. "I didn't mean to upset you. On the contrary, I've got a suggestion I thought you might like to consider. One which, if I may say so, would be a lot fairer to everyone than yours. It involves you leaving the country. You and your two friends, of course. I'd arrange

193

everything. Money. Everything. All you'd have to do is name the destination."

"You're mad."

"I don't think so."

"Out of your mind. Do you really think I went to all this trouble for a one-way ticket to nowhere?"

"Better than a one-way ticket to Wormwood Scrubs, don't you think?"

"Not with you in the next-door cell, my sweetheart. And Olivia up the road in Holloway."

"Don't count on it."

"I do. The girl'd convict herself. You know that. And as for you, when your country's not even meant to be trading *baked beans* with Rhodesia, what are they going to think of a guy who's been sending *guns* out there?"

The momentary impotent fury in Mannion's eyes was enough to give Michael the confidence needed to sit again. Having done so, he reached for his cigarettes, tipped one into the palm of his hand, placed it between his lips, and lit it. Outside the room, the false evening of the rainstorm was merging into real evening. Water drummed with dull persistence against the darkening skin of the earth.

"Yes," he said, "don't forget there's still that. Nothing's changed since Monday night. Rhodesia. It's not like South Africa. They may not have apartheid there. They may even treat their blacks a bit better than Vorster's lot do. But they *did* commit the unforgivable sin of telling Britain to go stuff herself and, as you know, we really can't put up with that sort of thing. So, 'No trading with you,' we said. 'Not until you tell us you're sorry and you'll do things the way we want you to again.' Sentiments, incidentally, I'd've thought you'd've rather approved of. But then, like we've agreed, you're a businessman. And it wasn't so difficult, was it, shipping your stuff to the Middle East for it to get lost a bit before carrying on to its real destination? No, all right, like I said before, I haven't got any proof on me. But I've got names and addresses and the proof's there all right, for anyone who cares to go looking. It's just that nobody's had any reason to, up till now."

"I suppose you got this—this story from your friend van der Walt. He was stirring things up in Rhodesia, too, for a while once, wasn't he?"

"It's not important who I got it from."

"No, it's not. Because I'm afraid not a word of it's true."

Mannion sat, as ever, upright in his chair. His fingers curled on his thighs. An aura of dove-gray silk encircled him, dissociating him from the garish orange of the kitchen walls and the Chinese restaurant calendar that drooped behind his head. Seeing this, Michael could not help thinking, What an armor.

If destruction was sweet, then sweeter still was the destruction of an object one admired.

He said, "It's all true. And you know it."

"*Even* if it were, and *even* if it could be proved, I think it's only fair to tell you that any maximum sentence imposed on me would be risible when compared with what you'd get."

"Don't be so bloody naïve, Mannion. Or don't try making out I am. What do you think? That you'd walk out of the Scrubs and back into your old way of life like you'd just been on a world cruise? Come off it. Even if you only got a fine, you'd be finished."

"There is that."

"Well, then?"

"You're still asking too much. Have you any idea of the cost of five hundred pounds weight of dynamite?"

"A pretty shrewd one, yeah. But then, cost is relative, isn't it?"

"And how am I supposed to explain all this to my partners?"

"You've only got one. And he's more like an office boy, from what I can gather."

"All right. But what guarantee have I got that you'll stop here? The deal's one-sided enough as it is, but it becomes ludicrous if I'm expected to go on supplying you with little packages month after month after month."

"You won't. There's no point my giving you my word on it, of course, but you must admit it'd be stupid of me to push you. If *I* go down, *you* go down. We've agreed on that. But the reverse is still true, isn't it?"

"Yes. We appear to be pretty dependent on each other. So once you've got what you want, neither myself nor my daughter ever sees or hears from you again? Is that what you're promising?"

"That's about it."

There was a silence. From the far side of the door came the tread of footsteps on stairs. Within the room, glass rattled and the pilot light of a water heater hissed.

"I'd better make sure you get it tonight, then," said Mannion.

"Tonight?"

"Yes. You'll be in, I imagine."

"But that's . . . I mean, how are you going to arrange everything so fast?"

"There's not much to arrange. Just a question of transport. As far as I know, there's no customs control between London and Kent as yet."

"Kent? Is that where the stuff is?"

"Yes, but I don't think we need bother with the exact address. Now, if I'm going to get it all fixed, I'd better leave you."

Mannion stood up. Michael copied him; within his stomach a curious emptiness floated, as though a lift had descended too fast for his body to follow, or as though after he had at last played a withheld ace, his opponent had put down a two.

"But won't you have to account for it sometime?" he asked. "Surely you're going to have to do a bit of paperwork, losing it?"

"Of course," said Mannion. "But that needn't concern you. Nor need it hold up the delivery. Well, I can't give you an exact time when the stuff'll be here, but I think we can safely say before midnight. You have got somewhere to put it, I hope?"

"Yeah, of course."

"Good. Well, I'll be off, then. Say goodbye to your friends for me and thank you for the hospitality."

He left. Michael followed him along the hallway, opened the front door for him, and watched him as he strode through the rain without even turning his collar up.

Once there had been a woman (an older, married woman) with whom Michael had had an affair. After a month or so of clandestine, afternoon beddings, Michael had felt that this woman was getting too possessive, too demanding, and had decided to break the relationship off. He had planned with care how he should do this, devising a speech unanswerable in its finality, yet humble, flattering, and (without being obvious) threatening enough to render impotent any thoughts of retaliation by which the slighted lover might have been tempted.

When he had finished his speech, the woman had smiled. She had lifted herself from the sofa on which she had been lying and said, "Not bad. Not bad for a nineteen-year-old. I particularly liked that bit about you 'never forgetting' me. Really touching, that was. And you don't have to worry. There won't be no hard feelings. Why, an old bag like me! I should be grateful a good-looking boy like you even *looked* at me. No, I mean it, Mike. You're going to go a long way. That's obvious. Only, while you're getting there . . . You don't mind me saying this, do you? While you're getting there, try not to lose too much on the way; or you may find it wasn't worth it. No, I'd better go now. It'd be daft for my old man to start getting jealous now there's nothing left for him to get jealous over, wouldn't it?"

Of course, Michael could no longer be certain that those had been her very words, but as Mannion's figure continued its independent, confident retreat, his own reaction to the speech (his sense of having been cheated, his suspicion of somehow having been tricked) returned with faultless clarity.

"How did it go, then?"

Malcolm had come up behind him. Michael shut the door.

"What do you mean?" he asked.

"How did it go? All right? You weren't just talking about the weather all that time."

"No. It went very well indeed."

"No problems?"

"A few protests, as a matter of form. But nothing serious. The stuff'll be here tonight."

"Tonight?"

"Well, that's all right by us, isn't it? And *he* doesn't stand to gain anything by holding on to it. So why not? Look, if he tries anything, he's done for. And he knows it. That pinstriped waistcoat of his doesn't make him invulnerable, however much he'd like you to think it does. All right? Well, then, relax, sweetheart. We're home and dry."

"I'm confident if you're confident."

"That's good," he said. Then, "Where's Barbara?"

"Upstairs. Lying down."

"Is she? Well, why don't you go and join her, eh? While I pop down to the telephone box. I've just had an idea. After all, there's no harm in being double sure, is there?"

48

"Shall I get it?" Simon asked.

The bell had been ringing for a quarter of a minute now and still Olivia showed no sign of answering it. When it had started, she had turned her face toward the hallway whence the sound came, but with the polite disinterest of a visitor in someone else's waiting room. Nor, thereafter, had her expression changed. She might have been listening to canned music, or to the gurglings of a familiar river, not to something that expected a response.

"It's probably your father," said Simon.

He left the room and lifted the receiver.

"Hello," he said.

"I'd like to speak to Olivia."

"Who's that?"

"It doesn't matter who it is. Just tell her I'd like to speak to her."

Then Simon knew—not because he recognized the voice, which (if he had heard it at all before) he had heard through the hubbub of a party, but because of the flash of childlike hatred that illuminated his mind long before thought could bring its slower, steadier light to bear. He drew back his lips to say something, ask something, but, once again, doubt gagged him. It was not only that he felt incapable of making a decision for himself; he didn't even want to be the cause of Olivia's making one. If a word of his might have the power to revitalize Olivia, to start her moving in God knew what direction, he preferred not to utter it.

"Are you still there? Look, stop pissing around and put me on to her, will you?"

"I think you must've got the wrong number," said Simon.

"Don't try that one on me. I know she's . . . Fuck it!"

Michael depressed the telephone cradle, waited a moment, released it, placed a second coin in the mouth of the slot and redialed Mannion's number. Waiting for the purring tone to stop, he drummed with his fingertips against the glass wall of the kiosk. On it, in lipstick, somebody had written, "N.F.'s a wanker."

He's not the only one, thought Michael. What does that . . . What's his name? Simon. The boyfriend. What the hell does he think he's playing at? Come on, man. I know you can hear me.

He wondered whether Olivia might not, after all, be in Chelsea. Yet if she was not, there was no reason for the boyfriend to have lied.

If she was, on the other hand, it seemed incredible that she should let the telephone ring this second time without either insisting that Simon answer it or answering it herself.

He contemplated scenes of physical restraint (of Olivia struggling in the arms of the effete young man whom he had last seen dancing at that hideous party in Kensington; of Olivia tied to a chair; of Olivia locked in a room), then dismissed them.

He thought, Maybe she's asleep.

He thought, Maybe they went out the moment he'd put the phone down.

He thought, Maybe I got the wrong number this time.

He was not, however, a man used to doubting his actions, nor did the first two solutions seem any more plausible than the third. The purring continued, however (bland, unhurried, capable of eternity), until, at last, Michael could listen to it no more and cut it off.

Ten years before, he might have vented his frustration on the machine that was the immediate cause of it. One week before, he might have done. Now he strolled back along the street to the house, his shoulders hunched against the

200

weather, his hands plunged into his jeans pockets, his tongue running back and forth along the coarse under edge of his mustache.

49

It being the rush hour, Edward had taken the underground to Victoria.

There, having made one out-of-town telephone call, he boarded a main-line train for the station in Kent in whose vicinity his government-approved explosives storehouse lay. As the train slipped free of its platforms and plunged into the open rain-swept plain of interweaving tracks beyond, the time was six-thirty-five.

50

At seven o'clock, Simon dropped the *Evening Standard* crossword that he had been attempting, finished his third glass of Martini, and stood up and said, "Look, Liv, I don't know what's happened to your father, but let's go and get something to eat, shall we?"

"All right."

Her answer startled him. He had expected either silence or a refusal.

"Well, where would you like to go?" he said.

Olivia felt for the arms of the chair in which she was sitting, pressed down on them, and levered her body upright. That Simon should offer her the choice of a place to eat as though it were important, as though it amounted to a release from captivity, was yet another joke from the comedy act that he and her father seemed to have perfected. The act, however, was no longer funny—never had been to its performers, she now realized.

She looked at Simon. He seemed to be standing a long way away from her. Although his plimsolled feet were less than a body's length from hers on the chocolate-brown wool carpet of the room, she had the impression of an untraversable distance between them, of a shimmering desert spanned by mirage roads that would disappear the moment one set foot upon them. Sadness engulfed her.

"What is there round here? There's that Italian place. Is that any good?"

She wished that he would not continue this pretense, this suggestion of unreal alternatives, now that their humor had died. She turned away from him and walked toward the front door, not doubting that his footsteps would follow her, or that when she opened the door and went out into the night, his body would hurry to be beside her, his arms to lift an umbrella above her head.

Simon had lied to her. He had told her that he was a member of no man's army and she had believed him. It was under this illusion that she had gone to him for sanctuary, to discover that (even if he did not wear a uniform) he was as much a conscript as she.

She didn't blame him for this. She felt no anger at his duplicity—only a tired, regretful sadness, a powerless feeling like nostalgia. She was not even certain that the boy knew what had happened to him, although she suspected that he must do. Such guilty knowledge would account for the new self-consciousness with which his old avoidance of dogmatism appeared to have become polluted.

"Are you sure this'll be okay?"

In their walking, they had reached the Fulham Road and the gold-lettered, plate-glass door of an Italian restaurant.

"We can have a hamburger, if you prefer. Or there's that

fish-and-chips place down the road, which isn't bad. I don't know. What do you think?"

"This is fine," said Olivia.

She knew as well as he must that *what* they ate and *where* they ate were unimportant variations on the theme of her father's parting words. Twitching his raincoat from its hook in the hall, shaking the creases out, and sliding his arms into the sleeves, he had said to Simon, "Stay with her till I get back. All right?" And had left.

Had he also, without Olivia's hearing it, asked him to insure that she did not speak with Michael? Or had the charade of the "wrong number" and the subsequent ignoring of the telephone bell been panic decisions of Simon's own? Either way (whether by obedience to explicit or implicit orders), the boy had confirmed what she had long suspected: the falsity of his claim to independence.

She felt no anger at this. Anger was too violent an emotion to achieve combustion now within the cooling embers of her being. There, what warmth there was was stale and secondary, a misery too vague for tears, a loneliness by custom made acceptable, a fear from which there was nowhere but fear to run. Soon these also might die and become cold. Olivia hoped so. She looked forward to the blow that would finally deaden her senses.

As her realization of Simon's treachery had killed any doubts she might have had about her *own* subjection to another's authority, as her awareness of the greater affiliation existing between her father and Michael than between either of them and herself had killed her understanding of right or wrong, so one more revelation might complete the extinction within her. She waited for it with passive expectation.

"Come on, Olivia, where do you want to sit? Here, by the

door? Or will that be too drafty for you? What about over there?"

Simon stood in the middle of the restaurant. It being early yet for dinner, only one of the dozen or so tables that lined the walls was occupied, and at each of the empty ones he pointed in turn, with the aimless gyration of a roulette wheel.

Oh, for God's sake! What difference does he think it makes *which* one we go to? If we were to sit on the floor now, or hang from the ceiling . . .

The idea hurt her. Like a spark brought to life by a chance breeze, it frightened her, but she squeezed the muscles of her forehead around it and soon it was extinguished. It was absurd that this pathetic insistence of Simon's on making a show of freedom (and whether he did it for her sake, or for his, or for both of theirs, Olivia was no longer certain) should be one thing that still had the power to touch her.

"Can I help you?"

A waiter, an elderly grizzle-haired patriarch with creased eyes and a powerful nose, had come up beside them.

"Thank you," said Simon. "Yes, we'd like a table for two."

"Of course. This way."

The waiter led them to a secluded corner of the room. He pulled out a chair for each of them to sit on. He unfolded a linen napkin and laid it on each of their laps.

Leaning forward to take a breadstick from its tall glass jar, Olivia relaxed her forehead.

51

"Oh, you're in here. What happened, then?"

"What do you mean, 'what happened'?"

Michael was sitting, with his feet on the kitchen table, in darkness. His arms hung loose to the floor and between the fingers of one hand a cigarette burned. An ashtray over-flowed beside his shoes.

Malcolm and Barbara stood in the doorway, he in front of her.

"I mean, what happened with the girl? Don't tell me it wasn't her you went to ring," said Malcolm.

"I didn't get to speak to her. Some bloody poofter boy-friend of hers answered the phone."

"Oh, I see."

Malcolm depressed the light switch and a malarial glow broke out across the room, uniting its three occupants against the night.

Barbara asked, "You haven't just been sitting here by your-self, have you, Michael?"

"No, of course not. The Solihull Glee Singers has been to tea while you was up there screwing."

"All right," said Barbara.

"It doesn't really matter, does it?" Malcolm asked, moving forward to hoist himself onto the table's edge and help him-self to one of Michael's cigarettes. "About the girl. It was only a double insurance, anyway."

"What do you mean?" asked Barbara.

"Michael went to ring Olivia up, to try and get her back here."

"Why?" asked Barbara. "Everything's okay, isn't it? I thought it was all settled. I thought it was all over. I thought the stuff was arriving any minute now."

"Don't squeak," said Michael. He lowered his chair from its tilting position and swung his feet through the air to land upon the floor. "It is," he said.

He looked at his watch, which read seven minutes to eight.

"In about an hour or two, at the most."

"Well, then? What do you want to drag Olivia back for? That was never part of the plan."

"He doesn't," said Malcolm. "It was just an idea. A double insurance, like I said."

"You're wrong, Malky-boy. I do. I do and I'm going to."

Michael had stood up. Now he turned his back toward the others and walked across the room to the French windows. The glass was moist with condensation, so that when he pressed against it with his fingertip and drew a circle, the figure remained.

Malcolm said, "Don't tell me you—how shall I put this?— fancy her?"

Michael, his voice soft (as, indeed, in contrast to his words, it had been since the others had entered the room), said, "Don't be stupid."

"You're telling me, 'don't be stupid'!" said Barbara. "He's never fancied anyone in his life. What is it? What do you want? Why can't you leave her alone now? Can't you imagine how she must be feeling? Raped! Raped, by you and by that father of hers and . . . I mean, *I* didn't like it, seeing that woman shot up. But when you'd told her that the gun wouldn't be loaded . . . And she must know now that it was all untrue, about raising money for Pieter's appeal. Mannion must've told her that. So don't you think it'd be more decent just to leave her in peace? Just to leave her to get over it, instead of dragging her back here just to satisfy some—some power hunger of yours?"

"Hey, hey," said Malcolm. "Who'd have thought the old girl to have so much life in her?"

Michael, however, did not immediately answer.

Since his return from the telephone kiosk (during the hour or more in which he had sat, undisturbed and alone, in the kitchen), he had thought only of the fact, not the reasons: that he wanted Olivia back with him, not why. Now, forced to locate his motives (if only to see how best he should misrepresent them), he was amused at the amount of tenderness involved. Not the vulgar tenderness that Malcolm had hinted

206

at, not the sentimental softness that people wrap around their sharper needs in order to make them tolerable, but a strong, clear, magnanimous current, upon whose back his reasoning rode like driftwood. Even his initial irritation at failing to speak with the girl had risen to the surface of this tide. He carried it as though it were weightless.

But then, he was the victor. Now, for the first time, he understood this. He had said it before. He had said to Malcolm: "Relax. We're home and dry." But at that point his intellect had been in advance of his emotions, as though the transition from fantasy to reality had been too sudden for both parts of him to accept simultaneously.

On the Monday of that week, he had stood within the shadows of the pillared doorway of a block of flats in Mayfair, his stomach knotted round itself, his nerves rubbed backward by a stale and irritating breeze, and (as a man marooned on an island too small for him, an island whose scant resources he knows cannot feed him) had prepared to dive into the sea.

Today it was Thursday. Today it was Thursday and he was still alive. Nor was this as a waterlogged, gasping shipwreck, but as a creature as much in his element as the white sharks and barracudas that swam with him. He had achieved what everyone (his parents, teachers, employers, and friends) had warned him was impossible. He had broken their laws of nature. It was not surprising that his heart had at first refused to believe what his head had told him.

When Mannion, his arrogance sodden by rain, had come to knock on his door, he had suspected the truth, but afterward the habit of losing had intervened and confused his view. It had not been alone for Malcolm's reassurance that he had said, "That pin-striped waistcoat doesn't make him invulnerable, however much he'd like you to think it does."

Now, however, as the rain continued to roll in dark streams down the window glass, as the summer-dried earth of the garden was beaten to winter mud, as the sky sagged lower and lower, its pale blue remoteness distended and heavy and black, Michael's heart caught up with his head. Nor was tenderness the only emotion to fill him—the most astonishing, the least expected, but by no means the only one. There was elation, too, and a strange perverse humility, an awful respect for himself and for what he had done.

He turned to face his inquisitors.

Malcolm still perched on the table's edge, his thumbs tucked under his armpits, but Barbara had moved from her place by the door to a chair, where she sat with the palms of her hands supporting her lowered forehead. Failure and second-rateness emanated from them like the smell of feet from a pair of old socks. Yet, for once, Michael did not resent this. On the contrary, a compassion flickered over him at the thought that soon he would have no more need of these two. There was no question of his retaining them. They were van der Walt's people, not his.

Olivia, on the other hand . . .

"You've got a perfect right to shout at me, Barbara," he said. "I don't blame you. It's been hard on the nerves, all of this. But we have got the best part of three thousand pounds upstairs and the other stuff'll be here any minute. Pieter wouldn't be too upset with that, I don't think. As for the girl —remember, I never *forced* her to do anything. She was lost, anyway. The whole setup was as much to her advantage as ours. And what do you think'll happen to her now if we 'leave her alone to get over it'? She'll be back where she was, only worse, with the old man tying her hand and foot with his blackmail. The way I see it, we rather *owe* it to her to get her back. We've rather got a *responsibility* to her."

"Oh, beautiful, beautiful! You've brought a lump to my throat, you really have." Malcolm leaped from the table, swiveled round, then closed his eyes and mimed the playing of a violin. "Come on, man. Who are you trying to fool?" he said when he had finished.

Michael said, "Not you, anyway. That's obvious."

"Not even Barbara. Does he, Barbara? Does he fool you? Do those noble, tear-jerking words sound like anything that might conceivably have come from the Machiavellian mind we know and love so well? What is it really, Michael? Do you still think Mannion might try something? Or have you decided he might be good for another go, later on?"

Michael blew with his lips like a horse. His face was as free from tension as his body. Even hatred, it appeared, could be borne without effort now.

"Well, it'd be naïve to overlook that possibility, wouldn't it?" he said.

Let Malcolm and Barbara think of him what they would. If they chose to turn his own cynicism against him, let them. They were the used spikes of his ascent, and whether they crumbled or snapped or rusted had become irrelevant to him.

Malcolm said, "That's more like it. You had me worried there."

Barbara said, "You mean you might use her again, to get more explosives?"

Malcolm said to her, "What's the matter? Why all this sudden concern for the girl, anyway? You've always hated her type."

"There's a difference between types and people."

"Oh, God! If you're going to start talking like that . . . Well, you should have thought of it sooner, that's all."

Michael looked at them. He wondered whether they had always been so stupid, so devoid of understanding. Their mediocrity made him feel sticky, like the dirt from a messy job. He longed to scrub it away.

Walking past them to the kitchen door, he said, "Mannion

can't get here for a bit yet. I'm going to try ringing her again."

Malcolm said, "Even if you get to talk to her, do you think you can really convince her to come?"

"Of course," said Michael.

52

"All right, then, Mr. Mannion! It's all loaded up!"

"Thank you!" Edward called.

Through the half-open door of the prefabricated office hut, he could hear the shuffling of feet, the sound of Ken, the old man, coughing and spitting phlegm. Rain still fell, but, for the last ten minutes, with less and less conviction aslant the white light of the newly uncovered moon. With the disintegration of the clouds, stars, too, had revealed themselves, and their sharpness reflected that of the night birds calling across the surrounding marshes.

Within the office, all was darkness except for the shifting oval that the beam of Edward's torch described. He had preferred not to turn on the lights. The place in which the storehouse was situated was, of necessity, remote, but there was no point in taking risks, no point in giving anybody the opportunity to notice an unusual light.

"Are you sure you don't need someone to help you drive this lot?"

The old man, Ken, stood on the threshold. He was sucking a boiled sweet and the smell of aniseed filtered out of him to mingle with the other smells of the night: of the rain, of the marshes, of dynamite.

"No, don't worry about that," said Edward. "I drove heavier things than that old van in the sappers."

"As you like."

"It'll be all right. I'll go carefully. Oh, listen—one more

thing, Ken. There isn't an old coat lying around and a cap, maybe?"

"There's that over there."

The man gesticulated toward a hook at the far end of the hut, where a navy-blue donkey jacket hung.

Edward said, "That'll be just the job. No hat, though?"

"I've one up at the cottage."

"Would you mind if I borrowed it?"

The man shrugged and left. As soon as he had done so, Edward opened the drawer of the table in front of which he was standing and took from it the three small objects that he had slipped there on hearing the other's approach. Then he put on the donkey jacket (which must have been overlarge for its owner, since it fitted him), dropped two of the objects into one pocket, and eased the third into the other. They caused no obvious bulge.

After a minute or two, the old man returned, with a greasy checked cap tucked in the waist of his trousers.

"Is that it?"

"That's it."

The garment was proffered, rolled up like a tobacco pouch. Although Ken's gestures were tight, his voice flat, his cracked, unshaven face expressionless, Edward had no fear that these were signs of hatred or resentment. Rather, he knew, they were the expression of a proud disinterest in the doings of others, a stubborn self-containment, which, in the circumstances, was far safer than the garrulous servility of a Mrs. Clifford.

When Edward had rung from Victoria and asked Ken to meet his train (but to park away from the station and wait for him there), he had agreed without curiosity, although always before his employer had been driven down by one of the men from the store, and rarely had he arrived at such an hour. Nor, when the nature of the business had been explained to him, had he offered criticism, or surprise. He would neither speculate nor gossip, nor, unless it was very much in his interest, concede information. That such reticence would not be the result of faithful devotion was irrelevant.

"Right, then," said Edward. "I'll be off. I've done all the necessary paperwork. Can you just go and open the gates?"

They left the office together, locking its door behind them. Then the old man trudged through the drizzle to the perimeter of the compound and Edward climbed into the driving seat of the van. From behind him, more concentrated than outside, came again the distinctive smell of the dynamite.

Edward studied the knobs and switches on the dashboard, stroked them with the tip of his fingers, moved his lips as though reciting a lesson learned long ago. Then he looked to the floor beside his seat and, with a strong, certain gesture, released the hand brake.

The vehicle did not move. He climbed out and pushed against the frame of the door until the wheels came unstuck and began to roll. Then he jumped back to his place behind the wheel as, with growing momentum, the van went down the slope that led to the gates.

Ken held one of the gates open. Against his legs, a couple of Alsatian dogs (not the frightened, hungry creatures that prowl around building sites at night, but broad-chested beasts with silvery hair, fine heads, and beautiful eyes) were pressed. These were Ken's dogs. He had owned them since puppyhood. At his command, they had not barked throughout the night's activities.

"Thank you, Ken," said Edward as he passed him.

"Night, Mr. Mannion," said the old man.

A path ran from the gates, through a flat, sheep-dotted field. Twenty yards along this, as the ground began to level out before rising toward a narrow country road, Edward ignited the van's engine and switched on its headlights.

Ten minutes later, he was on a wider road, being overtaken from time to time by cars heading northwest toward London.

53

"We're not going to be able to get back in. I haven't got the keys," said Olivia.

"It's okay, I left it on the latch. I reckoned the burglars'd never think that anyone'd be so stupid. Not in Chelsea, anyway," said Simon.

"Ah," said Olivia.

It was like the improvised dialogue between two actors who have been thrown by a wrong cue, for they were standing on the doorstep, and within the house the telephone was ringing, but they neither of them moved.

"You can just push it," said Simon. He did not tell her to do so, merely pointed out the possibility, for what had begun the afternoon as an unwillingness to influence the girl's behavior had, over the hours (and particularly over the last, storm-heavy hour they had spent in the restaurant), solidified into a mooring ring, to which, blind, yet feeling the cold lap, lap of danger against his ankles, he clung with dull, instinctive desperation. He must not drop. Help might yet come. The waves might yet reveal themselves as fantasies. He must not drop.

He waited to see what Olivia would do. It seemed possible that she would stand on the doorstep forever, her black woolen sweater spangled by rain drizzle, her face set, her small blue center-of-flame eyes compressed into slits. She did not, however. After five or six seconds, she reached out her hand and pushed the front door inward. Simon watched her enter the house and walk to the telephone table.

He said, "No, please, don't cut me off. It's important you listen to me. I can't explain if you don't listen, can I?"

To which she agreed.

He said, "How are you, anyway? You didn't get hurt, did you? You went under a car like I told you?"

She said that she had. He asked her how long she had stayed there and whether anyone had seen her.

He said, "You did bloody well, Olivia. Not just the way you stuck to the plan, but using your initiative, too. Not coming straight back here, in case you were seen and followed. But the others! Malcolm, I could—I don't know what I can say to you about that. It was inexcusable. He's a thug. A juvenile thug who gets his kicks from loud noises. It's my fault. I should've known better than to have trusted him. He *heard* me tell you the gun wouldn't be loaded, but he couldn't resist the temptation to play at gangsters. Well, we'll know next time."

"Next time?" said Olivia.

"Poor kid. But it's going to be all right. We'll have to be careful for a while, till the fuss has died down, but we'll be all right. You knew it wouldn't be roses all the way. You never expected that. We're up against the most powerful, callous force in the world, remember. The establishment. The South African government, the British government . . . Your father; you know he came to see me, of course."

"Yes," said Olivia.

"He told you why."

"He wanted to help you," said Olivia.

The words sounded strange, as though she were reading them (syllable by phonetic syllable) from a foreign phrase book. She did not know which of them meant what, which should be stressed and which passed over. She could not even be certain that any of them meant anything. The whole conversation had this quality: of one being conducted by people who do not speak each other's language.

214

There was no doubt, however, that Michael's was the language of the country. The way he was assuming her comprehension showed that. So she listened and made noises when he paused, waiting without hope for the sentence that she would recognize and that would indicate to her what it was that the others had been about.

"Help me?" he asked. "What do you mean? Those weren't his words, were they?"

"Not just you. All of you. And me."

"Okay, but what else? I mean, did he tell you . . ."

There was a pause. Olivia stared ahead of her, up the stairs, up the brown wool carpeting and stripped-pine banisters, to the place where they turned into shadow.

"Did he say *anything else,* about why he was coming here?"

"I don't think so," said Olivia.

"That's all right, then. No, it's just that I thought he might've told you some sort of story about . . ."

"Oh, I think *Simon* did. When I was in his flat."

It was odd, the way she was talking about Simon as though he were not there, when she knew that he must be standing somewhere behind her. But perhaps it was only to *her* that this seemed strange. It must have been, for there came no protest from *him.*

She said, "About you wanting explosives from Daddy and using me to make him give them to you. Is that what you mean?"

Michael said, "Yes, I thought you must know. Well, I can't say I'm sorry. You can guess how bloody awful it's been for me having to keep that from you. But the others insisted. And then, the 'using' part isn't true, is it? You know that. You did what you did because you wanted to and because it was right. Only, obviously, him being your father would've meant all sorts of emotional things if you'd known . . . You do? . . . He did tell you *that* bit, too, didn't he?"

"What bit?"

"The other side of the coin. The reason why it was your father, and not just anyone, we wanted the stuff from. He did tell you that, didn't he?"

"I'm not sure," said Olivia.

"Well, if he did, let me remind you. And if he didn't, which is a lot more likely, let me tell you."

He said that her father was selling arms and ammunition to Rhodesia, to the Rhodesian government, and that this, as she must realize, was not only immoral but illegal. He said that it was because of this that they (Barbara and Malcolm and he) had decided he should be the one to supply them with the explosives necessary to force Pieter van der Walt's release: as much in the interests of justice as of expediency. He said that it had never been their intention to involve her, Olivia, but that once she had insisted on *becoming* involved, it had seemed kindest to keep her in ignorance of her father's guilt, which was, after all, but a splinter of the establishment's more important, collective guilt.

She was surprised by none of this. Her father had slapped her across the mouth. He had also said, "It can't be helped," when told of her part in a woman's murder. There was no reason why he should not also be the illegal supplier of arms and explosives to a repressive minority government.

Michael said, "Don't you believe me? Think about it. Think about why your father *really* came to see me just now. To save your skin? Or his? Think about why he didn't go to the fuzz on Monday. There wasn't any need to protect *you* then."

"I expect you're right," said Olivia.

"Look, it's the truth. Just think about it and you'll know. I've lied to you, I admit it. But never to protect myself, have I? For *you*. So as not to make things too difficult for *you*. Not like your father, with his layer upon layer of respectable hypocrisy, his crookedness done up as enterprise, his immorality done up as laissez-faire."

Olivia relaxed one knee and rested her shoulder against the wall. She was tired from standing. A cold draft penetrated her sweater and she assumed that Simon had not yet closed the front door.

"Olivia! Are you still there?"

"Yes," she said.

Michael's explanations, his attempts to differentiate between one untruth and another, did not interest her. They seemed futile and energy-wasting, like the moves of an esoteric game. The only justification for his behavior, after all (for his and for her father's and for Simon's), was that truth did not exist, that even the word "green" was a suggestion, a sound capable of meaning either many things or none.

She would have put the receiver down, or dropped it to dangle from the length of its cord, were not the certainty still within her that there *was* a meaning underneath the nonsense words, that there *was* an intention for her to understand.

She tried to imagine what it might be. She tried to remember who Michael was, what emotions or thoughts he had once set alight in her, but the dull, cold almost painlessness remained untroubled.

Then he said, "Olivia, come on. Come back. I want you back here," and, without warning, without any constriction of the chest or throat, without any prickling along the lower eyelids, the tears began to flow out of her. They were so warm, so thick, so much more like blood than water. They ran down her cheeks, under her chin, and down her neck.

"You will, won't you?" he said. "Now?"

"Yes," she said, the word as independent of her crying as her body was. Her breathing had not altered its rhythm. Her muscles were not tense.

She replaced the receiver and turned round.

Simon stepped back against the door lintel. She was leaving. He had known that she would if she answered the telephone, if Michael was allowed to speak to her. What surprised him was that he felt no relief at this. He had expected the same lightness, the same floating freedom from guilt or responsibility that had bubbled up through him at their last two partings; instead of which, there was only anger and scorn, made stronger by their suppression.

He felt that he could have accepted it had Olivia decided of her own accord to return to the man. That she had waited for him to wheedle her back was what angered him. Did she think that *he* could not have done the same, could not have held her there with arguments and cajolery, had he allowed himself?

Her tears, as she came toward him down the hallway, filled him not with pity but disgust. There was a joyful, exalted light behind them that seemed like the ecstasy of a Christian martyr, his body erect with darts.

He said, "I gather you're going."

"Yes."

"I suppose you know what you're doing?"

She did not answer this.

He said, "There's no need me telling you he's a bastard? A ruthless, megalomaniac bastard? He'll put a gun in *your* hand next. Oh, a gun, a detonator . . . And you'll find reasons why it's not wrong to use them. He'll give you reasons. Or, more likely, he won't have to, because you won't be asking any questions. You won't dare. The more you get involved, the less you'll dare."

He could not prevent himself from speaking. He could contain the notes of his voice within the range prescribed for logical argument, he could restrain his body from moving to block the front doorway, but he could not be silent.

"You're selling yourself to the strongest bidder, Livvy. You're sacrificing yourself through fear. For God's sake, it's not as though you've never known how to think for yourself. With other people, who never have, it's different. But you've had years of . . . mental independence."

"Have I?"

"What? Yes, of course you have. More than most people, anyway. You know that perfectly well. And I just don't understand how you can let this man Michael persuade you that white is black and wrong is right and ugly's beautiful. If you'd just come back from South Africa, or something. If you'd seen a black servant shot by a white woman who 'thought he was going to rape her,' and seen the white woman get off with a caution. But you haven't. You've never been there. And yet you're prepared to kill?"

"This has got nothing to do with South Africa. Not really. I've never pretended that. Oh, for God's sake, you don't even begin to know what I'm talking about."

"You're right. I don't. But I do know this. If you'd gone straight from university into a job, an interesting job, I mean. Or if—if, say, I'd asked you to marry me, none of this would've happened. Now, that's a pretty sobering thought, isn't it?"

"Perhaps you ought to have married me, then."

Olivia was no longer crying, nor was it possible to see on her face signs that she ever had been.

"What do you think *that* would have done?" Simon asked. "My marrying you?"

"You've just said. Kept me a nice person. But you didn't, and I'm not any more. It's really quite simple, isn't it?"

"For God's sake, you're not serious?"

"I think so. Events seem to bear me out. As for you . . ."

She moved past him and began to descend the steps. When she had reached the pavement, the edge of the pavement nearest to the road, she turned back. Her high forehead (from which the hair was pulled back and tucked behind her ears) caught the light from a lamppost, or the moon, and shone with a dull glow. Her eyes were shadowed, seeming larger than usual, like craters.

Simon said, "Livvy," not in order to call her back—not, indeed, for any sensible reason—but as though, by saying her name, he might break down the stark lights and shadows into the human features (the small child's nose, the swollen mouth, the blue eyes trapped with a network of worry) of which he knew them to be composed.

"As for you . . ."

The girl's hands flung up to grip the opposite shoulders, so that her forearms made a cross upon her chest. She must have been very cold, for Simon felt her coldness. It lifted the skin on his shoulders and the back of his neck.

"As for you," she said, *"nothing* bears *you* out. Nothing but your own voice. Nothing but the consistency of your own words, like a diamond, immutable. Not even your actions support you. You talk about truth, but you lie like a secretary. You talk about freedom, but you obey authority without even thinking. You talk about 'self,' the respect due to 'self,' and all you mean, it turns out, is *your* self."

Olivia was not shouting. She was speaking as though Simon were three feet away from her rather than four yards. But the air, now that the rain had stopped, had a crystal quality through which her words came clearly.

Simon said, "You're not going to condemn me because I sometimes fail, are you?"

"I'm not condemning you. How can I? And it's not your failings, it's what you think you're trying to achieve. You know what it is? I think you hate so completely that it doesn't even show. There's no loving in you to show the hatred up. You hate Michael, of course, but the reason it's not as obvious as it would be with most people isn't because you're tolerant or broad-minded, no. It's because you also hate me, my father, your friends, everyone. Perhaps you, too. Perhaps you don't like yourself. Anyway, this 'philosophy' of yours, this

220

diamond flashing every time you open your mouth, is just . . . I don't know. An escape. A fantasy. A fantastic retreat from the real."

"It's an ideal, I know that, if that's what you mean. I don't pretend mankind's anywhere near it, or even that I am, a lot of the time."

"A lot of the time? You *never* are. Well, maybe in your head, when your head's isolated from outside contact. But, more important than all that, you never will be. You never can be. Nobody can be free the way you want it, or tolerant, or objective. It's as impossible as . . . It just cannot be. All the things that make us human deny it. Our bodies, our physical needs, the physical world we live in. Our ability to discriminate. Our power of imagination. Our emotions. Not to mention the other, peripheral needs we seem to have: for companionship and social order and so on. No, what you want's a contradiction of humanity, and that's not just pathetic, but dangerous."

"You're mad," said Simon. "Okay, I'm sorry, not 'mad.' That was a stupid word to use. But can you hear yourself?"

He dared to take a step toward her, imagining that because Olivia was speaking again, because she was arguing with him as she used to, she had returned to a former, familiar, touchable state. A gesture from her, however, stopped him. Or, rather, not so much a gesture as an inward traction of the body.

"Well, can't you?" he asked from the scarcely narrowed distance between them. "Can't you hear what you're sounding like? A romantic. A . . . a saccharine sentimentalist. It's awful! I never, never thought I'd live to hear you say things like that. Dragging out 'nature,' 'human nature,' as an excuse for glorifying the horrible."

"What horrible?"

A car turned in to the top end of the street, moving slowly, its driver searching for a space in which to park. In the middle of speaking, Olivia glanced at it and Simon was amazed at her lack of concentration.

"You see, I'm right: you are dangerous," she said, her face (normal with features now) rotating back toward him. "You'd have mankind believe he's so evil that his only redemption is to cease to exist, because anything he does, as a man, to improve himself is bound to be corrupt and therefore pointless. In other words—"

"In other words, you're calling me a reactionary. You don't have to say it. A conservative. The worst insult! Well, you know bloody well it's not true. You know bloody well you're just saying it so you can shut me in some pigeonhole with your father and forget about the both of us. Still, if that makes it easier for you . . . I only hope you manage to get rid of the 'danger' of your *own* intelligence as quickly. Or have you already done that?"

"Goodbye," said Olivia. "Stick to writing your poems. They suit you."

As she shifted her weight to walk away, the intrusive driver, having parked his car, passed between them and smiled at them in turn, with the tentative half-smile that strangers offer each other as a sign of non-aggression in otherwise deserted streets, at half past eight in the evening. Then he moved on and she moved on, and Simon was alone.

54

The first time that the owl had cried out, Edward had started and dropped his torch into the long, wet grass at the side of the road. The sound, the hooting, had been so human, so similar to that made by a man blowing into cupped hands, that he had thought it must be meant for him.

"Fool," he had told himself. "Fool. Even if it *is* someone, it's only a poacher." And the next time he had heard it, his body had resisted the temptation to react.

The place where he had stopped the van, in a lane half a mile from the A-20 trunk road, an hour from London, an hour and thirty minutes (at that time of night) from Wimbledon, was without sight of any habitation. Beyond the wooded western horizon, the sky was stained orange by the lights from a township. Closer to, however, there was nothing but star-scattered darkness and hedgerows and fields where small animals scuttled. The hum of traffic from the dual highway ahead of him was as unobtrusive here as the buzz of a refrigerator, or a central heating system, in a large house at night.

The dynamite had been packed in cases in the back of the van: forty sticks to a box. Edward took one of the cases from its place and stood it on the road. He opened it. He took off his watch and removed the straps. Then he extracted from the pockets of the donkey jacket the three objects he had put there; he knelt down, positioned his torch on the floor of the van so that it shone its narrow light where he wanted it, and began to work.

It was over thirty years since he had last performed an operation of this nature, and he was pleased at the ease with which the skill returned to him. Soldering, threading, crimping; involved and enchanted by the old-new talent in his fingers, he forgot where he was, and why. Smells of Burma invaded him, sounds of Burma, and the hopeful enthusiasm of youth.

When he had finished, it was twenty-five minutes to nine. With his fountain pen, he made a small mark on the case that he had removed from the van, then replaced it—not, however, in the same position whence he had taken it, but farther back, in the middle of the consignment.

55

On reaching South Kensington underground station, Olivia remembered that she had only a twopenny piece on her. Of the money that she had put in her jeans pocket that morning, all but this useless coin had been spent on making her way from the factory, from the robbery, to Simon's flat. She closed her eyes. A confused, incomplete map of London projected itself upon the inside curve of her skull. From it, she gathered that in order to reach Wimbledon she must move in a southwesterly direction and that she must cross the river. She began to walk.

56

Simon switched on the radio in Mr. Mannion's living room. He was surprised when the sounds (of a light classical opera) came at him in stereo from two speakers. He listened for a bit, then turned the tuning knob through various crackles to a pop-music station.

His glass of Martini stood where he had left it, on the table beside one of the black leather armchairs. He refilled it. Olivia and he had drunk mineral water in the Italian restaurant and had eaten little, her lack of appetite having affected the capacity of his. Now, however, he wanted to sate himself. There was a tin of cashew nuts beside the bottles of whisky and gin and apéritif. He opened the tin and began to cram his mouth with its contents.

He could have gone home. He could have returned to the underfurnished, silent flat that was his home. There was no reason for him not to, now that Olivia had left. Yet it was to *this* place, not *that,* that Mannion would eventually return and he had to speak with Mannion. He did not know why. He thought that it might be from politeness, to explain what had happened. He also thought that if he could not talk to someone, justify himself to someone, he might go mad.

Olivia's words fluttered and smashed like birds within his head, always missing the window that he held open for them. They made no sense. They had made no sense when she had spoken them. Yet the rejection of himself that had motored them, that had seeped in between them in thick, corrosive rivulets, was beyond misunderstanding.

"Why, though? Why, for God's sake?"

Martini glass between both hands, Simon strode from room's end to room's end. He swerved off course to take another handful of nuts. He lit a cigarette. He adjusted the volume of the radio.

"Why?"

It was not only incomprehension that thudded in dark waves against his brain, but fear.

During the last three days, Olivia had seemed to him the pitiable victim of deception, the innocent exploited by the guilty, and, as such, his feelings toward her (although varying from protectiveness to boredom) had all been tossed from a hill of superior enlightenment, a hill to which (or so he had assumed) she would one day, repentant, return.

This evening, his viewpoint had undergone a reversal. Olivia had revealed herself not as a victim but as a convert, and in so doing had presented to him the possibility that he might be wrong. Not the possibility of having failed in his endeavor, of which he had always been aware, but of attempting the wrong thing, of aiming at the wrong goal, of expending his energy on a dead, outdated idea. That, also, of right and wrong being not, as he had supposed, personal matters, nor, as was generally assumed, absolutes, but merely a reflection of that view held by the greatest number of people at any given time.

He refilled his glass. The sweetness of the drink, together with the fat of the cashew nuts, was beginning to make him feel sick. He picked up the *Evening Standard* and attempted to answer another clue from its crossword puzzle, then discarded it. He went to a narrow bookcase crammed with volumes of apparently unread classics: Shakespeare's plays, Tolstoy's novels, the poetry of Eliot, Donne, and Chaucer in leather-bound anthologies. He rested his face against the shelves, smelling the print, the paper, the hide.

Olivia despised words. Yet without them, without the hope that soon he would be using them with Mannion to give to his fears a shape, an acceptability, he might now be running after her and forcing her to stay. Was that what she wanted? Was that what O'Keefe had taught her to accept? A life in which emotional and physical needs, unchecked, wreaked their havoc, hurling and dragging one through chaos to the only inevitability: death?

His fingers closed upon the spine of a novel: E. M. Forster's *A Passage to India.* He opened the stiff covers.

"Chapter One," he read.

"Except for the Marabar Caves—and they are twenty miles off—the city of Chandrapore presents nothing extraordinary."

A joy leaped through him, a needle flame from his solar plexus to his head, for he had read the book before and knew that the Marabar Caves were mentioned *there,* in the first sentence, not by chance (as they might have been in a guidebook or a conversation) but because *they* were what the story was about.

He took the book with him to an armchair. Reading, he stretched out his hand to touch the sticky sides of his glass. But he drank more slowly now. He lit and extinguished cigarettes less often. Only his eyes were restless, traveling forward and backward, down and up. His limbs and torso sat detached, immune, isolated in their alibi from all that might be happening on earth or in Wimbledon.

57

"Where is he, for Christ's sake? It's getting on for ten o'clock."

"He'll come," said Michael. "He didn't say which part of Kent he had to get to, did he?"

"You mean to say he's gone there himself?"

"That was the impression I got. Anyway, he wouldn't want to tell more people than was necessary about it, would he?"

They had returned to the living room, the three of them. From there they could see the road.

Malcolm said, "I can't imagine him driving. I shouldn't've thought he could've got from Piccadilly Circus to the Ritz without a chauffeur."

"Then that's stupid of you," said Michael.

"But what about Olivia?" Barbara asked. "You said *she* was coming."

"She is."

"Well, how long can it take her to get from Chelsea? It was a good deal more than an hour ago you rang her."

"I've told you, she's coming," said Michael.

He knew that she was. He knew that they both, father and daughter both, were coming. His only anxiety on that level was whether they might not now arrive together, which would be inconvenient.

On another level, however, there stirred a current far colder than strategic anxiety or the anticipation of inconvenience (both of which he was not only used to, but enjoyed). This was a new feeling, at the same time numbing and painful. It swirled around his mind like fumes of dry ice, affecting parts that he had long since thought protected from such an assault.

Throughout the telephone conversation with Olivia, it had grown, each of her dead, angerless replies increasing it. At first, he had assumed that it was the disappointment of a huntsman on seeing the fox sit down and wait to be caught, as he had sent out his ingenious arguments and heard them returned, unnecessary. Then, when, without meaning to, he had said "Come back. I want you back here," and she, in the same blank hopeless voice as that in which she had answered his calls to her reason, had replied, "Yes," he had understood the real extent of the coldness, the dread, within him.

It was not just annoyance. It was not just disappointment with the girl for demanding no explanation from him, for ceding on an accidental, emotional point. It was an understanding of the reasons for, the inevitability of, such a state of affairs: that the end of the hunt must always be inglorious, that the fox must always be trembling, exhausted, and stained, that the flame that excited hounds in the morning must always be dull and extinguished at the kill, for the kill does not take place until this is so.

"Yes," she had said, and he did not doubt that she would come. Only, there had been a time when he had wanted her to, when he had looked forward to her coming with an excitement that had seemed like a new strength.

Now he stared at the crude floral pattern of the living-room carpet and had difficulty in keeping his temper with the boy who lay on his back on a sofa and the woman who lifted and dropped, lifted and dropped, the net curtains.

He wondered whether Mannion had anticipated (and enjoyed the anticipation of) this moment. Or had he overestimated Michael? Had he credited him with more understanding of the loneliness, the emptiness, of power than he had, until that evening, possessed?

"Hey, look! Is this him?"

Barbara's voice was shrill. Her contorted neck was blotched red with excitement.

"How can I tell? It might be."

Michael pushed himself away from the sideboard against which he had been leaning and walked, as did Malcolm, to the window. An anonymous, colorless van had drawn up in front of the house and, from the offside, a man in a flat cap and heavy laborer's jacket was climbing.

"I don't know," said Michael. "It's not . . ."

"It is, you know," said Malcolm, punching him between the shoulder blades, laughing. "That's Mannion, all right. My God, what a ham the old bastard is. He's even put on drag for the occasion."

"Pull yourself together," said Michael. "What did you think? That he was going to risk being seen in his Burberry raincoat? Go on. Go and open the door for him."

As the boy left, Barbara said, "What's the matter, Michael? Did you have to speak to him like that?"

"I'll speak to him however I want. And you, stop pulling at your clothes like some village idiot. Come and help us unload."

One by one, the boxes were taken from the van to the house, where they were stacked in careful piles inside the cupboard beneath the stairs.

The street was empty, noiseless except for the backward and forward tread of feet and the puffing of strained breath. Nonetheless, before each journey, at least three of the carriers looked to the left and right of them, peering into the darkened interiors of cars, the shadowed porchways of houses. A break in the rhythm of the unseen High Street traffic made them catch their breath. The sudden blaring of a television program's theme music caused them to stop in their tracks and stare at each other, faces frozen.

When the job was over, the van empty, the broom cupboard almost full, Mannion said, "Okay, close the front door. Now, I don't suppose I'm going to get a receipt for this lot, but hadn't you better check it?"

"That's all right," said Michael. "If it's not all there, we know where to get in touch with you."

"No, come on. I'd rather know now if you're not happy. I don't intend carrying out a prolonged after-care service."

He walked past them and removed the top box from the front pile.

"Open it," he said. "And count. There should be forty sticks in there."

"We'll take your word for it," said Michael.

"*I'll* count them," said Malcolm.

"Good."

The lid of the box was pried off, to reveal ten candlelike cylinders, each approximately six inches long and each wrapped in a thick, greasy, gray-brown piece of paper.

Mannion said, "Don't breathe in too deeply, or you'll start feeling sick. Now, look. Two, four, six, eight, ten. And there's four layers like that in every case."

"Thanks, but you did say to check," said Malcolm.

He wriggled one hand beneath the upper, visible sticks and began to grope with his fingers. Michael felt the irritation tighten within him at the youth's lack of dignity, at the greed that spilled from his Latin gigolo's eyes. Mannion, in spite of the absurdity of his costume, in spite of the ignominy of his defeated position, excited greater respect than the arrogant creature grubbing at his feet.

He said, "For Christ's sake, do you want them analyzed as well? Look, what's the risk of these things going off if they're handled too much?"

"Not very great," said Mannion. "They're quite low explosive. Let him look if he wants to. Would you like the next box down?"

"That's okay," said Malcolm. "I'm just about capable of multiplying by forty."

Barbara, from her hunched and isolated position in the middle of the hallway, said, "Does anyone want some coffee or something?"

Nobody replied. The atmosphere had become that of a party overextended; of an official reception, the speeches all made, the champagne long finished or flat.

Never, in imagining this moment, had Michael thought that it might be filled with so much desolation. He would have liked then to have escaped to a pub; not to a southern pub, but to a vulgar, noisy, gut-smelling Midlands pub, with a bad drag artist and a loud rock group and tankards of strong, stunning beer. Such flight, however, was impossible. There was still Olivia's arrival to cope with and certain arrangements to be completed with a man whose telephone number was composed of multiples of three and . . .

Then a light leaped across Michael's brain: a zigzag blue sparkle like wild electricity, splitting his thoughts apart. And, immediately, he could not understand whither or why he had wanted to run. There was so much still to be done, so much still to be gained. He must have been mad. He . . .

"O'Keefe?"

He focused his vision once more. Barbara was jerking her head and saying, "He's going."

Mannion was saying, "Unless there's anything you think we haven't settled."

"No," said Michael. "No, I think that's all satisfactory."

Then, as though testing a new or rediscovered ability, he added, "Only, don't go having a change of heart, will you? I mean, don't go deciding to do something clever. Because you do know the small print on the contract, don't you?"

Mannion's eyes narrowed—not much, but enough to confirm and strengthen the flow of energy singing in Michael's nerves, enough to make him think, Yes, lovely, lovely. In spite of his cool, he hates it. And he can't do a single thing about it. God, if only he knew . . .

He found that he wanted to laugh, and did so.

"Well, it's been a pleasure doing business with you," he said, still laughing, stepping forward with exaggerated politeness to open the front door.

"I'm so glad you think so," said Mannion. "Just bear in mind that things are never as much fun a second time round, won't you?"

He came toward Michael and, as he did so, the tone of his voice changed.

"In other words, I'm not ever to see you or hear from you again. You understand?" he said.

"Oh, but you won't, sir. You have my word on it."

"Yes. Well . . . Oh, how stupid of me. I almost forgot. My daughter's bag. A velvet pouch affair."

"What about it?"

Michael's laughter paused.

"Could I have it?" Mannion asked.

"You think of everything, don't you? Barbara! It's upstairs, I think. In the bedroom."

The woman went. Until she returned, nobody spoke. Then Mannion said, "Thank you."

"A pleasure," said Michael, the laughter rising all the stronger for its rest. "It wouldn't have done to have left that here, would it? Well, goodbye again. And drive carefully. All right?"

58

It was not the first time that Olivia had walked a long distance through London at night. It was, however, the first time that she had done so merely through lack of money. Before, when she had not had the necessary cash to pay for a taxi or a bus, she had hitched a lift, reserving her walking for those occasions when anger drove her from a place—or anticipation drove her toward one—with too great a force to be satisfied by anything but the relentless locomotion of her legs.

Tonight there had been no such urgency. Had she had more than the twopence in her pocket, she would have waited without restlessness at whatever underground station or bus stop was necessary. She had not had more; therefore she had walked. But her progress through the lamplit yellow streets—from Chelsea, down the King's Road, over Putney Bridge (beneath which the Thames at high tide had shone and lapped with a rich, oily blackness), up Putney Hill, past the dark expanses of Wimbledon Common, and into Wimbledon High Street—had been casual and slow, as though the journey were one that might, if it chose, take forever.

Indeed, Olivia no longer saw the house toward which she was moving as a goal, as an end, at all. When Michael had said "Come on. Come back. I want you back here," his words had not reignited the ashes within her. Such a thing would have been impossible. What they *had* done had been to reveal an area of comparative warmth, an area (in the ice field across which she wandered) more close to thawing point than any other.

She went toward it not in the hope that it would at once revive her, not in the certainty that it ever would, but because of the chance that those words "I want you" uttered with such unwillingness over the telephone, dragged from unfathomable depths in order to win an argument, might, one day, be confident and strong enough to take their rightful place upon the surface. It was a small chance, she knew, but in taking it she was not gambling. The alternatives were no longer accessible to her.

She stood on the corner made by Wimbledon High Street and the street in which the house was. On the far side of the road from her, a cluster of young boys eating chips outside a late-night take-out called, "Come over 'ere, darling. We've got something to show you."

Beside her, in the recessed doorway of a bookshop, an elderly man stood shuffling his feet and beating his waist with crossed hands.

A sports car drew to a halt against the pavement and a girl climbed out.

From round a bend in the side street, a gray van appeared, changed gear, then turned too fast in to the main road, heading in the same direction as that from which she had come.

59

The first clock that he noticed was above a chemist's shop in Putney and it said quarter past ten. Seeing this, Edward made a rapid calculation, smiled, then relaxed his foot on the accelerator. In the driving mirror, there was nothing extraordinary: a fast saloon car pulling out to overtake him, a becapped cyclist, head bent, feet pounding to keep up with the natural downward velocity of the hill.

He increased his smile and, once again, the speed of the van. He crossed the traffic lights before the bridge as they changed from amber to red.

Once over the river, he intended driving straight to the office and parking the van in the street outside the main door, where it was not unusual for it to be. The chances of anyone seeing him leave it there were scant, the area being non-residential, but even if someone did so, and even *remembered* doing so, it didn't matter. No one would ever think the information relevant.

Having performed this operation, he would then take a taxi (or perhaps a bus and a taxi, there being no harm in playing safe) back to Chelsea, where he would have to deal with the secondary problem of Olivia. It occurred to him that it might be best if she were to go abroad for a while. Driving along the Fulham Palace Road, he made a mental list of people he knew in Paris, or Milan, or Munich, who might be willing to offer his daughter a job.

60

He had been frightened that she might touch him. He had been frightened that she might run toward him and throw her body against him. He had a suspicion that something he had said on the telephone might have given her reason to think such behavior acceptable.

When she didn't, he was both relieved and troubled.

"Hello," she said, coming into the kitchen with Barbara behind her.

"Olivia."

He stood up. They faced each other across the cold, stale, untidy room, he with his shoulders hunched forward, uncertain, she relaxed and soft and still.

"She walked all the way," said Barbara.

"Did she? Why? There was no need to do that."

"I didn't have any money."

"Well, couldn't you . . . Look, sit down. Give her a chair."

She sat and Michael looked at her.

For one moment, seeing her thus, her pale, heavy face

drained of its previous mobility, her eyes made old by the pouches of tiredness beneath them, her brown hair (always untidy) now dank and lifeless and sprinkled with dry, flaking skin, he felt a push of pity against the newly formed crust of his determination. Then pity became (or was transformed into) despising.

It occurred to him how lucky it was that he *had* thought to get her back. In her present condition, she would have been as plasticine beneath her father's fingers. Her softness, her malleability, shocked him. Yet it shouldn't have done. Had he not always known these qualities to be hers?

He remembered that he had once, twice, made love with this girl and the feeling of scorn spread out to include revulsion; not just against her, but against himself, for having lost his objectivity, for having allowed himself to accept a mediocre definition of pleasure.

He removed his eyes from her. He took a cigarette, then pushed the packet away from him across the table.

"Have one," he said.

"Thanks."

Their hands didn't touch, yet he felt as though they had. Scorn and revulsion sprang backward into anger.

He said, "I suppose there's no point asking whether anyone knows you're here. You probably had to get your boyfriend's permission before you set out."

"He knows where I am."

"Of course he does. I'm surprised he didn't bring you over in a taxi."

"When he told you you'd got the wrong number, he was just doing what he thought was best, that's all."

"Oh, I'm glad to hear that. Let's just hope he doesn't suddenly decide it's best to come chasing after you and take you home. What with you and your father and him, we'll have a regular footpath leading here soon. I don't know why we didn't wear identity cards this morning, instead of masks."

He checked himself. The words were coming too fast, spinning from the top of his head. He was frightened of what they might reveal were they to unravel themselves completely.

He said, "Anyway, you're here. So that's all right. And tomorrow we'll be moving on."

"Is that all fixed, then?" Malcolm asked, from his position on the drainboard. The note of challenge was strong in his voice that evening.

Michael said, "There's nothing *to* fix. I've told you, I've got friends up in the Midlands. We'll be okay there for a while."

"Oh, those junkies you were supplying when we first met you. Well, if you say it's all right . . ."

Michael stood up.

"Okay," he said. "Okay. I'll go. I'll go and make a phone call. I wouldn't want you telling Pieter I'd neglected you in any way. I wouldn't want him to think I hadn't your best interests at heart. And why don't you get the cards out and have a game of snap while I'm gone? I mean, unless you fancied doing the washing-up, or something useful like that. No? Well, it doesn't matter. Whatever you want."

He was careful not to look at Olivia as he spoke, although he didn't know why he should be. She was, after all, no less deserving of his anger than either Barbara or Malcolm. Yet there was something, some knowledge, some apprehension of knowledge, that prevented him from focusing again on her defeated features.

"Right," he said. "I shan't be long. Try to be good while I'm away, won't you?"

"Michael . . ."

He ignored it, the voice that neither asked nor expected, but merely came and went like that of a patient on a mechanical lung. He ignored it as he ignored the face, preferring the familiar sounds of Malcolm's insubordination and Barbara's plaintive whine.

"I'll be back in a couple of minutes," he said.

61

"Good evening."

Like an answer-phone record, he was always there. Michael would dial the number composed of multiples of three, the bell would ring once, twice at the most, and always he would answer it, as though he had nothing else in the world to do. It was quarter to eleven at night. Why was he not out having dinner somewhere, or making love to a woman?

Michael pressed the coin into the slot.

"It's O'Keefe here," he said.

"My dear boy, I've been waiting to hear from you."

"Yeah, well, I've got it."

"Good! Splendid!"

"Five hundred pounds of it."

"I see. That's even better than you promised. How nice to know that my faith in you wasn't misplaced. When can I have it?"

"You'll have to come and fetch it."

"Shall I?"

"Look, I haven't got any transport. But it's here. It's ready for you."

"Yes. Well, I'm sure we can arrange something. It would help if I knew where 'here' was, though."

"Yeah. Of course."

Michael gave the address and, when he had done so, said, "How soon do you think you can get over here?"

"How soon would you like me? Immediately?"

"Well . . ."

"No, I was joking. Tomorrow morning?"

"Yeah, that's better. But not *too* early. I mean . . ."

"Just give me a time, dear boy."

"I don't know. . . ."

"Ten o'clock? Eleven o'clock? Twelve o'clock? This is beginning to sound like an old song."

"Okay. Twelve'll do just fine. I've got . . . I've got things to arrange, that's all. No, twelve. Twelve'll be fine. And you will have the money, won't you?"

"It won't be *me* who'll be coming, of course. But whoever I send . . . You'll be wanting slightly more than we originally agreed on, I imagine."

"A quarter as much again," said Michael.

There was a pause, then, "Yes. Of course. Quite right. Um, there *will* have to be a small deduction, though, for the inconvenience of collecting."

"I never said I'd deliver."

"It's normally understood."

"Is it? Yeah, yeah, okay. Okay. You'd just better make sure it *is* small, though. That's all. You're not doing me any favors, you know, buying this stuff from me. You'd be hard put to get any cheaper, and you bloody well know it. If I weren't in a bit of a hurry . . ."

"I know, I know. And I must thank you *so* much for considering me in the first place. It was Pieter you got my name from, wasn't it? Didn't you say? Well, if ever you're visiting him, do thank him, too. Oh, no, of course, I don't suppose he knows. . . . No, of course he doesn't. . . . Anyway, thank *you*. And *à demain*, Mr. O'Keefe. Yes?"

"Yes," said Michael. As soon as the other had done so, he replaced the receiver, then tipped his body forward, bowed his head, pressed his hands against the glass wall of the kiosk, and held his arms rigid at right angles, so that they supported his weight.

"Fuck him," he said. "The bastard. Fuck him."

He took a deep breath, then let it go slowly, staring at his reflection in the dirty glass.

"Still, just let him wait," he said. "He'll be next. I'll get you next, you sod."

Within a minute, humiliation had retreated, pressed backward by the twin visions of eventual revenge and immediate financial compensation.

Michael smiled. He straightened his body and began to push himself up from the leaning position.

Then he stopped, as the glass walls of the kiosk burst into light around him.

62

The night had come—for the moment, at least—to rest. After the clatter battery of the rain (the side-swept gusts of water hitting and bouncing and folding with their wetness, the rush in gutters and drainpipes, the smashing of surfaces, the movement, and the noise), the air was blanketed in a peace all the softer for what had preceded it.

Clouds trailed in front of the moon, not hiding it but netting and diffusing its white brightness. Amongst the high, hard stars, the red and green lights of a homing airplane blinked. Sound traveled across vast distances, modulated only by the varying directions of the wind. A heavy-goods lorry rumbled. A cat screeched. A burglar-alarm bell rang and rang and rang, unanswered.

There was a threat in the air, a promise. Such clarity could only be the forerunner of frost. Nothing but freezing could emerge from so brittle a stillness. Yet, for the moment, the threat withheld itself, as though sure enough of its inevitability not to have to hurry.

Stepping out from his taxi, Edward didn't bother to button his raincoat, but allowed it to hang open in folds like a flag lying limp between battles. He reached into the inner pocket of his suit and from it took his wallet.

"How much?" He said, bending his knees to peer into the driver's cab.

"Ninety-five pence, sir."

He proffered a note and some coins.

"Thank you, sir. Good night, sir."

"Good night," he said.

From his drawing-room window, a bar of yellow slashed down the front of his house and out across the pavement. The soft sound of music followed it: of drums and of a wailing jazz trumpet. Edward pressed his lips together.

He had decided that his first move must be to apologize to Olivia for having hit her, though he would have preferred to do so at breakfast, on a new day. If, however, she was still up, he supposed that he would have to confront her now. He straightened the collar of his shirt and climbed the steps.

Turning the key in the lock, he heard a male voice. The boy must still be there. Edward was glad that he had stayed, but he would have to be sent away before the conversation with Olivia took place, for it appeared that he had the habit (common to many ineffectual people) of playing the devil's advocate. One could only be certain of his allegiance if one were losing an argument.

A hint of tiredness nudged at the back of Edward's eyes. There was always so much to be thought of, so much to be taken into consideration, so many niggling, unnecessary impediments to one's plans.

Once, Caroline had said to him, "Look, darling, I've got an idea. Why don't you just hand the whole business over to Dick Hastings for a couple of months and let's us two go abroad somewhere? Or, better still, give it up completely. Find something that doesn't take up so much of your time. We don't need *so* much money." And he had smiled, knowing better than she how little she would have relished financial restrictions; how little, also, she would have respected a husband who was merely an employee, a wage earner (she whose mother still referred to him as "that young parvenu"). But, more important, he had *enjoyed* working then, had enjoyed scheming and plotting and outwitting his rivals, had enjoyed creating an empire of power. Every movement had been a movement forward and up. Now he sometimes knew that he was moving simply in order that he might remain in one place, and it was this knowledge, rather than a lessening of strength, that tired him.

He closed his eyes. He tightened the muscles of his back. Then he opened the door and stepped inside his house.

"Oh, hang on. Just a second," said Simon. "Mr. Mannion's just come in."

He covered the mouthpiece with the palm of his hand.

"It's for you," he said. "A Mr. Hastings. I think it's quite important. He was round here earlier trying to find you."

Mr. Mannion said, "Thank you," and took the receiver from him.

Simon stepped back, uncertain which would be less impolite: to stay and listen to the conversation, or to return to the drawing room and his almost finished book.

"Yes, Dick, I know. I know," said Mr. Mannion. "I've been out all evening. I've been busy. Well, you can tell me now, can't you?"

He squeezed the bridge of his nose between the thumb and index finger of his left hand.

"Yes," he said. "The fellow up in Finchley. Well, what did he have to say? Yes. I see. I see. Oh, really? Well, well, well! Why on *earth* didn't I—? I should've guessed."

For the first time since he had entered, he looked into Simon's eyes, watching him as he listened to Hastings. Mannion was smiling. His left hand dropped from his face to hang, relaxed, by his side.

"Yes," he said. "Of course I know him, the old crook. Let's just hope *he* doesn't know where O'Keefe got— What? No. Don't worry. It's not your fault if I wasn't here. All right.

Thank you. Yes, I'll see you tomorrow. Oh, and, Dick, give Sally my love?

"So . . ."

Having dismissed the other, he swung the full beam of his attention onto Simon.

"So," he said. "Where's that daughter of mine?"

He jerked his head toward the drawing-room door, whence the moan of a blues tune came.

"In there, listening to that horrible noise?"

He took a step forward.

"Er, no," said Simon. "No."

"Where is she? I've just learned something I think might interest her."

Then he laughed, with a harsh, involuntary sound like a cough, and said, "You know that fellow, that O'Keefe? The great, angry anarchist? The Che Guevara of South West London whose disciple my daughter was so keen to be? Well, I've just been told—and I wish to God I'd known sooner—that those explosives he wanted from me *weren't* for blowing holes in the establishment, *not* for sowing terror amongst the bourgeoisie, but for selling. For *reselling!* Isn't it wonderful? The fellow was a confidence trickster, not a Communist. A cheap, dirty, money-grubbing swindler. Well! . . . Look, where is she? Where is Olivia? I really think she ought to hear this."

Simon said, "She isn't here."

He had expected to feel nervous, embarrassed, on imparting this information. Now such feelings were no longer large enough to fill the vacuum of his emotions.

"I'm sorry. What did you say?"

Mannion's face still smiled. Like a chicken that continues to run after its head has been chopped off, his face maintained the lines and creases of amusement after Simon had spoken.

"She isn't here," repeated Simon.

"Where is she?"

"She went . . . She *said* she was going back to O'Keefe."

"How long ago was this?"

The questions slipped like a social inquiry between the up-curved lips.

Simon rubbed the palms of his hands with his fingertips. They were wet.

"About three, three and a half hours ago," he said.

"Three and a half hours ago? No, I don't think . . ." The smile faltered, but did not fail. "I don't think that can be right. I was with O'Keefe myself until ten and she certainly wasn't there then."

"Well, that *is* when she left. I mean, perhaps she decided not to go there in the end, but—"

"You bloody, bloody idiot!"

The words ripped before the pressure of their hatred.

"You stupid fool! You meddling, interfering— Look, she'd just better not've gone there, that's all. What did you think? Serves Daddy right for not having been nicer to her? Serves him right for not having kissed her and made her better?"

"No, that's not—"

"Shut up! You make me ill. People like you should be put down at birth. The most irresponsible *child* could've seen that that girl wasn't in a fit state to go wandering off alone, but *you*, with your blancmange sentimentality, just sit back and let her go trotting off to—to a murderer!"

"That's not—"

"I asked you to look after her, fuck it! Couldn't you even do that?"

"I'm not—"

"You're not *anything*. Oh, God, I could . . . Why? Why, in Christ's name, couldn't you've just done what you were told?"

It was a silence that interrupted them: a silence from the

244

drawing room where had been the lament of music. Then, through the silence, came the voice of a radio disk jockey saying, "And now it's exactly midnight and time to go over to Matthew Atkin at the news desk."

As though Simon had ceased to exist, Mannion's body slumped from its fury and began to move, or to be moved, toward the source of the sound. His face had become unrecognizable, like that of an aging film star seen, by mistake, without make-up. Simon stepped to one side and let the old man pass by him into the room.

"Reactions are still pouring in to the Prime Minister's statement, this morning, on price controls. The Director of the C.B.I., addressing a meeting of small shopkeepers in . . ."

Mannion's head was resting against the right-hand speaker, as though it were a pillow. His breathing was audible. His Adam's apple swelled and shrank behind the skin of his neck. Simon stared at him, with the same revulsion, the same fascination, the same awe as that in which one watches any spectacle one does not understand but whose climax one knows must be horrible.

". . . been settled by the weekend, they shall call upon the other unions to support them in their claim. And now to some news that's just come in, of an explosion in a house in Wimbledon. Police searching the wreckage of the house say that they've found signs of a large quantity of explosives having been stored there. They've also found the remains of three bodies, as yet unidentifiable, but thought to be those of two women and one man. None of the houses on either side . . ."

"Switch it off!"

"I don't understand."

"Switch it . . . Damn you! Not even that?"

Mannion stumbled across the room to the radio control box and, with hands grown suddenly too large, floundered among its knobs. Sound blared and screamed. Music erupted through words and, through the music, laughter.

Then there was a click.

Following which, a balloon of silence that bloated and stretched and intensified until all but the rasping of air dragged in and out of lungs had been suffocated by it. Nor was this a silence like the other, the prelude, the pause before the newscaster's announcement. This one was merciless.

Simon gripped his forehead. By force, he tried to stanch the flow of knowledge that was throbbing, throbbing its pulse within his brain. Not a flow of facts, nor of implications from facts. These had yet to impress themselves upon him. But knowledge that bound him, beat by beat, with the suffering in that room; that spun his soul into strands and wove it, like Penelope, relentless, into the voice of the man on the radio and Mannion's unuttered cry.

"What did he say?"

Simon opened his eyes. Mannion had moved away to the window and stood with his back three-quarters turned on the room.

"What?" Simon asked.

"I said, what did he say? He said 'two women and one man,' didn't he? 'Two women and *one* man,' isn't that what he said?"

"Yes. Yes, I think he did," said Simon.

Mannion swung round. He no longer looked old. He no longer looked clumsy or impotent.

"Then O'Keefe wasn't there," he said.

"I don't know."

Simon felt behind him for something to lean on, for something to stop him running. He prayed that anger might come soon enough to help him.

Mannion said, "Well, *I* know. And if O'Keefe wasn't there, then O'Keefe's still somewhere alive. And he knows . . ." The pause was infinitesimal. "I . . . I'm sorry. I'm just . . . It's been such a ghastly shock, that's all. I don't know what I'm saying.

I . . . And it might not even have been them. We can't be certain. We just . . . We both of us . . . leaped to the conclusion, of course. But we can't be sure."

Then anger came. At this, at the father's abdication of his right to mourn his daughter, anger came. And Simon was surprised at how hard it was, how heavy and dull and cold. He had expected a flashing, ephemeral sword.

"We can't be sure," said Mannion.

Simon answered, "Don't. Don't open your mouth to me again, or I swear before God I'll fill it with the shreds of your daughter's body. In the name of reason, what *are* you? And did you really think I'd—? Oh, no, you're horrible.

"But you're finished. You understand that? O'Keefe you could have silenced and no one would've cared. But me?

"Come on, it was easy enough with Olivia. You wiped *her* out between supper and bedtime. Now, how are you going to silence me?"